THE DOCTOR'S CONVENIENT MARRIAGE

SECOND CHANCES IN HARMONY SPRINGS ~ BOOK THREE

LAURALYN KELLER

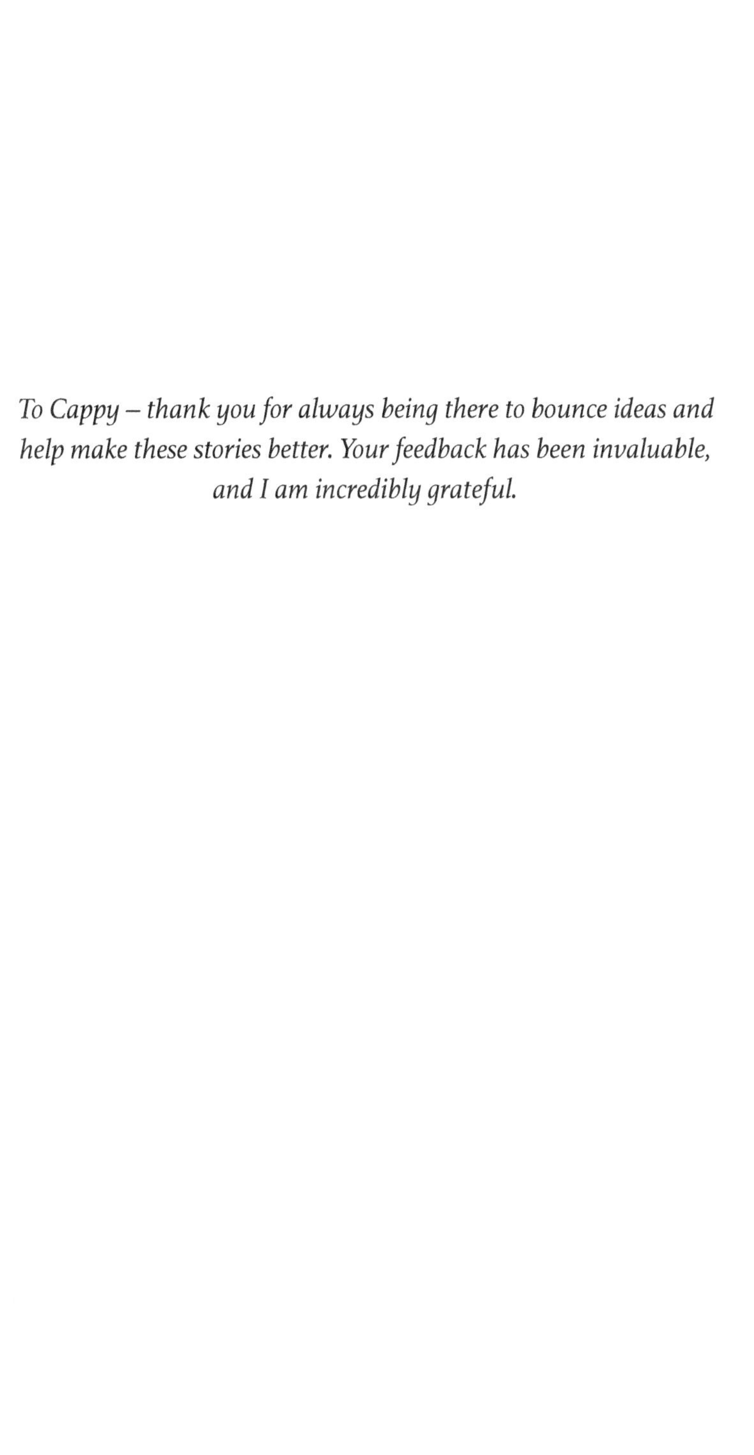

To Cappy — thank you for always being there to bounce ideas and help make these stories better. Your feedback has been invaluable, and I am incredibly grateful.

CHAPTER 1

"*I*'m sorry, Miss Mountbatten. We have no current openings for a physician."

Tori inhaled a deep breath and counted to three, clenching her fists in her lap. She forced her voice to remain even. "There is a sign in the window that claims otherwise, Dr. Burns."

The doctor leaned back in his chair and folded his hands over an ample belly. "We can't help you. I'm sorry."

Liar.

Tori bit her tongue, then winced at the metallic taste of blood. Everything about Dr. Burns—from his half smirk to his perfectly pomaded salt-and-pepper hair—sent her stomach roiling. Yet another self-satisfied man who didn't think women capable of being in his profession.

She rose, smoothing the ruffles on her deep-green dress.

Dr. Burns stood with that blasted smirk etched on his face, casting a smug glance at her emerald earbobs. "If I may, Miss Mountbatten. A lovely society lady like yourself shouldn't be searching for a career. One snap of those pretty fingers and you'd have dozens of men at your door." He leaned forward. "I have a son…"

"Good day, Dr. Burns."

Spinning on her heel, Tori marched to the door, ignoring the deep chuckle behind her. She didn't stop until she pushed through the double doors onto the busy Boston sidewalk. Tori turned into an alley and pressed her back against the wall, inhaling deep breaths.

The nerve!

She put white-gloved hands against her cheeks. Warm.

Botheration. Her face likely matched her fiery red hair. She tugged on a tightly coiled curl. A color to match her temper, as her mother constantly opined.

Why did arrogant men like Dr. Burns get under her skin so easily?

Tori growled, letting the curl spring back into place. She'd never be able to open her own practice if she couldn't find a doctor to train under first. At least a year. That's what the stipulation on her medical diploma stated. She was technically a doctor but had to work under a more experienced physician before she could take on patients by herself.

But no one would hire her. She'd been looking for weeks, and not a single doctor took her seriously. Most laughed when she applied. Others said women doctors had no place in medicine.

With another growl, Tori shoved off the wall and stomped down the alley, the heels of her walking boots clicking against the cobblestone. The late-morning sun shone warm and bright. People called to one another as they hurried to and fro, going about their daily business. She kept her head ducked to avoid talking with anyone. Too soon, she reached the south slope of Beacon Hill. Tori stared at the opulent homes, her own included, and shuddered.

Fancy prisons, the lot of them.

Maybe now was a good time to visit the hospital in...

"There you are, Victoria."

Tori groaned under her breath. That syrupy, condescending voice belonged to only one person. "Hello, Mother."

Her mother floated down the sidewalk, parasol held over her head. Tori was certain Crystalline Mountbatten's skin had never felt the sun. That milky white complexion wasn't easy to accomplish as a redhead, but her mother religiously used her silly parasol no matter the season or weather.

Tori never used one and had the freckles to prove it. Freckles she was rather fond of.

"You really should use your parasol."

Perhaps Mother was a mind reader. Tori rolled her eyes heavenward, praying for strength as she often did around Mother. "We've been over this."

"Yet you refuse to take my advice." Mother sniffed, somehow managing to look down on Tori even being several inches shorter. "No self-respecting man will want a woman with freckles."

"Excellent." Tori smiled wide. She lifted her chin to the sky, letting the sun hit her full force. "This feels divine. You should try it."

Her mother gasped, one hand flying to her chest. "Victoria!"

Time to make her escape. "It was nice seeing you, Mother, but I must be going."

"Not so fast, young lady. I'm going to tea with Mrs. Williamson. You should join us."

The request sounded like a demand. Mrs. Williamson had a son—and the two families seemed determined to bring their children together. Kenneth Williamson was an arrogant, womanizing cad who thought himself God's gift to the world.

With a grunt, she fisted one hand against her hip. "No, thank you. I'm still looking for a job."

Mother's face hardened, showing off the lines around her

eyes and mouth. "Women do not belong in medicine. It's been over a month, Victoria. Give it up and take your place in society like a respectable lady." She gripped Tori's arm. "Come along. Kenneth mentioned he wanted to see you again."

Tori laughed, pulling away. Best to ignore the Kenneth comment. "If women don't belong in medicine, why did you and Father pay for my schooling?"

"You were supposed to get that out of your system in school," Mother muttered. She squared her shoulders and looked Tori in the eye. "We didn't think you'd be this determined to have a career once you knew all it entailed."

Proof that her parents didn't know her at all. Tori tossed her head, curls bouncing. "I'll see you later."

"You will never find a doctor to take you on."

"You underestimate my abilities."

Mother smirked, looking far too similar to Dr. Burns. "You underestimate your father's influence."

Tori narrowed her eyes. A shiver slid down her spine. "What does that mean?"

"I'm late. I'll give Mrs. Williamson and Kenneth your regards." Mother waved a gloved hand. "Speak to your father, Victoria. It might be enlightening."

A sick feeling settled in Tori's stomach. Father hadn't used his machinations on her in a couple years, ever since her sister, Ella, left for the Montana Territory to escape his tyranny and her ex-fiancé's abuse. Tori had wanted to go with Ella, but she needed to finish medical school. Suspecting Father would turn his manipulative ways on her, she'd been surprised when he willingly paid her tuition. Now, it seemed he'd just been biding his time to flex his control over her.

Tori gritted her teeth. She bolted back the way she'd come, past building after building on the cobblestone street, not stopping until she reached her father's office. The three-story brick structure loomed over her. It was the first Monday in June, and

Father never took clients on Mondays—which meant no interruptions. She pushed through the front door and strode down the hallway, past the receptionist, and burst into his personal office.

Father acknowledged her presence with a lift of his bushy brows. He swept back his graying brown hair and frowned, green eyes flashing with annoyance. "What are you doing here?"

No one would accuse him of beating around the bush. It was perhaps the only thing she'd inherited from him. "Looking for answers."

He sat back in his chair and crossed his arms. "Theatrics won't get you anywhere, Victoria. Speak plainly."

She mimicked his position, plopping into a chair with her arms pulled in tight against her chest. "Mother insinuated you're the reason I haven't found a position as a doctor. Is that true?"

Father chuckled, the derision in the sound slicing through her. "For someone who thinks she's so smart, it took far too long for you to catch on."

Dread curled in her stomach. She stared at her father, clenching the material of her skirt. "Why did you pay for my schooling if you had no intention of me practicing medicine?"

He snorted. "The tuition was mere pennies. Your mother and I knew we'd have less of a fight from you if we indulged your little venture. Now that you've graduated, it's time to take your place in society. No daughter of mine is going to have a profession." His face twisted. "It's bad enough your crazed sister ran off and married a rancher..."

"Ella is not crazed." Tori stood, hands fisted at her sides. "She escaped the dysfunction of this family."

Father's eyes sparked, and his face became dangerously calm. "Careful."

As if his threats ever deterred her. "Or what? You'll block

me from becoming a physician? It seems you've already decided on that." She planted her palms on his desk, learning forward with a sneer. "You can't cow me the way you do your clients. Unlike them, I see you for who you are. A calculating, manipulative man who cares nothing for others, who will stop at nothing to get what he wants." She straightened, burning rage pulsing through her. "You won't win. I'll find a way to fulfill my dream. Count on it."

Pushing back his chair, her father rose slowly, gaze locked on hers. "I've had enough of your rebellion. You had your time in medical school. That part of your life is now over. No doctor in Boston will take you on. I've made sure of that."

A surge of heat exploded in Tori's stomach. She slammed a hand on his desk. "How dare you!"

"I dare more." Father's lips curved in a cruel smile. "As of now, you're cut off from family funds. Until you marry a suitable man, you will have no resources. Understood?"

She stared, heart hammering an erratic pulse. "What?"

"And if you're not married within three months, you no longer have a home at our residence. You'll have to fend for yourself, though it'll be hard to do so without money."

"That's blackmail!"

"Call it what you will. My decision is made." Her father lowered back into his chair, a satisfied grin on his face. "I believe Kenneth Williamson is looking for a wife. You should consider him."

And he dared label Ella the crazed one.

"Never."

Father shrugged and riffled through papers on his desk. "It's no concern of mine who you choose, so long as he comes from wealth and status. For your sake, I hope you find a husband soon."

For her sake, indeed. Nothing about this was for her. Father craved control, and he'd never liked how Tori bucked his rule.

Now, by cutting her off from money and career hopes, he knew she'd have no choice but to follow his directive.

Spine going rigid, Tori backed out of the office and slammed the door behind her without a glance behind.

No. He wouldn't win.

She'd find a way out of this mess.

$\sim$

*H*arrison Blake stared at the calendar on his office wall. June sixth. His thirtieth birthday loomed just four months away, and with it, the requirement that he marry.

"Ridiculous stipulation for an inheritance," he muttered. What had great-aunt Lucille been thinking? He was already set to inherit his father's wealth one day, but with the funds his aunt left him, he could finally move west and build a hospital— his life-long dream.

The one he'd never breathed to a single soul.

His parents would have a conniption if they knew their son wanted out of society life. They already lamented the fact that he'd become a doctor instead of a gentleman of leisure. If he told them he wanted to leave Boston, they'd think he'd lost his mind.

He wanted the money, but his aunt also stated his future wife must be a society lady. What socialite would want to leave Boston for the wilds of the west?

With a sigh, Harrison left the office. He had patients to see, and thinking of his aunt's requirements for his future gave him a headache.

He passed through the lobby. A young couple sat with their infant on one of the settees. They spoke in low tones, but he caught their whispered words in Italian. The woman bit her lip as he walked by, her gaze darting to the floor. Harrison paused.

The immigrants in Boston were not treated well by the general population. If only he could ease the woman's fear, but trust took time to develop.

The door of the clinic opened as he passed, drawing his gaze up from the young couple. Victoria Mountbatten, daughter of Boston's most influential business mogul, marched inside. Her red hair gleamed under her hat, and he tried to ignore the slight hitch in his breath. They'd formed something of a friendship over the past few years, and he admired her spirit and determination to do good. "Good afternoon, Dr. Mountbatten."

She rolled her eyes. "What good is the title if I can't find work as one?"

"You've not found someone to train under?"

She stiffened, brown eyes glittering with…rage? "No."

The word was clipped and harsh. Harrison frowned, moving closer. "Is something wrong, Victoria?"

"Yes." She plunked her hands on her hips and glared at him. "Why are men determined to control women's lives?"

"Uh—"

A bit of the fight faded from her eyes. "Not you personally. You're actually one of the few men I find somewhat trustworthy."

His brows lifted. "Somewhat? You've volunteered here for three years, helping me with patients, and I'm only *somewhat* trustworthy?"

She waved a hand. "Don't take offense. I don't trust easily, as you might have noticed."

He had but wasn't about to confirm it.

"Anyway…" Victoria released a deep sigh. "I don't suppose your superior will change his mind about letting me train under him?"

"I'm afraid not. He claims he's already got his hands full training me."

She eyed him. "Haven't you been a physician for six years?"

"I have." He'd been one of the youngest men to gain that honor, but his age also meant people didn't easily take to him as a doctor. They preferred his mentor, Dr. Carrington, who'd been practicing for over forty years.

"You're fully trained, then."

"Yes."

"Could I train under you?"

With a smile, Harrison motioned toward the examination room. "You know I'd need my own practice."

She fell into step beside him. "Do you intend to have one?"

"I hope to, but I doubt you'd be interested in helping with that."

"Oh?" One perfect eyebrow rose. Two stray red curls brushed her cheeks as she spun toward him. "Why do you say that?"

Might as well tell someone. "Because I hope to go west. Boston holds no appeal for me. I want to establish and run a hospital in a place that needs one."

Victoria froze. She grabbed his arm.

Harrison stopped walking, his brow furrowing. "What?"

She stared at him, pink lips hanging open. He shuffled his feet and cleared his throat. Maybe it hadn't been the best idea to share his dream. "Did I shock you?"

"N-no." Her eyes narrowed, the look almost calculating. Harrison started to ask what was on her mind, but she tugged him toward the examination room. "Let's see our patient."

They went through their familiar routine—him doing the bulk of the examination but allowing Victoria time to practice her own skills. She was a talented doctor. In truth, if he had been the head doctor of this clinic, she'd have easily gotten the hours needed learning under him to open her own practice.

Unfortunately, that wasn't the case. And he'd heard rumors that her father threatened any doctor who took her under his care with financial ruin. He wasn't sure how the man would accomplish that, but Archibald Mountbatten had a reputation not to be crossed.

Victoria was feisty, yes but how had such a manipulative father produced a daughter as kind-hearted as she was?

"That's all for today," Harrison said to her once their final patient left. "Thanks for your help. As usual, you did great."

She regarded him with a little frown, chewing her bottom lip. Harrison's gaze tracked the motion but quickly snapped back up to her eyes. The calculating look was back. He—a grown man—wanted to squirm under her intense scrutiny.

"You said you wanted to move west. Where, exactly?"

He blinked at the abrupt words. "Uh—well, there were a few places I considered, but the one that calls to me is Montana Territory."

Her mouth fell open again.

Before she could speak, Harrison rushed on. "It's nothing but a dream, Victoria. I have no funds of my own, and I can't just move to Montana and build a hospital without money."

"I thought your great-aunt recently left you a fortune."

He grimaced. So Boston society knew of his inheritance. "She did, but there was a stipulation to receiving it."

Victoria gave him an expectant look.

Harrison sighed. "I have to get married to a society lady before I turn thirty in October."

"That's four months away."

He barked a bleak laugh. "I'm aware. It's a hopeless situation. I can't ask a woman to marry me for money, then turn around and take her from her family and home to the unknown in the west. It's unfair."

Victoria drew in a long breath. She stepped closer to him. "What if the woman gained something from the marriage as well?"

He frowned. "I'm not sure what she could possibly gain..."

"I do."

"Oh?"

She nodded, taking another step toward him, so close he could smell her jasmine perfume. "Freedom, Harrison." She grasped his hands, her next words nearly knocking him over. "Marry me."

CHAPTER 2

"*J*...beg your pardon?"

Tori would have laughed if the situation were different. Harrison blinked at her, dark-brown eyes wide in disbelief. His hands hung limp in hers.

She'd shocked him, but she couldn't let this opportunity pass. Her father had been insufferable over the past three days since his declaration. Now a way out of her predicament had fallen in her lap, and she planned to grab it and run.

If she could convince Harrison to agree.

"Marry me," she repeated, "and both our problems are solved."

He kept blinking. "Maybe you didn't hear what I said. I want to move west. There's no high society there, Victoria."

An unladylike snort escaped. "Please tell me you don't think I actually care about society."

"Not caring and not living in it are two completely different things."

Tori released one of his hands, using the other to tug him toward some chairs. "Let's discuss this, shall we?"

He settled into one and ran his fingers through his hair. The color reminded Tori of dark chocolate, and it matched the neatly trimmed beard he wore. He really was a striking man. Why hadn't he found someone to marry on his own? Surely, lots of women would be willing to tie themselves to a handsome man from money who only wanted to help others.

Not that they'd have a chance now if Tori got her way.

She leaned forward, propping her elbows on her knees. "My father gave me an ultimatum this week. He blocked my chance at being a doctor, and he cut me off financially. I'm dependent on him for everything." She scowled. "He even managed to freeze my bank account, one I'd set up separate from him."

Harrison's brow furrowed. "Isn't that illegal?"

"Not if you're Archibald Mountbatten," she muttered.

"I still don't see…"

"I'm getting there." Tori exhaled, rubbing a finger over her forehead. "Father says I must marry within three months or be kicked out. Naturally, I'm not thrilled at the thought of being homeless with no prospects for supporting myself. I'd also rather walk through fire than marry one of the pompous windbags my parents will consider a suitable husband."

Lips twitching, Harrison leaned back. "I take it I'm exempt from that class of men?"

"Without a doubt. From what I can tell, you're one of the good ones. Which is the only reason I'm suggesting we marry. You won't stand in the way of me becoming a doctor, will you?"

"Of course not. You'd make an excellent physician."

She smiled. "You see, that's why I like you."

He chuckled. "Is that the only reason?"

"No." She studied him a moment. "You're a perfectionist, but you're kind. Patients trust you. You're working in this clinic and not taking much money because the immigrants you serve can't afford it. You believe women can make good doctors, and you don't care what society thinks of you." She nodded, satisfied with her analysis. "Yes, you'll do nicely as a husband."

"You make me sound like a prized horse at auction."

"I never claimed to be a romantic. This union would be convenient for us both. With the funds from your aunt, you fulfill your dream of moving west and building a hospital, and I get out from under my father's thumb and train under you to become a physician. It's a win no matter how you look at it."

"You seem eager to go west yourself." Harrison eyed her. "Is there a reason for that?"

"My sister lives in a small Montana town. Harmony Springs." She reached for her reticule, pulling out a letter. "This is from Ella. I happen to know that town desperately needs a doctor. She asked me to come, but I didn't feel comfortable practicing medicine without any formal training. But if we went together, that would solve their problem and give us a chance to start that hospital."

His brows quirked. "Us?"

"I'd be helping you, of course. We'd have a partnership. And I should be clear, this will only work if we end up in Harmony Springs." She tucked the letter back in her reticule.

"I'm not opposed to that. You would be a good partner." He crossed his arms. "But what would our marriage look like? You make it sound transactional."

"It is transactional. It's not as though we're marrying for love. If we join our lives, it's to get something we both want. Love—or the idea of love—just complicates things."

Harrison tilted his head, gaze piercing her. "You don't believe in love?"

"Love is for fairy tales. A few people find it, but most just end up disappointed."

"That's rather cynical."

She shrugged. "It's reality."

With a sigh, Harrison nodded. "I admit, I haven't seen many

couples find love. Most in our circle marry for status, money, or both. Happiness doesn't seem to be a factor." He drew in a breath. "What about children?"

Her heart slammed against her ribs. "Children?"

He regarded her with a steady gaze. "Yeah, you know, miniature versions of us. Would you want any?"

She clutched her skirt. "Would you?"

"Yes."

Swallowing, Tori's grip on her skirt tightened. "Um…I guess we could consider that…once we're settled."

Very, very settled—preferably for several years.

"I don't mean to make you uncomfortable, Victoria. But if we do this, you should know children are another dream of mine. I've always wanted to be a father."

She wouldn't be the reason he lost that dream, even if the thought of such vulnerability with a man terrified her. She'd simply have to get over it. Women had been doing that for centuries, after all. Surely, she could manage.

"I suppose I can get used to the idea of motherhood."

A grin split Harrison's face. Hope lit inside. Was he considering her offer?

She held her breath. "So…what do you think? Should we marry and make our dreams come true?"

Harrison held up a hand. "Victoria, this isn't a decision to be made lightly. I need to pray on it, to weigh reasons for and against a marriage between us. Can I have a week?"

Shoulders slumping, Tori nodded. "That's fine."

He shook his head. "You don't think it's fine. You want an answer now."

"Well…yes. I'm a little desperate."

Chuckling, Harrison got to his feet. "That's another reason I want a week—for your sake. You might decide this decision was too impulsive and seek another way to solve your problem."

Tori shook her head, curls bouncing. "I won't change my

mind. Marrying you means I'd be able to live near my sister. That alone seals my decision, more so than escaping my father." She paused before standing. "If we did this, we would move to Harmony Springs, right?"

"Yes."

His simple answer calmed her. Tori twisted her fingers together, chewing on her lip as she regarded him. "Then I guess all that's left to do is wait."

He took her hands, just as she had earlier. "Wait and pray."

She inhaled a long breath. "Will this make our working together awkward over the next week?"

"I don't think so. We'll work as we always have, and I'll call on you at your home when I have an answer."

"All right." Tori stepped back, and Harrison released her hands. She swallowed and gave him a shaky smile.

This week would be the longest of her life.

~

Tori paced in her family's parlor. She'd never liked this room. It felt opulent and stuffy with its deep-red tapestries, matching furniture covers, and dark wood paneling. All for show.

She glanced at the clock. Thirty minutes before the infernal visiting hours were over. Who'd decided at-home social visits were a good idea? Four ladies and three gentlemen had already stopped by for refreshments and gossip, and Tori felt like jumping out of her own skin. All three men had insinuated they'd like to court her. Her parents' doing, no doubt. They'd likely told all their friends and acquaintances that their daughter was ready to choose a husband.

Ready, indeed. Rolling her eyes, Tori clamped her lips together. Forced, more like. She swung around to make her way to the other side of the parlor. Hopefully, Harrison agreed to her proposal. That would solve all their problems. Unfortunately, it had been five days, and he hadn't yet given her an answer. Their work at the clinic continued as always, but the topic of marriage hadn't come up again.

That didn't bode well. If she had to marry one of these peacocks her mother kept parading before her, she'd be trapped in society life and unable to fulfill her dreams—not to mention being miserable.

The skirt of her deep-blue dress rustled as she turned again, earning her a sharp glare from her mother.

"For goodness' sake, Victoria, sit down like a proper young lady."

"I prefer to stand, thank you."

Mother folded her hands. "Have I taught you nothing about manners and decorum?"

Tori swallowed the smart reply that sprang to her lips. *Don't rise to her baiting.* Instead, she drew in a deep breath and sank onto the loveseat.

"There now." Mother nodded, approval in her eyes. "Was that so hard?"

Biting her tongue, Tori gave Mother a thin smile and kept quiet.

"Ahem." Their butler, Hanson, stood in the doorway. "Madam, Mrs. Williamson and her son are here to see you."

Knots twisted in Tori's stomach as Mother's smile stretched wide. "Excellent. Show them in." Her gaze shifted to Tori. "Behave yourself, young lady."

Tori stood. "Why are they—"

Mrs. Williamson glided into the room. "Crystalline, dearest, it's been far too long." She air-kissed Mother's cheeks as Kenneth ambled in behind her. His dark-blond hair was pomaded to perfection, and his navy waistcoat brought out the color of his eyes. A square jaw and strong cheekbones framed a straight nose and practiced smile. The man was undeniably handsome—and he knew it.

He bowed to Mother, one hand behind his back. "Mrs. Mountbatten, thank you for receiving us."

Mother preened. "It's our pleasure, Kenneth. Isn't it, Victoria?"

"Hello, Mrs. Williamson, Mr. Williamson."

There. Her voice sounded civil enough.

"Ah, Victoria." Kenneth's cat-like smile widened as he stepped her way. "You look lovelier every time I see you. The summer air agrees with your complexion."

Tori choked back a snort. She inclined her head and searched for the right words. "I appreciate the compliment, Mr. Williamson."

"Come, now, it's 'Kenneth,' darling." He whipped his hand from behind his back, flourishing a bouquet of roses under her nose. "For my sweet Boston rose."

Disgust churned inside. Mother and Mrs. Williamson watched the interaction with unconcealed delight. Tori schooled her features as best she could and accepted the bouquet. "What a...kind...gesture." She raised a hand for Hanson, who remained hovering in the doorway. "Hanson, would you please find a vase for these?"

"Of course, miss."

Once he'd taken the flowers, Tori's mother clapped her hands. "Shall I send for tea?"

"Actually, Mrs. Mountbatten, might I be so bold as to request an audience with Victoria alone? I have a particular question I'd like to ask her." Kenneth's eyes never left Tori as he spoke. His gaze reminded her of a lion's with a gazelle in its sight.

She shook her head. "I don't think that's necessary. Anything you have to say to me..."

"Nonsense, Victoria. Hear the young man out." Mother rose gracefully. "Mrs. Williamson and I will take a nice, long walk in the garden."

The gleam in her mother's eyes and the grin on Mrs. Williamson's face told her they knew what this interview was about. Tori's stomach dropped as they left the room and clicked the door shut behind them, leaving her alone with Kenneth.

She plopped onto the loveseat with a groan. "What do you want?"

He tutted. Sitting beside her, he gripped her hands in his. "Is that any way to speak to your adoring suitor?"

Tori yanked her hands away and shot to her feet. "You are too familiar, sir. I did not give you permission to touch me, and we are not courting."

"I would like to change that." He rose to his feet, his gaze locked on hers as he took purposeful steps toward her. "I spoke to your father this morning, Victoria. He gave his blessing for us."

She backed away. "I don't see how—"

"Marry me, darling."

Her jaw dropped open. It hadn't been a request, but a demand. The audacity! "Absolutely not."

He chuckled low. "Why not? Your father tells me you've found yourself in a rather delicate situation. You need a husband, or you face being disowned with no way to support yourself."

Father told him that? Tori's cheeks flushed, and her heart thumped heavy in her chest. "I'll manage."

"You don't have to manage." Kenneth loomed closer. "Marry me, and you'll never have financial concerns." His gaze raked over her body. "My parents love the idea of joining families with yours. Imagine the sheer wealth between us."

Greed proved a powerful motivator for members of their class. Tori had no doubt the only reason Kenneth wanted to marry her was for her substantial dowry and social standing. She'd be left on her own, while he scurried around town with his multiple mistresses. Rumor had it he'd fathered eight children already. She had no intention of being another feather in his cap.

"No."

"No?"

His brow arched. Amusement etched over his face. "Do you have a better option?"

His arrogance made her bristle. Tori lifted her chin even as she took another few steps back. "As a matter of fact, I do."

Kenneth's confidence wavered. His eyes narrowed. "You're just saying that."

"No, I'm not. There's already been a proposal."

Never mind that she'd been the one to propose.

Something sinister flickered on his face. "And it's been accepted?"

She faltered. "Not...exactly. My father isn't aware of it yet."

Kenneth scoffed. "What kind of man asks a woman to marry him before getting permission from her father?" He laughed, the sound derisive. "He's not suitable, is he?"

"It's none of your concern."

A slow smile spread over his face. "So you're not engaged."

"No, but—"

Kenneth lunged forward. Tori jerked back. Fear slithered through her as his hands clamped over her arms. He pinned her arms behind her and pressed her into the wall with his body.

She was trapped.

Panic threatened. Tori struggled, but his vice grip didn't loosen. "Let go of me!"

"And let an opportunity to kiss a beautiful woman pass by? I don't think so." Warm breath puffed in her ear as he whispered against it. "Relax. You'll enjoy this."

"I doubt it." She sneered. "Now unhand me at once, or I'll scream."

He laughed, gripping both her wrists in one hand while his other moved to her face. "I like feisty women. Makes taming them that much more satisfying."

Before she could react, his lips crashed onto hers. Revulsion filled her. She struggled again, but he pressed her harder into the wall, his hand holding her face captive, his lips insistent.

He thrived on domination. Just like her father.

But if she'd learned anything in the years under Father's roof, it was that apparent submission appeased him. An idea sprang to mind, one that disgusted her but might work. She stopped struggling and forced her body to relax. Then, instead of resisting his kiss, she kissed him back.

He chuckled low in his throat. "I knew you'd like it," he whispered against her lips.

Tori wanted to gag, but she purred out the answer he wanted. "You were right." Then she kissed him again, pressing forward slightly.

He stumbled back a couple steps, dropping her wrists and pulling her into his arms. With her body free from the wall and her hands loose, Tori gripped his upper arms. Being a doctor gave her excellent knowledge of human anatomy. Using her grip on him for leverage, she jerked her knee upward hard.

Kenneth ripped away with a curse, then doubled over and crumpled to the floor.

Tori ran to the door and flung it open. "Hanson!"

The butler materialized at once. "Yes, miss?"

She jerked her head at a prone Kenneth. "Get Bates and escort Mr. Williamson from the house. He's not welcome."

Hanson's gaze took in her features, which no doubt included swollen lips and messy hair. His eyes hardened. "Did he—"

"Yes, but he's no longer a threat. I incapacitated him. At least temporarily."

"Good." Hanson gave a sharp nod. "I'll just be a moment."

"Thank you."

Tori walked back to Kenneth. He glared up at her, then groaned. She shoved him to his back. "If you *ever* try something like that again, I will make sure you never father another child. Understand?"

"You made a big mistake," he wheezed.

"You made the mistake." Tori crossed her arms. "And in case it wasn't crystal clear, I will *never* marry you."

Hanson arrived with Bates, the household manservant who used to be a bodyguard. He'd once saved Ella from a situation much worse than the one Tori just endured. She waved a hand at Kenneth. "Get him out."

Bates nodded. "Yes, miss." He hauled Kenneth to his feet. "Let's go, Mr. Williamson."

"I can walk myself," Kenneth grumbled. He shot Tori a nasty look as he left the room.

She ignored it and grasped Hanson's hand. "Thank you for coming right away."

"Of course, miss. Is there anything else I can do?"

"Yes. Please tell my mother and Mrs. Williamson that Kenneth had to leave. I'll be in my room."

"I'll let them know."

Tori clenched her trembling hands. Suddenly cold, she exhaled a long breath and followed Hanson into the hall. She stopped abruptly. Kenneth's flowers sat on the table just outside the parlor.

"Hanson, one more thing, please."

He raised a brow.

Tori pointed at the offending bouquet. "Get rid of those."

He grinned. "Very good, miss."

As he took the flowers from the room, Tori settled her hands over her stomach. Her body trembled. She leaned against the wall, swallowing hard as her bravado fled. Harrison had to accept her proposal. If not...

What would she do?

CHAPTER 3

Harrison pinched his nose as he walked down the street at a rapid pace. The humid morning air did nothing to calm him. His week was almost up, and he felt no closer to an answer than when Victoria first proposed marriage.

He still couldn't believe how gutsy she'd been. Desperation could drive a person to strange things, but he'd never pictured the determined, feisty Victoria Mountbatten being brought to such measures. She'd asked him to marry her for the sake of freedom, and after hearing her story, he couldn't blame her.

If they married, everything he hoped for would come true. His aunt's money would be his. He could leave Boston and establish a practice of his own, build a hospital. He'd have his wife as a partnering physician, and they would live in the west. No more expectations from high society, just the freedom to live out their lives in a manner they wanted.

Even so, part of him wished for a love match, no matter how unlikely. If he married Victoria, that hope would die. He'd seen the panic in her eyes when he brought up children. She might have agreed to it in a fit of desperation, but he wouldn't force her into anything she didn't want. And he hadn't been brave enough to bring up his desire for love. Could he give those up?

A deep sigh escaped. He glanced toward the heavens. "What do I do, Lord? I need Your guidance."

He turned a corner and ran into someone. A feminine *oomph* had him reaching to steady the woman. "My apologies, miss. I wasn't watching my steps."

She chuckled low. "Something on your mind, Harrison? I do hope this is a sign you plan to marry me."

He stepped back, hands still at her waist. Victoria gazed up at him. Humor sparkled in her eyes, eyes turned amber by sunlight. Something zipped through his stomach. Attraction? They'd worked together for three years, and while he found her beautiful, he'd never felt butterflies before. It must be her proposal playing with his mind.

Dropping his hands, he took another step back. "I'm still considering it."

The humor vanished from her gaze. She glanced behind her, worrying her lower lip. "Let me know as soon as you can. My parents have been hounding me to marry, and if you won't do it, I need to find another plan."

"That eager to get rid of me, are you?"

Her shoulders drooped. "You're the best option, but I can't live under my parents' thumb. I will do whatever it takes to be rid of their control."

"Victoria! Where are you?"

The male voice sounded close at hand. Victoria winced. "I should go. Father doesn't like it when I disappear from sight."

Harrison frowned. "I thought you didn't care what he thought."

"I don't, but I'm playing the dutiful daughter while I plot my escape." She straightened her shoulders and tossed him a smile. "See? I can be a good actress. Maybe that should be my plan if all else fails."

He started to laugh, then paused. "Are you serious?"

She met his gaze, resignation on her face. "If I must."

Still unsure if she meant it, Harrison tipped his hat. "I'll have an answer for you tomorrow when you come to the clinic."

"Thank you."

Victoria glanced over her shoulder again, then hopped backward. "Goodbye, Harrison."

He tracked her movements as she hurried around the corner once more. Unease ate at his gut when a harsh male voice spoke from somewhere in the direction she'd gone. He peered around the corner.

Victoria stood with a man and woman about twenty yards away, her posture submissive. He'd never seen her like that before. His unease grew. He recognized Mr. Mountbatten, and he didn't like the way the man was berating his daughter.

Before he realized what he was doing, Harrison rounded the corner, walking with purposeful steps toward the Mountbatten family. He knew what he had to do.

Victoria caught sight of him first. Her eyes widened. Harrison didn't slow until he stood at her side. Looping his arm through hers, he gave her a soft smile. "Hello, my dear. Fancy running into you like this."

Her father eyed him with suspicion. "Mr. Blake, what are you doing?"

"Greeting my beautiful fiancée, of course."

Victoria's small gasp was drowned by Mr. Mountbatten's sharp exclamation. Mrs. Mountbatten also gasped, her hands going to her throat. "Victoria, why didn't you tell us you were engaged to Harrison Blake? No wonder you turned down Kenneth. A Williamson is nothing to a Blake. Your wedding will be the society event of the year!"

She'd turned down Kenneth Williamson?

His new fiancée rose to full height. "Mother, you know full well I don't want a big wedding, regardless of who I marry."

"But…"

"Wait just a minute," Mr. Mountbatten boomed. Silence descended over their little group. His angry gaze darted between Harrison and Victoria. "Is this a ploy?"

Victoria's hand tightened on Harrison's arm. "No, Father, it is not. We fully intend to wed. The sooner the better."

"He's a doctor."

Harrison shifted his body, shielding Victoria from her father's venomous gaze. "Sir, your daughter and I already work together. Our marriage will simply be a continuation of that."

Mr. Mountbatten turned purple. "What do you mean, you already work together?"

Harrison glanced at Victoria. What had he said wrong? The man's anger seemed to have multiplied exponentially at that innocent statement.

Victoria lifted her chin. "I volunteer at Harrison's clinic every Tuesday and Friday. You know that, Father."

His expression eased the smallest bit. "You mean Dr. Carrington's clinic?"

"Yes, Dr. Carrington is my mentor," Harrison said. "I've worked under him for six years."

"So you don't have your own practice?"

Something gleamed in the man's eyes that Harrison didn't like, but he refused to respond to the unknown bait. "That is correct."

"Hmph." Mr. Mountbatten leaned on his showy cane. "Then I suppose this could work." He peered at Victoria, brows lowering. "But if I discover this is a sham or a trick…"

"It's neither," Harrison cut in. He pulled Victoria closer, placing his hand over hers where it rested on his arm. "Why would you think such a thing?"

Mr. Mountbatten's mouth opened and closed like a fish's.

"Never mind." He thumped his cane against the ground. "We'll have the wedding in six weeks. Starting the planning, Crystalline. Between you and Mrs. Blake, I trust it will indeed be an event for the ages."

Harrison tugged his collar. He would have to break the news to his parents tonight. "Umm...this engagement is still new. We hadn't told either family yet."

Waving a hand, Mrs. Mountbatten beamed. "Katharine will be thrilled. She's long talked of you finally settling down. It will be fun planning a wedding with her."

Mr. Mountbatten glared at Victoria. "And no arguments from you, young lady. Your mother was denied a wedding for Ariella. She's getting one for you."

Victoria's smile seemed as genuine as fool's gold. "I didn't plan to argue."

"That's a first," her father muttered.

Harrison had never particularly liked Mr. Mountbatten, but his dislike grew by the second. "If you don't mind, *sir*, I'd like a moment alone with Victoria."

"Suit yourself." The man shrugged. "She'll be your problem soon enough."

As the Mountbattens walked away, Harrison stared after them. He turned back to Victoria with a shake of his head. "I can see why..."

She launched herself into his arms. "Thank you."

He stumbled back a step before wrapping her in a loose embrace. Jasmine permeated his senses, momentarily rendering him mute. Why did it feel so good to hold her?

He didn't dare analyze that.

She pulled away seconds later. Her brows hitched upward. "So...we're truly getting married?"

"If you still want it."

"I do."

Harrison pulled in a slow breath. "Then I guess we'll be

man and wife in a few short weeks." He tilted his head. "Though your mother said you had an offer from Kenneth Williamson. Are you sure you want to marry me instead? Maybe he can offer you love..."

Her face went stone hard. "You can't be ignorant of his dalliances around town."

"Well...no."

"Then you know why I turned him down. I expect fidelity in marriage, regardless of type." She eyed him. "You will be faithful, won't you?"

"I'm insulted you have to ask."

Victoria crossed her arms. "That's not an answer."

Maybe playfulness hadn't been the correct response. He laid a hand on her shoulder. "I will be faithful, Victoria. You have my word."

She studied him for a moment. Her face softened. "Good. Then we're officially engaged."

No backing out now. They'd get married and travel west, chasing their dreams.

What could possibly go wrong?

~

Six weeks passed far too slowly for Tori's liking. Her mother was consumed with wedding plans, barely asking Tori her opinion on anything. Which was fine. As far as she was concerned, her mother could make this wedding whatever she wanted. Katharine Blake did just as much planning, and Tori often came home to find the two women in the parlor, gushing over their children's impending marriage.

She'd let them have their fun. Once the wedding was complete, Harrison could access his aunt's funds, and they would leave Boston for good.

Tori couldn't wait.

Harrison had already wired Harmony Springs, asking to take the open position for doctor. The reply had been immediate—an enthusiastic yes. Harrison simply mentioned he'd be bringing a wife, respecting Tori's wish to remain anonymous until they arrived in town. She wanted to surprise Ella.

Now it was nearing the end of July. The wedding would take place tomorrow. With a skip in her step, Tori made her way to Harrison's clinic. Perhaps she should call it Dr. Carrington's clinic, but since she volunteered on the days he had off, she rarely saw him.

So much the better. She didn't trust him, not when he didn't have the backbone to train her because of her father's threats.

Coward.

She pushed the door to the clinic open. Harrison met her in the lobby. His hair was mussed and his shirt wrinkled. Tori blinked, unused to seeing him in such disarray. "You look frazzled."

He ran his hands through his hair, making it stick up at odd angles. "There's so much paperwork to finish before the wedding. I can't leave it all to Dr. Carrington. He's used to me doing it, and—"

"Hold on." Tori gripped his arm. "Isn't he the head physician?"

"Yes, but he's already stressed with me leaving. I'd like to relieve him of whatever I can."

Her eyes widened. "You told him about leaving?"

"Of course." He eyed her, brow wrinkling. "I couldn't just disappear, Victoria. That wouldn't be fair to him. The man took me under his wing for six years. I asked him to keep it quiet, and he's done so."

Maybe Carrington wasn't as cowardly as she'd thought. Or maybe he saw no reason to mention their imminent departure to her father. They certainly didn't run in the same circles. She exhaled a breath. "That's fair." A subject change was in order. "Do we have patients?"

"No. Would you like to help me with the paperwork?"

Wrinkling her nose, Tori shrugged. "It's not my favorite pastime, but I suppose I'll have to get used to it as a doctor. Lead the way, Harry."

He froze, his eyes bugging. "Don't call me Harry."

Sheer delight coursed through her. Tori grinned, sidling closer. "Why not? Harrison sounds stuffy."

Crossing his arms, Harrison shook his head so fast, his hair flopped. "I can't stand the nickname. Boys used to call me that in school, knowing I hated it."

Tori's grin grew. "You realize that gives me ammunition, right?"

He groaned. "Forget I said anything."

"Nope. Be on your guard, Harrison. That nickname might show up when you least expect it." She chuckled at his eye roll. "Now, about that paperwork…"

"This way."

He led her to his office. Curiosity burned in her as she followed. The two offices were the only rooms she'd never seen, as she hadn't been there to help with paperwork or filing. As she stepped into Harrison's office, she figured it'd be pristine. The room held a desk, a couple chairs, and more papers than she'd seen in her life.

Tori gaped at the mountain of white. "Where did all those come from?"

"Dr. Carrington's office."

"These aren't even yours?"

He snorted. "I wouldn't be able to handle this kind of mess. A lack of order makes me twitchy." As he eyed the papers, and a muscle in his jaw demonstrated that they did indeed make him twitch.

Tori smothered a laugh. She grabbed a stack of papers and

paged through them. Her mirth fell away. "Harrison, these are months of backlogged patient information."

"I know." He rubbed a thumb across his forehead, the V between his brows pronounced. "That's why I have to get this done before our wedding."

"Which is tomorrow."

A strangled sigh left him. "Yes."

She frowned, stepping toward him. "Why are you doing this?"

"Dr. Carrington has done so much for me. He took me in, trained me, made me the doctor I am today. If I can take some stress from him, I will."

"Most men would leave such work to their secretary."

"Uh..." His smile didn't reach his eyes. "That's why there's so much paperwork here. Dr. Carrington relied heavily on his secretary. When she got married four months ago, well..." He waved at the desk. "This happened. I wish he'd told me how disorganized he was. Maybe I could have done the paperwork once his secretary left. Then he wouldn't be in this mess."

"You realize once you leave, he'll just let paperwork pile up again, right?"

"Ugh." Harrison winced, his shoulders drooping. "You're probably right, but I can't leave this unfinished. I just...can't."

Tori rolled her eyes, pushing up her sleeves. "Perfectionism strikes again."

He reared back, blinking. "What?"

She attacked the pile of papers, sorting them into stacks. "I've seen the difference between your patient room and Dr. Carrington's. Yours is immaculate. Everything is organized just so. Your office is the same."

With a smirk, she bumped the paperweight sitting on the edge of his desk. It went askew. Harrison stared at it a moment before reaching over to right it again.

"You just proved my point," Tori said.

Red crept up his neck. Harrison dragged a hand over his cheek, his beard rustling slightly. He tugged at his collar. "Shall we get to it, then?"

They worked in silence for several long minutes. Tori made it through four stacks before coming to a sheet that looked different from the others. A newspaper? She scanned the contents and gasped. Her gaze shot to Harrison. "When did this happen?"

His forehead wrinkled in confusion. He accepted the paper and looked it over. Face going ashen, he dropped the page to the desk. "W-what's that doing in there?"

Were his hands shaking? Tori picked up the paper again. "A structure fire where people died? I don't remember hearing about that. Usually the Boston papers..."

"Don't care where immigrants are concerned."

Harrison's voice sounded faint but hard. Tori's gaze met his. He stood, pacing the small space between his desk and the wall. When he didn't speak, Tori stood as well. "What happened?"

"No one knows. They never discovered a cause." His hands tightened into fists. "Since it was three Italian workers who died, no one cared to investigate fully." Breaths coming fast, he refused to look at her. "It's my fault they're gone."

"Your fault?" Tori tipped her head, eyes narrowing. "I doubt that."

His Adam's apple bobbed as he swallowed. "I'm a physician, Victoria. It's my job to help people, to heal them. I happened to be in the North End that night soon after the fire broke out. I heard screams from men inside. Only a couple bystanders ran inside to try and help them—but I couldn't. I stood there, paralyzed with fear. And all three of them died because of it."

"Harrison, you might have died, too, if you—"

He shook his head, slicing a hand through the air. "I was a coward."

Words failed her. Tori stared at Harrison, watching as he continued to pace. If only she knew how to comfort him.

Finally, he sighed, dropping into his chair once more. "I'll finish up here. You can go home." His smile didn't reach his eyes. "I'll see you at the church tomorrow."

Was it wise to leave him in such a state? Tori bit her lip, studying him. "Harrison—"

"Please. I'll be fine. I...I just need some time."

The brokenness in his voice touched a part of her heart she didn't realize existed. She slid a hand over his and gave it a gentle squeeze. "Are you sure? It seems to me you need a friend right now."

His breaths came faster, and his eyes shone with unshed tears. "A friend...would be nice."

Tori slipped her arms around him. Harrison heaved out a short breath and hugged her back, resting his head against hers. His chest rose and fell in quick bursts as if trying to control the emotion inside. Tori held him close and closed her eyes.

Warmth pierced the hard shell around her heart. Her stomach fluttered as their embrace lengthened on. When Harrison pulled back to look at her, sparks ignited in her gut.

"Thanks, Victoria."

"You're welcome."

Her voice cracked as she spoke. Tori cleared her throat. "I guess I'll see you tomorrow."

This time, his smile did reach his eyes. "See you then."

She turned and walked out of the office, her mind in a tangle of confusion.

What just happened?

CHAPTER 4

Harrison tried to ignore the stares from the assembled wedding guests. He stood at the altar with his head held high. People packed the church, murmurs echoing through the vast sanctuary. They had to be surprised at the sudden nature of his wedding to Victoria. There had been no courtship, just an engagement announcement. He'd heard more than one disparaging comment in passing over the past six weeks about the reason for their quick nuptials.

Victoria scoffed at the opinions of society, so he let it go, even when he wanted nothing more than to defend her honor. She told him it wasn't worth it. People would think the worst, but as long as the two of them knew the truth, that was all that mattered.

He'd even heard her own father doubt her character, asking if she was in the family way when he thought Harrison out of earshot.

None of it bothered Victoria. How she managed to ignore society and its harsh judgment, he didn't know, but he admired her for it.

Organ music began playing. Harrison straightened, his gaze

snapping to the back of the church. His older sister walked through the double doors. She wore a flouncy dress, deep burgundy with lace trim, her dark hair twisted into an elegant updo. A genuine smile tugged at her lips when their eyes met. He and Temperance might not be confidantes, but he'd always looked up to her.

He'd miss her when he left town. Just as he'd miss his parents.

Temperance took her assigned spot. Harrison's gaze went back to the church doors.

The organ swelled into the wedding march made popular by England's Queen Victoria when her granddaughter married a few decades ago. His lips twisted with the irony. How appropriate as he prepared to marry his own Victoria.

She'd probably spear him with words if he dared call her *his* to her face.

Smothering a smile, he waited for his bride to appear. Then she did, on her father's arm, and Harrison lost the ability to breathe properly.

She wore a long-sleeved white dress, the fabric smooth and shiny. It cinched at her waist—no doubt to quell any rumors of a baby. The lacy veil that covered her head couldn't hide her bright red hair, twisted into a braided crown with pearls woven throughout. A few curls lay against her cheeks. The sapphires at her throat gleamed in the sunlight pouring through stained glass windows.

How had he failed to notice her radiant beauty before?

Something stirred inside, a feeling he didn't want to welcome. She was so much more than a pretty face. He'd known that for a while, but yesterday, her concern in his office cemented it. The fact that she'd offered comfort touched him deeply.

His hand moved without conscious thought, rubbing at the hidden scars under his expensive suit. He jerked his hand down again as Victoria joined him. Pushing the memories away, he smiled at his bride. She smiled back, though it looked tight.

Mr. Mountbatten placed her hand in Harrison's. No emotion clouded the older man's face. He turned and stoically stood beside his wife.

Victoria relaxed. Her smile softened, her hand steady in Harrison's. He let his gaze roam her face as the pastor began the ceremony. She must have powder on because he couldn't see a single freckle.

What a shame. He liked her freckles.

The pastor's booming voice rang out through the church. "And now for the vows." He turned to Harrison. "Repeat after me."

"I, Harrison Blake, take you, Victoria Mountbatten, to be my wife, to have and to hold from this day forward, for better, for worse, for richer, for poorer, in sickness and in health, to love and to cherish, till death us do part, according to God's holy law, and this is my solemn vow."

This is my solemn vow.

The words played over and again in his mind as Victoria spoke hers. A solemn vow. To have and to hold in all life's circumstances, to love and to cherish until death parted them.

And he'd vowed to do that before God and man.

Sweat broke out on his brow. Why hadn't he paid closer attention to wedding vows before? He'd just promised to love his wife.

Victoria's gaze remained calm and collected. She smiled at him, and his stomach flipped.

Oh no.

As they exchanged rings, Harrison prayed his hands remain steady. He slipped the ring on her finger. The diamonds sparkled, winking up at him.

"I now pronounce you husband and wife. You may kiss the bride."

Harrison nearly choked on air. He gulped. Victoria eyed him with a smirk on those pretty lips. Lips he'd soon be kissing, apparently.

He leaned forward. She met him halfway, their lips colliding in a short, perfunctory kiss that nevertheless turned his knees to mush.

Blast it all. His knees had no business doing that. *Victoria doesn't believe in love, remember? Pull yourself together!*

The crowd burst into polite applause as Harrison and Victoria faced them. The preacher introduced them as a married couple. Mind still hazy, Harrison led his new wife down the aisle. He didn't stop until they were secluded in a small room outside the sanctuary.

Victoria tilted her head, an amused smile dancing on her lips. "Not that I'm complaining, but aren't we supposed to greet the guests?"

"You want to stand on ceremony?"

Her smirk deepened. "Absolutely not, but we need to play the society game for another day or so. Then we'll be free."

"In a moment. I have something for you."

Her eyes lit up with interest. Harrison reached into his suit's inner pocket, producing two tickets. "I purchased these a few days ago."

Victoria took them, glee written on her face. She glanced at the date stamped onto the paper. "We're leaving tomorrow?"

"If that's acceptable."

She chuckled. "Harrison, I'd leave right now if we could." Handing the tickets back to him, she brushed a wayward red curl back. "What about the money from your aunt?"

"I directed my solicitor to send the funds to the bank in Harmony Springs once they're released. It should be there before we are."

Victoria expelled a long breath. Her brown eyes shone.

"This time next week, we'll be in our new home. Wherever that may be. I can't wait."

He liked the sound of *our home* a little too much. Extending his arm, he tried to block the thought from his mind. "Shall we see to our guests?"

She slid her hand into the crook of his elbow. "Our final foray into society." A grin split her face. "Lead the way."

~

"*Y*ou're *what?*"

The purple hue on Father's face made Tori grin. Wedding guests milled about the lavish reception at the Mountbatten home, meaning he wouldn't yell, but his shock and displeasure couldn't be hidden. He lowered his voice and leaned closer, his words coming in a hiss. "What do you mean, you're moving to the Montana Territory? Have you lost your mind?"

"Just what I said. Harrison and I leave tomorrow morning."

The color on Father's face grew darker. "Victoria, this is nonsense. You need to settle down, have children, and take your place with society matrons. That's the whole point of this marriage."

"No, the point of this marriage was freedom. Harrison and I both needed something from each other, so we made a deal." She tapped her chin with a finger. "Isn't that what your business is all about? Contractual relationships?"

"I forbid you—"

"You can't forbid anything. I'm no longer under your control. That honor belongs to my husband."

The words felt bitter in her mouth, but the expression on her father's face was worth it. He slapped his hands together. "We'll annul the union and find you a more acceptable—"

"There will be no annulment. You have no power over our

affairs. We're married, and we'll remain married." Tori scanned the room, catching sight of Harrison with his parents at one of the tables. "Excuse me, Father. I'm going to speak with my husband." She gave him a brittle smile. "Feel free to tell Mother that we're leaving in the morning."

Flouncing away, she left her past behind. Sweet relief poured through her. She could now live life on her own terms, her own way.

Someone latched onto her arm and pulled her into an alcove. Tori gasped, almost losing her balance in her voluminous dress. She straightened with a huff. "What in the world —?" When she saw the man's face, she almost gasped again.

Kenneth.

His grip on her arm became painfully tight. "Hello, Victoria."

She glared at him. "Let go of me. Or do I need to knee you again?"

Eyes narrowing, he backed away slightly while keeping hold of her. "I told you that was a mistake."

Harrison's voice sounded behind her, hard and stiff. "Williamson. Is there a reason you're holding onto my wife?"

The protectiveness behind his words had Tori's knees going weak. Kenneth dropped her arm as Harrison's hand came to rest on her lower back. "Congratulations, Blake. You snagged the catch of the season. Be careful, though—she's a handful."

Tori's jaw tensed. Her fingers itched to smack that arrogant smile off Kenneth's face. How dare he insinuate such rot?

Harrison's hand slid around her waist and pulled her close. Blinking, she looked up to see him smiling at her tenderly. "She's perfect." He leaned down and placed a soft kiss on her lips. When he pulled back, he ran a finger down her cheek. "I'm a fortunate man."

Currents of heat zipped through her.

Kenneth cleared his throat. "Yes, well..."

Harrison side-eyed him, wrapping Tori fully in his arms. "If you don't mind, I'd like a moment with my wife. Alone." His gaze returned to her as if she were the most precious thing in the world. For a moment, she forgot how to breathe.

"Of course." Kenneth slipped around them as malice burned in his eyes. He smiled tightly, giving her a short salute. "I'm sure we'll talk again soon."

Not if I'm in Harmony Springs.

Harrison nuzzled her neck. Tori gasped, all thoughts of Kenneth vaporizing. "Wh-what are you doing?"

He lifted his head and looked over her shoulder. "Is he gone?"

Disappointment hung heavy in her stomach. Her shoulders drooped. "You were acting."

"I thought I did quite a good job. For all he knows, we wanted this alcove to ourselves for a little romantic rendezvous." His serious gaze searched hers. "I'm sorry for taking liberties like that, Victoria. I should have thought of something else to get rid of him."

"It's fine. I'm glad you got him to leave." She shuddered, thankful to still be in her husband's arms. There was something comforting about them. "He trapped me before at my home."

Harrison's body went rigid. He stared at her, fire flashing in his eyes. "What did he do?"

"Proposed marriage, wouldn't take no for an answer, then forced a kiss on me."

"That disgusting, licentious weasel. I ought to—"

Tori rested her hand on his chest. Harrison stilled, his gaze meeting hers. She smiled, rubbing her thumb against the soft fabric of his formal waistcoat. "Thank you for getting rid of him."

His jaw twitched. "Men like that should be locked up." His face fell and his gaze dropped. "Though I'm not much better. I just kissed you without warning."

"Don't compare your kiss to his. For one, we're married. There's nothing untoward about kisses." Her stomach slowly flipped as his gaze found hers again. "Second, his was about domination and power. Yours was gentle, protective. Never apologize for that."

A twinkle lit in his eyes. "So you were fine with it?"

Her stomach danced again. Ignoring the strange sensation, Tori shrugged. "It served its purpose."

"There you two are!"

Tori jolted out of Harrison's arms and swung to see his sister smirking at them. Temperance shook a finger at her brother and linked arms with Tori. "You lovebirds can have alone time later. Mother and Father would like to speak with you."

"Both of us?" Harrison asked.

"Yes." Temperance's face went solemn. "They heard a rather distressing rumor from the Mountbattens."

Harrison muttered under his breath, running a hand through his hair. He grabbed Tori's free hand. "That's not how I wanted them to find out."

Temperance followed them out of the alcove. "It's true?" Her voice trembled. "You're leaving?"

"We are."

"Why didn't you say something sooner?" Hurt flashed over her face, her lips forming a perfect pout.

Harrison sighed. "I'll explain once we're all together."

They made their way across the room. Mr. and Mrs. Blake stood to receive them, matching looks of disappointment etched across their features. Mrs. Blake spoke before they'd stopped walking. "Darling, what's this nonsense about a move to the territories?"

Temperance sat at the table, and Harrison's grip on Tori's hand tightened. "Would you like a drink first, Mother?"

"No, thank you. Please explain yourself."

Mr. Blake put a hand on his wife's back. "Katharine, why

don't we all sit? I'm sure there's a logical explanation. Right, son?"

"There is." Harrison pulled out Tori's chair. Once she sat, he took the chair beside her. With a long exhale, he folded his hands on the table. "Mother, Father, you know being a doctor is important to me."

"Yes." His mother sniffed. "An occupation we don't understand. Is this what's taking you away from us?"

"I'm afraid so. Victoria and I are moving to the Montana Territory to build a hospital and provide medical care to residents on the frontier."

His parents fell silent. Tori waited for the shouting, the demands to abandon such a plan.

They never came. Instead, Mr. Blake took a sip of champagne before speaking. "Son, where did this idea come from? You've never said a thing about living outside of Boston."

"I know it seems sudden, but I've dreamed of this for years. Ever since medical school."

Mrs. Blake frowned. "Medical school? That was years ago."

"Yes. I never had an opportunity to make it happen. Now, though, with the inheritance Aunt Lucille left me, I can afford to build and finance a hospital for years."

Temperance broke in. "Why Montana Territory, Harrison? Why not build a hospital here in Boston? There are plenty in need of your services."

"There are lots of doctors here. The territories are often lacking in medical care because infirmaries are few and far between, much less hospitals." He leaned forward, passion burning in his eyes. "People there die from illness or disease that are treatable with the right care, medication, and hygiene. I have the resources to help. Isn't that the right thing to do?"

Tori stared at him. She'd known Harrison for years, but she'd never seen him so alight with purpose. It was quite attractive.

Not that our relationship is like that.

Nor did she want it to be. But working together, knowing that kind of passion drove him? They'd get along just fine.

Mr. Blake cleared his throat. He downed another gulp of champagne. "That's a noble endeavor, Harrison. I commend you for wanting to help others. You take Christian charity seriously. However, think of what you're giving up. You have never known the hardships of life in the territories. Everything has been handed to you. Do you think it's going to be easy establishing yourself in a new, unknown place? What if the residents of the town you move to don't want your help?"

"They do," Tori said. "My sister lives there, and they've been wanting a doctor for some time."

All three members of his family looked at her. Mrs. Blake tilted her head. "You're moving to the same town as Ariella?"

"Harmony Springs. It's a beautiful place, with friendly people. I think Harrison and I will be happy there."

"Still..." Mrs. Blake sighed. "Our only son is moving so far away. What about seeing our grandchildren grow up?"

Tori coughed, air sticking in her throat.

Harrison covered her hand with his. A smile played on his lips. "Mother, when grandchildren come, we'll be sure to visit. And you're welcome to visit Harmony Springs anytime. We'd love to have you."

Mr. Blake studied them both. His brows lowered as he leaned back. "You're determined to do this."

"Yes, sir." Harrison straightened. "We leave on the morning train."

"What?" Mrs. Blake's hand flew to her chest. She stared at him, mouth opening and closing. "Tomorrow? We have no time to send you off properly!"

"We don't want fanfare." Tori turned to her new mother-in-law. How to ease the woman's distress? "Perhaps we can enjoy breakfast together before Harrison and I depart?"

"That would be wonderful." Mr. Blake patted her free hand. He exhaled slowly. "If my son decides it's best to move across the country, I'm glad he'll at least have you at his side. A good companion makes life easier."

Tori nodded, giving Harrison a smile. "It'll be an adventure."

Companionship was a good way to describe their relationship. But something deep inside rebelled at the thought, whispering that marriage was meant to be more.

She buried the thought deeper. Having a companion for life would be good. They'd continue to grow their friendship, and there would be no need for messy feelings.

Her gaze met Harrison's, and the spark that shot through her at the sight of his warm brown eyes said she might be in trouble.

CHAPTER 5

They'd done it.

Tori bounced in her seat, watching the countryside pass by through the train window. Harrison slept upright beside her, his head bobbing against the seat. Four days of travel left him exhausted, but she only felt exhilaration. In a few short hours, they would be in Harmony Springs.

Her new life awaited. Opening a medical practice, living in the same town as her sister, and being free of her parents. Surely, it would be glorious.

A half snore from her new husband had her eyes turning to him. Even traveling, he managed to keep his beard well-trimmed. Was it as soft as it looked? Tori reached out, but Harrison's head slipped to the side, landing with a thud on her shoulder. She froze. He grunted but didn't wake. Tori tucked her hand under her leg to prevent another wayward desire to touch his face.

What was wrong with her? She'd never had a desire to touch a man before. Harrison might be her husband, but that didn't mean she should be caressing his face while he slept.

Her gaze landed on his lips. Their two kisses had been

unexpectedly pleasant. She'd been kissed a few times in her life —Kenneth's being the worst—but none made her feel the way Harrison's did. Both his kisses were gentle and ended too soon.

Tori snorted. *Too soon?* She rolled her eyes and crossed her arms, jerking her gaze back to the rolling hills outside. That was quite enough thoughts about kissing. It wasn't something they'd be repeating anytime soon.

Why not?

The soft whisper through her heart made her eyes widen. *No. Absolutely not.*

Harrison's head fell forward. He righted himself with a small gasp, his eyes blinking open. "How long was I asleep?"

His already deep voice took on a raspy quality after his nap. Tori's stomach swooped and dipped. "A few hours. We should be arriving soon."

"Good." Harrison stretched. "I can't wait to get off this train and properly stretch my legs."

Tori chuckled, praying her warm cheeks weren't too pink. "What's wrong, Harry? Can't handle being in a moving conveyance for a few days?"

His brown eyes bored into her. "Don't call me Harry."

That took care of the pesky butterflies that invaded her stomach. She grinned, tapping his shoulder. "The more you react..."

His growl faded as the conductor walked by their compartment. The elderly gentleman poked his head inside. "We'll be arriving in fifteen minutes, folks. We appreciate you traveling with us."

Harrison thanked him.

Tori clasped her hands with a squeal. "Wonderful. Ella will be so surprised."

"On more than one count, I'd wager," Harrison said, brows raised. "How are you going to explain our marriage?"

Tori waved a hand. "Ella married to escape our parents as

well. She'll understand. Though she probably never thought I'd stoop to such a thing."

"'Stoop'?" Harrison's brows shot higher. "First, I'm only somewhat trustworthy, and now I'm someone you *stoop* to marry?"

"Well, I certainly wouldn't have married you at all if I wasn't desperate."

Harrison slapped a hand over his heart. "You wound me, Victoria."

The sparkle in his eyes told her otherwise. She chuckled. "Face it—you wouldn't have married me, either, if you'd had another choice."

"Perhaps not, but here we are, man and wife, with an inheritance that will build and run a hospital in Harmony Springs for years." He shrugged. "Seems a good deal to me."

"At least we're friendly." She reached for the lace gloves in her lap, tugging them on. "That'll make this marriage tolerable."

Laughter danced in his eyes. "Tolerable?"

"Quite so."

He leaned closer, his voice dropping to a whisper. "What if we aimed for happy instead?"

Those dratted butterflies took flight once more. "W-what?"

His gaze held hers, those chocolate depths making it impossible to look away. "We did this to take control of our future. Why not choose happiness as well?"

Wonderful. She couldn't think straight with him looking at her like that. Tori grasped onto the first thing that came to mind. "Happiness in marriage is entirely a matter of chance."

Harrison laughed. "Did you just quote *Pride and Prejudice*?"

"Charlotte Lucas was right. Most people are lucky if they find happiness with their spouse." Her eyes narrowed. "How did you know that's from *Pride and Prejudice*?"

"I have a sister obsessed with Miss Austen's books." He

rubbed his beard. "She used to quote that to me when I said I wanted to fall in love."

A prick of unease stabbed her heart. He'd wanted to fall in love? She swallowed. "I'm sorry I took that chance from you."

He regarded her for a few moments without speaking. Finally, he glanced away. "We'll see," he murmured.

Her limbs tingled. What did that mean? Before she could ask, the train slowed.

Excitement pushed out her confusion over Harrison's muttered comment. She took in the small town from her window, relishing the sight of its familiar streets. Though she hadn't been back here in two years, Harmony Springs made an impression. From its quaint wooden buildings to the friendly people, it left Boston in its dust.

She could be happy here.

When the train screeched to a halt, she bounced up and grabbed her bag. "Let's go!"

Harrison stood. He peered into the corridor. "If we hurry, we can be the first ones off."

Without another thought, Tori raced into the corridor and toward the door. As they stepped onto the platform, the warm summer air filled her lungs, smelling of sweet flowers, horse, and pine. What a unique combination.

She smiled, inhaling deeply. "Isn't it glorious?"

Harrison looked around, his gaze darting left, right, and back again. "It's something." He straightened and pointed to an empty lot across from the livery. "That might be the perfect spot for our hospital."

"You can tell already?"

He smiled, a sheepish expression on his face. "I might be a little excited to get started."

"Clearly." She patted his shoulder. "I like that about you. Once you put your mind to something, you see it through."

His ears turned red. "Thanks." Offering her his arm, he smiled. "Shall we check in at the hotel?"

They walked along the boardwalk until they reached the hotel on the opposite side of Main Street. Harrison looked between the hotel and the train station. "I'm surprised they're not closer."

Tori shrugged. "The hotel probably existed before the railroad built tracks here."

Just before they reached the doors, a man walked by, the star on his chest denoting his profession. Tori broke into a grin. She knew him well. "Travis!"

Travis Doyle stopped in his tracks. His gaze swept over her face, and his mouth dropped open. "Tori?"

She laughed, dropping her bag and Harrison's arm, and launched herself at her old friend.

~

Harrison stood frozen, watching his wife embrace another man in the middle of town. A sheriff, no less.

What had he called her? Tori?

A strange burning sensation curled through his gut. How did Victoria know this man, and why were they on such familiar terms?

When the two pulled apart, Victoria's face glowed. "It's so good to see you."

The man pushed back his cowboy hat, revealing brown hair that matched the beard on his face. His hazel eyes twinkled with good humor. "Good to see you too. Ella's gonna be thrilled. Did she know you were coming today?"

He spoke with a light Irish accent. Harrison had seen many women taken in by an accent. He clenched his teeth together as

Victoria giggled. "Oh no," she said, "we planned to surprise her."

"'We'?" The sheriff's eyes turned to Harrison, narrowing slightly. "Howdy. I don't believe we've met. How do you know Tori?"

Harrison glared back. "How do *you* know Victoria?"

"'Victoria'?" The sheriff laughed, turning to the woman in question. "I haven't heard you called that in ages." He looked at Harrison once more. "We're old friends. I lived in Boston like her family, was on the police force for a while, and helped Ella and Tori with a school for immigrant girls."

Harrison's indignation faded a bit. "I see." He took his wife's arm. "Why does he call you Tori?"

"It's what those close to me use." She shrugged. "My way of rebelling, I suppose. Tori isn't exactly a high society name."

It stung more than it should that she didn't consider him close enough to use her nickname.

"How rude of me," Tori said, slapping her forehead. "Harrison, this is Sheriff Travis Doyle. Travis, this is my husband, Harrison Blake."

"A Blake, huh? I've heard of your family." Travis's eyes went wide. He stared at Victoria before his gaze shot back to Harrison. "Husband? You got hitched?"

"About a week ago." Victoria slipped her arm through Harrison's again. "It's a long story."

"Wait." Travis's brows furrowed. "Harrison Blake—that's the name of the doctor coming to town."

"Guilty as charged."

The sheriff's lips twitched at the horrible pun. He clapped Harrison on the shoulder. "I think I'm gonna like you. If Tori agreed to marry you, you must be one of the good ones."

"He is." Victoria grinned up at him before speaking to Travis again. "There's a story there, one you'll hear at some point. Suffice it to say we both had good reason to marry and move out here."

"I'm glad for it. We've been needing a doctor something awful. Now we have two."

Victoria shook her head. "I still need a year of training—"

"You're a doctor. You have the degree." Harrison nudged her. "The training is a formality."

She glanced up, her brown eyes softer than he'd seen them before. "Which I'll have thanks to you."

His stomach flipped.

Travis plunked his hands on his hips. "Why don't you two stay with me and Cassie until you find a place to live permanently? We'd be happy to have you." He smiled at Harrison. "Cassie's my wife. Best cook this side of the Rockies. Feeding people is her love language."

The sheriff was married. Harrison suddenly liked him a lot more. "We couldn't impose…"

"Oh, yes, we could," Victoria said with a laugh. "One thing you'll learn quick about this town, Harrison—family and friends watch out for one another."

Harrison rubbed a hand over the back of his neck. "I suppose so. Can we pay you for your trouble?"

Something flickered in Travis's eyes. "No. But that reminds me, I have something I'd like to discuss with you." He stepped closer, gaze darting around while he lowered his voice. "It involves the money you transferred here."

Worry tingled up Harrison's spine. "Was it intercepted?"

"No, nothing like that." Travis picked up Victoria's discarded bag. "If you'll follow me, we can talk at the house."

As they walked, someone called Travis. He fell into step with the man while still leading Harrison and Victoria.

Harrison leaned down to his wife. "Tori?"

Her step stuttered. "It's strange hearing you call me that."

An ache began in his chest. "Do you want me to keep calling you 'Victoria'?"

"No." She regarded him for a moment, her forehead creasing. "Victoria reminds me of society and people's expectations of what's proper. Here, I just want to be Tori."

He took her in, from her tightly coiled ringlets to her adorable freckles, and a smile tugged at his lips. "The name suits you."

She scrunched her nose. "I don't know why I never thought to ask you to call me that. Ella and Travis were the only ones who used it in Boston. I guess I assumed you wouldn't like it."

"I do like it. Though I think Victoria is beautiful as well."

A low chuckle left her. "Want to know something? I don't hate it when you call me by my full name."

"Is that so?" The tension in his chest eased. His smile grew into a grin. "Maybe I'll still use Victoria from time to time."

His wife laughed. "I suppose that's acceptable." Her eyes twinkled. "Especially since I intend to call you 'Harry' from time to time."

"Ugh."

Travis said goodbye to the man walking with him and looked back at Harrison and Victoria—Tori. "Sorry about that. We're almost home."

Two minutes later, they stood in front of a two-story, clapboard house, painted white with green trim. Travis led them up the steps to the front door. He pulled it open. "Cass, I'm home. We've got company."

A petite blonde with striking blue eyes met them in the hall. She grinned at her husband. "What kind of company?"

"The kind that will need a room until they find a home." He stepped to the side, waving an arm at Harrison and Tori with a flourish. "Cassie, meet the Blakes."

Cassie gave them a warm smile. "Welcome, both of you. It's so nice to..." She gasped, her gaze locked on Tori. "Oh!"

Travis looked on with a grin, as if he enjoyed surprising his wife with someone she knew.

"Hi, Cassie," Tori said, moving forward to embrace the woman.

"Oh my word!" Cassie pulled back, eyes wide. "I can't believe you're here. Ella didn't say a word."

"She doesn't know."

Cassie laughed, the sound like tinkling bells. "Planning on surprising her, too, huh?"

"Yep."

Tori threaded her arm through Harrison's, pulling him forward. "Cassie, I'd like you to meet my husband, Harrison Blake."

"Husband?" Cassie's gaze assessed him, and Harrison fought a momentary desire to fidget. Her eyes swung back to Tori. "You got married?"

"Sure did. He's a doctor, and we plan to work together to build a hospital here in town."

"I heard about that." Cassie clasped Harrison's hand in hers. "Forgive me for being rude. Welcome to Harmony Springs."

"Thanks, ma'am."

"It's Cassie, please." She looked between him and Tori. "You must be starved. I've got some sandwiches made up in the ice box. Why don't I show you to your room, and then you can eat?"

"That sounds wonderful, Cassie. Thank you," Tori said, her face relaxed with a large smile.

Harrison had never seen her quite so at ease. Boston society must have taken a bigger toll on her than she'd let on. They'd worked together for years, and he never saw it.

Rocks settled in his stomach.

Travis clapped a hand on his shoulder. "While Cass shows Tori the room, why don't we have that chat?"

Tori and Cassie walked toward the stairs, heads bent

together, talking rapidly. At least Tori had friends in this town. That would help her feel at home.

Whether he felt the same was yet to be determined.

Squaring his shoulders, he nodded at Travis. "Let's talk."

The sheriff led him to the kitchen. Yellow curtains hung at the windows, making the room appear bright. Harrison's shoulders loosened a tension he hadn't realized existed.

Travis motioned to a mug. "Would you like some coffee? I can make a pot."

"Sure."

"Take a seat. I'll have this ready soon."

As Harrison pulled out a chair, Travis began grinding the beans. The sheriff got right to the point. "I'm worried about the amount of money you transferred to our bank."

"Worried?"

Travis put some water on the stove to boil. He faced Harrison, arms crossed. "You have more money than the folks of this entire town put together. My concern is word might get out. There's been an uptick in outlaw activity over the past five years. Bank robberies aren't common, but if someone knows there's that much cash in Harmony Springs, we could become a target."

Something Harrison should have considered before transferring his inheritance. "Do you have much of a police force here?"

Travis spread his arms. "You're looking at the police force. I don't even have a deputy."

Drumming his fingers against the table, Harrison mulled over possible solutions.

Travis finished making the coffee and brought it to the table. "I'm glad you're here, Dr. Blake, especially with this hospital proposal of yours. As I said, bank robberies are not typical. Your money should be safe."

"There's a 'but' in there, I presume?"

"Yeah." Travis handed Harrison a mug. The earthy aroma of the coffee tickled Harrison's nose, reminding him he hadn't had a decent cup since leaving Boston. He sipped slowly, the smooth, bitter flavor coating his tongue.

Travis continued. "There's a notorious gang sniffing around these parts, the Otterson brothers. They usually target trains or stagecoaches. Nothing has happened near Harmony Springs. The closest they've been is forty miles away in Helena. It might be nothing, but all it takes is one wrong person discovering that cash, and we could be in trouble."

"Does anyone know about it? Other than you and the banker?"

"The postmaster knows, but I think that's it. We'll have to tell him and Mr. Collier at the bank this needs to remain quiet." Travis took a long drink of coffee. "This might be overly cautious, and I hope nothing comes of it—but it's my job to make sure the people of this town are safe. Yourself included."

"Thank you. I prefer over preparedness to the alternative."

"I thought you might." Travis leaned back, his lips turning upward. "Now, tell me your vision for this hospital."

Harrison grinned. The hospital—a dream about to come true. He rubbed his hands together. "I'm so glad you asked..."

CHAPTER 6

ind whipped Tori's hair as her husband drove a small buggy toward the outskirts of town. She pushed flyaway strands out of her eyes and fidgeted in her seat. In less than thirty minutes, she would see Ella again.

Had she really let two years go by without seeing her beloved sister? Tori shook her head. She should have made it a point to visit Ella and her family more. Her newest niece was nearly a year and a half, and Tori still hadn't met her.

Focusing on the passing landscape, she took a deep breath of country air. Flowers dotted the grass in hues of purple, yellow, and blue, while majestic mountains rose high in the distance.

Beautiful. Much better than the congestion and fancy buildings in Boston.

Harrison's deep voice broke into her thoughts. "What's your plan?"

She blinked. Side-eying him, Tori tilted her head. "Plan?"

"For surprising your sister."

"I don't have a plan."

"Really?" A furrow appeared between his brows.

Tori chuckled. "Not everything has to be planned, Harrison. It's more fun to make something up in the moment."

"If you say so."

She turned to see him better. His mouth set in a firm line, a muscle in his jaw twitching.

Tori scooted a little closer. "What's wrong?"

He glanced at her before returning his attention to driving. For a few moments, he remained silent. When he spoke, his voice was quiet, controlled. "I'm nervous about meeting your sister."

"Ella?" Tori frowned. "Why? You knew each other in Boston."

"I wasn't your husband in Boston."

Understanding dawned. "You're afraid of her reaction?"

"Something like that." He released a long breath. "She's clearly important to you. I want to make a good impression but am worried a surprise marriage announcement will have the opposite effect."

Why did that simple statement warm her inside? Probably because no other suitor had shown interest in her family except for financial reasons.

Suitor?

Tori smothered a snort. Harrison wasn't a suitor. He was her husband, and he married her to gain his inheritance. His reasons had been financial.

Still...

"Tori?"

Drat. She'd been woolgathering rather than answer him. Turning to face Harrison, she looked him in the eye. "Just be yourself, and I'm sure you'll make a fine impression. Ella won't judge either of us for marrying. She married her husband to escape our family, too, so she understands."

Though her sister would likely be shocked Tori took the same route.

Her husband's brow remained wrinkled, but he shrugged. "I hope you're right."

The silence over the next few minutes had Tori clenching her hands. She blew out a breath. "Is it really bothering you?"

"Yes."

"Why?"

He pulled the horse to a stop. For another minute, they sat in silence, Harrison's jaw working as he stared out over the prairie. Finally, he faced her. "I told you why. Your sister is important to you, so it's important to me that she approves."

Crossing her arms, Tori studied her husband. No guile lay in his expression. If anything, he seemed earnest. Her arms fell to her sides. "You're serious."

"You doubt me?"

Guilt pooled in her stomach at the hurt in his eyes. She stared down at her hands, clutching the material of her sapphire blue skirt. "I don't want to."

Birds sang into the silence pulsing between them. The happy sound contrasted with the tense sensation in her gut.

The buggy creaked slightly. Tori jumped when Harrison's hand landed on her shoulder. She glanced up, her breath catching at how close he was. His dark gaze bored into hers, heat from his hand searing through her dress. "Victoria, you can trust me. I despise lying. It might take some time for you to believe that, but it's the truth."

Her full name falling from his lips did funny things to her heart. Tori wasn't sure if it felt more like flipping or seizing. His words had even more impact. She swallowed hard, forcing her gaze to remain on him. "Everything you've done over the past years indicates that, Harrison. But my experience with men in general..." She shook her head, no longer able to look him in the eye. "It's not good."

He released a long breath. The buggy creaked again as he

moved back to his spot. "I'm committed to this relationship. If that means I need to keep earning your trust, I'll do it."

Tori closed her eyes. He shouldn't have to. She knew him better than any other man, and he was honorable. Trustworthy. Good.

And yet...

Her father's face sneered in her mind's eye. She shuddered, shoving the image away.

Harrison was not her father.

He slapped the reins, urging the horse into a brisk walk. The wind felt good against Tori's warm face. A glance at Harrison showed his lips still compressed, a vein ticking in his neck. Throwing caution aside, she moved close until she could thread her arm through his. His gaze brushed hers, surprise dancing through it.

"Thank you for being patient with me, Harrison. It means a lot." She squeezed his arm. "I'm sorry for doubting you. For what it's worth, I think my sister will like you once she gets over her shock."

His lips inched up. "How shocked do you think she'll be?"

"We'll find out soon." Tori pointed ahead, where a two-story log house stood near a large red barn. "There it is."

Tears burned her eyes. She pressed her hands to her mouth, taking in her sister's home. As they drew closer, she could see chickens roaming the yard, scratching for bugs. They scattered when Harrison pulled the buggy to a halt in front of the house. He jumped down, then rounded the conveyance to assist Tori. She accepted his hand, sparks shooting up her arm. Her foot caught in her skirt. Tumbling forward, she shrieked.

Harrison's arms wrapped around her, bracing her tight against his chest. "Are you all right?"

No. No, she was not. Tori couldn't breathe. Harrison's subtle scent permeated her senses, a combination of pine and cloves.

His solid chest pressed against her cheek. A swarm of butter-flies took flight inside of her.

Great. Attraction was the last thing she needed. It would only cloud her focus.

Tori pushed back, her face heating. "Th-thanks," she mumbled.

A strange rumble escaped her husband. He stepped back, raking a hand through his hair with a short nod.

She turned to the house and climbed the porch steps. Heavy footsteps behind her proved Harrison followed her lead. Tori straightened her shoulders and rapped three times on the front door.

It swung open, revealing a girl about six or seven with black curls and wide hazel eyes. "Hi. Who're you?"

Blinking, Tori stared at the child. This wasn't Ella's daughter. Had her sister moved?

Another child came running to the door, a boy with floppy, sandy hair. "Ruby, Mama wants to know who's here."

Relief flooded Tori. She recognized him. "Hi, Isaiah."

He eyed her, brown eyes narrowed. "Do I know you?"

"Don't be rude," the little girl whispered, elbowing him in the side. She smiled up at Tori. "Isaiah needs a snack. Mrs. Brooks says he gets grumpy when he's hungry, like his papa."

Tori smothered a laugh.

"Humph." Isaiah crossed his arms and stuck his tongue out at the girl. His gaze swung back to Tori. "This is Ruby. She's my friend." He tilted his head. "You look familiar. Kinda like my mama."

She crouched in front of him, arms out. "I'm your mother's sister. You don't remember me?"

"Aunt Tori?"

Isaiah gaped, then threw his arms around her. "Mama said you were coming this summer, but we didn't know when."

Tori hugged him close. "You've grown so much. I'll bet you're almost as tall as your papa."

"Gettin' there." Isaiah pulled back and beamed. "Papa says I can take over the ranch someday if I want to."

Ruby tugged his arm. "Shouldn't we let your mama know she's here?"

"Yeah. C'mon, Aunt Tori." Isaiah grabbed her arm. His gaze went behind her. "Hey, who's he?"

Before Tori could respond, her sister's voice sounded from the hall. "Children? Are you going to welcome our guest inside?"

Ella came into view, red hair plaited in a simple braid, her green dress overlaid with an apron. She wiped her hands on the white material, a smile on her lips. "Sorry about that. Won't you come in and..." As she stopped in her tracks, Ella's green eyes went wide. "Tori?" she whispered.

"Surprise." Tori rushed forward and enveloped Ella in an embrace. "It's so good to see you."

Tori's hair muffled Ella's laughter. "You goose! I thought you'd write before coming." She pulled back and smiled fondly. "Not that we mind, of course. Where are you staying?"

"With Travis and Cassie."

"I wish you could stay with us. We have the space, but you'd be too far from the infirmary."

"I don't mind. It's nice just being nearby."

"How long will you be here?"

"Permanently."

Ella cocked her head, brow furrowing. "I'm sorry, I thought you said..."

Isaiah's voice cut her off. "Hey, Mama, this man says he knows you."

The two women looked back in tandem. Isaiah and Ruby stood on either side of Harrison, Ruby gazing up at him in awe, and Isaiah with confusion.

Squinting, Ella gripped Tori's hand. "You brought a man with you?"

Time to drop her second surprise. Tori threaded her fingers around Ella's and pulled her to the porch. "You'll probably recognize him."

Sunlight streamed onto the porch, bathing them all in a golden glow. Ella shaded her eyes and looked up at Harrison. Her forehead scrunched before smoothing out. "Dr. Blake?"

He smiled with a little bow. "Hello, Miss Mountbatten." A crease formed between his brows. "Or rather, Mrs...?"

"Mrs. Brooks," Ella supplied. Her gaze darted between Tori and Harrison. "You two are here...together?"

A muscle twitched in Harrison's cheek. The strangest urge to smooth it with her fingers prodded Tori. Her hand lifted of its own accord. Moments before touching his skin, she jerked it back down.

Ella's gaze tracked the motion. She shot Tori a questioning look.

Tori grinned, moving to Harrison's side. She slipped an arm around his waist, ignoring the jolt of attraction, and feigned as much confidence as she could. "Ella, say hello to my new husband."

~

That could have gone better.

Harrison hadn't expected Tori to blurt out their news, but at least Mrs. Brooks didn't faint on the spot. She'd gone pale but invited them inside for tea. The parlor had two windows that provided plenty of natural light, and the settee he sat on was worn but comfortable.

He accepted a cup from Mrs. Brooks. "Thank you, ma'am."

"Call me 'Ella.' It seems we're family now."

She didn't sound particularly pleased. He gulped a scalding swallow from his cup. "Yes, ma'am. You can call me Harrison."

Tori plopped onto the seat beside him. "For goodness' sake, Ella, you're making the poor man nervous. I promise there's a very good reason for all this."

"Please, enlighten me."

Ella sat in a chair across from them, one eyebrow arched higher than the other. Harrison felt as if he were a schoolboy caught dipping a girl's braids in ink again.

Tori leaned back against the sofa. She folded her hands and smiled at her sister. "It's quite simple, really. I married Harrison for the same reason you married Cody."

Understanding flashed over Ella's face. "To get away from Father."

"That, and to practice medicine." Tori's eyes hardened. "He let me get my degree, let me get within reach of my dreams, then tried to take it all away. No doctor would take me on." She shrugged. "Harrison provided a way out."

That couldn't be less romantic, even if it was true.

Ella studied him, her gaze unwavering. "What did you gain from this arrangement, Harrison?"

"My aunt left me a substantial inheritance but stipulated that I be married by thirty to gain it."

"Ah." Ella's eyes glittered. "So you married her for money."

"Essentially, yes."

Tori faced him. Her brows rose, a challenge in her smile. "You aren't going to tell her why you wanted that money?"

He tugged his collar, face heating. "Uh—"

A stampede of feet interrupted them. Children spilled into the room, one after another. Harrison's mouth fell open. How many kids did his sister-in-law have? He counted at least six.

Isaiah led the pack. He grinned. "See? Told ya. We've got a new uncle."

Another little boy around five came closer. His blue eyes

widened under a mop of sandy hair. "I thought you were joshin'."

Tori chuckled. "Harrison, meet Jonah. He's the middle child." Her gaze swept over the four girls, two of whom were toddlers with bright blue eyes. Pointing to a child under three, she gasped softly. "You must be Addie."

The girl nodded, her brown curls bouncing. She opened and closed her fist in a sweet wave.

Tori hugged her. "Look how grown up you are."

Addie giggled. She pulled back and grabbed the hand of the youngest child, an adorable strawberry blonde with plump cheeks. "'Dis Wosie."

"Rosie," Tori breathed. She reached for the tiny girl, lifting her up onto her lap, then shook her head, throat working. "Ella, I'm sorry I've been gone for so long. I should have visited sooner."

"You're here now. That's what matters." Ella smiled, her features relaxing. "Earlier you said you were staying permanently?"

She phrased it as a question. Tori nodded, her cheek smooshed against Rosie's. "Yes. Harrison is the new doctor. That's why he wanted the inheritance, to be able to start a new life out west and build a hospital."

Surprise colored Ella's face once more. She tipped her head and turned to Harrison. "Is that so?"

"Yes, ma'am."

Ruby's eyes lit up. "We have a doctor again? He's gonna take care of the sick people?"

Something about the girl's innocence set Harrison at ease. He leaned forward with a wink. "I sure am. So is Dr. Tori."

The four older children whooped. Jonah grabbed Harrison's hand. "Aunt Tori's a doctor too?"

"She sure is. A very good one. I couldn't ask for a better partner."

Tori blushed.

Harrison chuckled. "What? It's true."

Ella watched them from her chair, a contemplative look on her face. Something soft crept into her eyes, and she smiled fully for the first time since Harrison saw her. "Children, why don't you play in the yard while the grownups talk?"

"Aww, but I wanna talk, too," Isaiah said.

"You can talk with them at supper." Ella turned to Tori. "That is, if you'll stay?"

"Of course we will." Tori set Rosie on the floor. As the children ran from the room amid giggles and goodbyes, her gaze fell on the quiet blond girl. "Who's she?"

"That's Alice. She and Ruby are adoptive sisters. Lydia Jefferson married our pastor, and they took the girls in. Do you remember Lydia?"

"Of course. She saved you from Howard."

The pure venom in Tori's voice as she said the name, combined with Ella's grimace, made Harrison pause. He'd heard rumors in Boston—how Ella's fiancé, Howard Archambeau, refused to let her go when she left town, even going so far as to chase after her. He'd been killed in an attack, but no one in Boston seemed to know exactly what happened.

"I see the questions in your eyes." Ella's wry tone combined with a small smile.

Harrison flushed. "Sorry, ma'am. I don't want to pry. Everyone knew how unhappy you were with Howard when you left town and married someone else. People talked for months."

"I'm sure they did. Which made my parents furious." Ella picked up her teacup and took a sip. Her gaze slid to Tori. "You didn't give him the details?"

"It's not my story to tell."

Ella smiled. "I appreciate that. Consider this my permission to tell him everything when you want." She looked at Harrison again. "I'll give you the short version of events. Howard was a cruel, manipulative man in private. Things got so bad one night, I left and came here, marrying Cody within a week, both to protect myself and to give his adopted children a mother. Howard hired someone from back home to scare me, and when that didn't work, he came for me himself, kidnapping me and taking me to Helena, where he planned to catch a train to Boston. My husband and Travis chased after us, and there was a fight. In the end, I shot Howard. He died later from an infection."

She sipped her tea again. Harrison stared at her, the information she'd given whirling around in his brain. His thoughts locked on one fact. There had been two men present in the fight, but... "*You* shot him?"

One side of Ella's mouth turned up. She nodded. "Howard had shot Cody and stunned Travis with a blow to the head. He was about to kill Travis. I did what I had to."

"She's a crack shot," a deep voice proclaimed from somewhere behind Harrison.

He stood to face the newcomer. A man came into the room, cowboy hat in hand, blond hair wind-mussed. His blue eyes twinkled as he stopped beside Ella. "Hello, darlin'." He leaned down, pressing a kiss to her hair. "The kids gave me an earful just now. What's this about Tori being married?"

Tori leapt to her feet. "Cody!"

The man met her with a short embrace. "Hi, Tori. Good to see you again. Especially since you don't have a rifle aimed at my heart this time."

What?

Harrison sputtered. It took a few moments for his voice to work. "Do all the women in this family shoot?" Disbelief colored his words.

Tori chuckled. She smacked the cowboy in the chest before pulling back. "Ella was in danger. I had to be sure this guy wasn't a rogue. Turns out, he was the best thing that ever happened to her." She smiled. "Cody, I'd like you to meet my husband, Dr. Harrison Blake."

Cody's roughened hand clasped Harrison's firmly. "I heard we were gettin' a new doc. Happy to meet you." He grinned. "Never thought I'd see the day my sister-in-law married. You must be a good man."

"He is," Tori proclaimed, just as Harrison said, "I try."

Amusement danced in Cody's eyes. "Look at you two, already acting like an old married couple. I'm glad you found love, Tori. You deserve happiness."

An awkward silence descended on the room. Cody fidgeted with his hat, gaze darting from person to person. "Did I say something wrong?"

"Uh...this isn't exactly a...love match," Harrison stammered. He rubbed his neck, the skin hot against his palm.

"Oh. Well, love can grow." Cody's eyes grew soft as he placed a hand on his wife's shoulder. "Sometimes it just needs a little nurturing."

An ache started in Harrison's heart. He looked at Tori. She possessed a fiery spirit, a good heart, and clearly loved those she let in. Would he ever be one of those fortunate few?

Her gaze collided with his. As her teeth sank into her bottom lip, Tori's cheeks turned a lovely shade of pink, but her eyes remained focused. Just when he thought the tension between them might snap, Cody's voice broke into the silence.

"So...you two staying for supper?"

CHAPTER 7

Morning light poured in through the windows in the Doyles' guest room, warming Tori's face and pulling her from a deep sleep. She stretched with a yawn. Snuggling deeper into the bed, she sighed.

What a lovely way to wake up.

An interrupted snore sounded from the floor.

Tori's eyes flew open and she jolted upright. The quilt puddled around her lap. Peering over the side of the bed, she remembered where she was.

And who she was with.

Harrison lay sprawled on a nest of blankets, dark eyelashes fluttering against his cheeks.

Tori crept from the bed. Reaching for her robe, she shrugged into it and secured it shut just as her husband opened his eyes. The dark brown depths clouded with confusion before clearing. He sat up, running one hand through his disheveled hair. "Good morning."

She clutched the neckline of her robe. The low rumble in his voice, roughed by sleep, had butterflies beating against her stomach.

That wouldn't do.

Squaring her shoulders, Tori produced a smile. "Morning. I think we should try finding a house today. Preferably one with two bedrooms so you don't have to sleep on the floor."

He chuckled low, rising to his feet and stretching his back. "A bed would be nice. It turns out there's an apartment above the infirmary in town. Travis told me about it last night. Said we can move in anytime."

"Really?"

"It's been empty for a while. We'll have to clean it up, but Travis said there are two bedrooms, a kitchen, and a parlor. It'll be much cozier than either of us are used to."

"I prefer cozy and free over an opulent prison."

"Home was that bad?"

Tori crossed her arms, suddenly chilled despite the warmth of the room. "Yes."

He stepped toward her. "You'd tell me if I ever made you feel imprisoned, right?"

His hands came to rest on her upper arms. Tori sucked in a breath, caught in his earnest gaze. Cody's comment from last night chose that moment to march through her mind.

Love can grow.

Did she want it to? Wasn't falling in love its own form of imprisonment? Better to keep her heart locked secure.

"Tori?"

Harrison moved another step closer. He dipped his head, his eyes searching hers. His breath puffed against her mouth. Of its own accord, her gaze fell to his lips. What would it be like to kiss him again? The one at their wedding had been nice—

Harrison nudged her chin with his knuckles. "My eyes are up here, Victoria."

Heat pulsed over her in waves. Warmth from the way he said her full name, embarrassment at being caught staring at his mouth. That was bad enough, but for him to call her on it? Tori covered her face with her hands. "Sorry."

He laughed and tugged her hands down. "Don't be." His grin spread wide. "Were you going to kiss me?"

She jerked back, face flaming. "What? No, of course not."

"Because if you wanted to, I wouldn't object."

The teasing expression on his face made her gape. Was he *flirting* with her? And gracious...was he saying he wanted her to kiss him?

This man was a walking riddle. One moment he was quiet and grave, the next teasing and laid back. Though she'd never seen this level of ease from him. Talking about kisses? No one did that.

Well...maybe married couples did.

Harrison cupped her face in his hands. His carefree look fell away. In its place stood his serious mien. "You never answered my question."

She couldn't think with him so close. "Wh-what question?"

"Would you tell me"—he came another step toward her, effectively banishing any space between them—"if you felt imprisoned"—his hands tightened slightly—"with me?"

Fighting for control, Tori rested her hands on his chest, whether to push him away or feel connected, she wasn't sure. "You've known me for years, Harrison. Have I ever been one to hide my thoughts?"

"No. It's one of the things I admire about you. In fact..." He rested his forehead against hers. "I wish I could be more like you. Confident. Unafraid to speak my mind." His eyes hooded, his gaze slipping to her lips. "Unafraid to—"

A loud thump made them jump apart. Muffled exclamations sounded from downstairs.

Harrison raked both hands through his hair. "I suppose we should ready ourselves for the day. We've got a lot to do between setting up the infirmary and our new home."

Going through her morning ablutions helped Tori feel herself again. Whatever those strange feelings Harrison provoked in her, they were firmly set away as the two of them made their way to the infirmary after breakfast.

The clapboard building sat at the edge of town across from the saloon. Tori eyed the other establishment with distaste. Nothing good came of imbibing alcohol in excess. "When we build that hospital, can it be in a more desirable location?"

"Absolutely." Harrison opened the infirmary door. "Once we're settled here, Travis is going to show us a few plots of land for sale close to town. We need a place that's easily accessible but large enough to support the size of our hospital." He swept out his hand. "After you."

Tori walked through the door. The infirmary was one large room. A staircase near the door led up to the apartment they would call home. An old desk sat in one corner. Four beds lined the far wall. Five large crates were stacked near the door, the ones they'd had shipped from Boston. Shelves graced every wall, ready for supplies, along with some cabinets.

And dust. Thick, heavy, and oppressive.

Tori sneezed three times. "My word. Look at all this dust." Her steps left footprints on the ground. A thick layer of grime covered the shelves and cabinets. "We've got a lot of work to do."

"At least we just need to clean. All our supplies are packed in those crates, so we'll be able to arrange them once we have this room in order." Harrison walked to one of the sheet-covered beds and pushed down, sending a cloud of grayish-white particles into the air. "These mattresses seem serviceable."

"Should we see if the apartment upstairs is also in need of a deep clean?"

"Might as well."

They climbed the stairs that led to their new living quarters.

Their steps disturbed the dust, causing Tori to sneeze again. Harrison tucked a handkerchief into her hand. "Hold this over your nose and mouth."

"Thank—choo!—you."

Tori pressed the white cloth over her lower face. Her eyes watered as more dust gathered there. "Ugh. It'll be good to have this place washed clean."

Harrison pushed open the door to their apartment. They stepped into a cozy parlor, which featured a sofa, two chairs, a couple side tables, and a coal stove to heat the room. There was no divider between the parlor and kitchen. A small, four-person dining table sat between the two spaces. The kitchen had an icebox, water barrel, oven, another coal stove, and a few shelves and counters. Two windows in each room provided substantial light, which was a nice surprise.

Off the parlor ran a short hallway, at the end of which were the two bedrooms. They were nearly identical, both with another two windows, a bed, small bedside tables, and a sturdy-looking wardrobe.

And dust. So much dust.

Despite the cloth, Tori sneezed again.

Harrison shot her a regretful glance. "We'll get it cleaned up. Why don't we start by opening all the windows?"

Within five minutes, the windows in both the apartment and the infirmary were open, summer air freshening the place instantly. Tori breathed a bit easier. "Where do we start?"

Harrison glanced around the infirmary. He rolled his shirt-sleeves to the elbows. "Might as well start here. We can stay with Travis and Cassie until our apartment is ready. I think having the infirmary cleaned out and open for patients should be our priority. What do you think?"

He asked her opinion instead of telling her what they would do. Tori swallowed, her heart beating a bit faster. "I think that's a brilliant idea."

"Then let's get to it."

~

By the third day of cleaning, Harrison's back ached, and he'd done more manual labor than ever before. No wonder his family had servants back home who took care of the cleaning, cooking, and household upkeep. It was a lot of work.

But he'd also never experienced the sense of pride that rushed through him as he stood in the immaculate, organized infirmary.

His wife spun around the room, arms extended, laughter floating on the air. She turned in a little skip, eyes bright. "Step one is finished. The infirmary is open once again."

"And we're set to look over potential sites for the hospital in about an hour. Should we be done cleaning for today or start on our apartment?"

Tori grimaced. "Just the thought of rags and water and soap is unpleasant. Let's save that for tomorrow." She stretched, hands at her lower back. "Why don't we get lunch at the café? Cassie said her special today is fried chicken."

"Have you ever had fried chicken?"

"No, but I hear it's delicious."

He winced, shaking his head. "Some say so."

"You don't like it?"

"It just sounds strange."

Tori's lips pressed together while amusement danced in her eyes. "So you haven't eaten it."

"No."

"Well, there's a first time for everything." She linked her arm through his and pulled him toward the door. "C'mon, Harry. Let's expand your palate."

They entered the café, Harrison debating internally

whether he should try the fried chicken or stick with roasted. His nose picked up the rich aromas of gravy and chicken. Something sweet lingered in the air as well, as though a chocolate cake had just been pulled from the oven.

Cassie greeted them with a smile. She waved a hand at the tables, where people chatted and laughed. "Find an open spot. Josephine will take your order in a moment."

"Thanks, Cassie." Tori led Harrison to a table against the wall.

A waitress with long, dark hair—presumably Josephine—came over with a smile, plunking a hand on her hip. "Howdy, folks. Welcome in. What can I get you?"

"Two orders of fried chicken, mashed potatoes, gravy, and string beans, please." Tori smiled and leaned forward, her gaze never leaving Josephine's. "My husband has never had fried chicken."

Josephine clucked with a shake of her head. "You've been missing out, young man. It's delicious."

Harrison held back his protest. It couldn't hurt to try the meal once. He leaned back in his chair, crossing his arms. "Can that be packed up in a basket?"

"Sure. You want anything to drink with that?"

"Lemonade would be great. Thanks, Josephine."

Tori's head tipped to the side. "A basket?"

"You'll see."

Once their food had been packed up and Harrison paid, he led Tori back outside. They walked down the street. His wife shot him glances as they left the main thoroughfare. "Where are we going?"

"It's a surprise."

Tori tucked her hand into the crook of his elbow. "If I didn't know any better, Harrison Blake, I'd think you were taking me on a picnic, which would be suspiciously like an act of courtship."

"Maybe it is."

Tori sputtered, and Harrison hid a grin. "What's wrong, Victoria? Are you opposed to courtship in general or from me specifically?"

With a toss of her curls, Tori huffed. She pulled her arm from his and leveled her gaze at his. "Harrison, we're here to build a hospital and provide care for the people of this town. Courtship has no place in our relationship."

"No? Seems to me it could make our marriage more fun." He leaned closer. "And if you're so against this, why is your face a deep shade of pink?"

Tori's hands flew to her cheeks. She averted her eyes, her pace increasing. Harrison chuckled. "You don't know where we're going, remember?"

His wife muttered something under her breath. It was probably good he couldn't make it out. Fighting another chuckle, Harrison sauntered closer. "Come on. We're almost there."

They crossed an open field about a quarter mile from town. Wildflowers dotted the grass, their sweet scent rising in the hot midday air. Harrison stopped under a large tree. "Here we are."

"It's a pretty spot, Harrison, but why are we here?"

"To eat lunch."

She shook her head, a tiny smile appearing on her lips. "There's more to it than that, isn't there?"

"Let's get settled, then I'll answer that."

The cool grass was soft and lush, providing a nice place to sit. Harrison handed Tori her plate before taking his in hand. Delicious aromas wafted from inside the basket. His mouth watered.

Tori arched a brow, amusement gleaming in her eyes. "Smells good, huh?"

"Indeed."

He served the food. The chicken was browned to perfection, the potatoes white and creamy, the gravy smooth and dappled with pepper, the string beans crisp and bright green. It looked as good as it smelled. His stomach rumbled in appreciation.

Tori took a big bite of chicken. "Mmm." She pointed the drumstick at him. "You'll never go back once you try this. It's incredible."

Harrison lifted his chicken from the plate. It felt firm and crisp between his fingers. He bit into it, his teeth sinking through a crunchy layer before reaching the succulent, tender meat beneath. Peppery, salty, rich—he'd never tasted anything so good.

"Told you so," Tori said in a sing-song tone. Her brown eyes sparkled with good humor.

"It's amazing."

She sat back against the tree, regarding him as she took another few bites. Harrison dug into the potatoes, finding them every bit as creamy and luscious as they looked. His wife's stare brought his gaze back to hers. "What?"

"You admit when you're wrong." A crinkle appeared between her brows. She looked over the field, shaking her head. "You're different."

Something in her tone said that was good. He smiled, his eyes on his food. Words like that from Tori meant more than heaps of compliments from other women.

"So why'd you choose to make this lunch a picnic?" Tori asked, snapping a string bean in half and popping both into her mouth.

"This piece of land happens to be for sale. It's one of the potential locations for the hospital."

Tori lowered her fork. Her gaze returned to the land around them, this time calculating. A soft smile appeared on her lips. Her head bobbed up and down as she turned it to and fro. "It's a worthy spot. Close to town, lots of space, peaceful. I like it, Harrison." She put her plate down and perched her chin on a closed fist. "Are the other possibilities this nice?"

"I don't know. I only knew of this one because Mr. Peterson at the mercantile mentioned it. I wanted to come out here with you so we could form an opinion together."

She blinked three times in succession. "You didn't look at it first?"

"No."

Tori shook her head, picking up the box once more. "Yeah. You're different."

He'd take it.

CHAPTER 8

"You and Harrison decided to purchase the land you picnicked on?" Ella asked, rubbing a sleepy Rosie's back.

"We did." It had been three days since they bought the land, and Tori couldn't be happier with the choice. "The deed was transferred to Harrison, and we just need the town's approval before we begin construction." Tori sipped her tea, the lemon flavor sweet and tart. "Travis said he'll call a town council this weekend." She lifted a plate and held it out to her sister. "Cookie?"

Ella eyed the offering. "Are those chocolate cookies?"

"Of course they are. What else?"

The sisters chuckled. Ella selected one before sitting back in her chair. Her gaze swung around Tori's apartment, taking in the mopped floors, clean furniture, and sparkling windows. "I must say, you and Harrison did a wonderful job with the place. It looks brand new."

"It took a lot of work, but it's been worth it. We've been here a week, and this place feels more like home than Boston ever did."

"I know that feeling. I'm happy you're here." Ella's piercing green eyes focused on Tori. "But are you happy?"

"Very."

"Even in your marriage?"

Tori swallowed another gulp of tea. "It's serving its purpose."

"That's not what I meant."

Plunking the teacup on its saucer, Tori squared her shoulders. "This marriage was never about love, Ella. Harrison and I are just two people who saw an opportunity in each other and took it."

Her sister leaned back with a smirk. "I never said anything about love. But now you mention it…"

"Ella."

Laughing, Ella raised her free hand. "I'm your older sister. It's my job to worry about you. Besides, I always hoped you would find love. You have so much to give."

"And I will. To you and your children, to my patients."

"Hmm." Ella laid Rosie on the sofa, then reached for her tea. "Do you like Harrison?"

"Of course, I like him. We worked together for three years. He's a good man."

"Which is why you were comfortable marrying him."

"It's why I proposed to him."

Ella coughed. Tea seeped from her mouth. She grabbed a napkin and dabbed her chin, gaze never leaving Tori. "*You*? I thought it was his idea."

Chuckling, Tori shrugged. "I don't think the thought would have occurred to him. Not for marrying me, at least."

Her sister sat blinking wide eyes.

Tori's chuckle turned into a laugh. "How surprising can this be? You basically proposed to Cody. I'd say that was more out of character than me doing so to Harrison."

"That's different. Cody was talking about needing a wife, so I volunteered for the job."

"That's exactly what happened with me. Harrison was talking about needing a wife to gain his inheritance, so, as you put it, I volunteered for the job." She folded her arms with a grin. "You see? We had very similar circumstances."

Ella's lips pulled into a sly smile. "Then maybe the outcome will be the same."

"The outcome is the same. We're all married."

"You know I meant falling in love."

Tori's insides itched. "Love tends to make people weak. I don't have time for such nonsense."

Rolling her eyes, Ella set her cup down on a small side table. She stood, going to the window. "Come here."

When Tori joined her, Ella pointed outside. "You see how Cody is playing with our children, keeping them entertained while you and I visit?"

The big cowboy was indeed running around the yard behind the infirmary, chasing his three active kids like a lumbering bear. With a jolt, Tori realized Harrison had also joined in the play. He laughed as he scooped a giggling Jonah into his arms and swung him high.

Her heart skipped a beat. Traitorous organ.

She crossed her arms over her stomach. "What of it?"

"He's a good man, Tori." Ella slipped an arm around Tori's shoulders. "A good man worthy of love. I suspect Harrison is the same." She gave a quick squeeze. "You're worthy of love as well. And you and Harrison can only find that with each other now that you've made vows. Why not see if love can grow?"

Tori turned away from the window. She plopped into her chair with a huff and lifted her teacup from the table. "It sounds like a dream, Ella, not real life. Love's not for me."

"Why not?" Her sister remained at the window, but her gaze locked on Tori.

Why would anyone love a terror like you?

The memory rose up, cold and ugly—herself at seven years old, asking her father if he loved her the way her schoolmates' dads loved them. He'd sneered and told her to be on her way. When she insisted he answer, those hurtful words pierced her little soul.

Tears burned her eyes. She'd forgotten about that day. Why did it resurface now?

"Tori?"

Ella's concerned voice sounded right beside her. Forcing a laugh, Tori swiped at the tears slipping down her cheeks. "It's nothing."

"Are you sure?" Ella sat and hugged her. "You never cry."

And she didn't intend to make a habit of it. Tori pulled back, grabbing a napkin from the table to wipe away the evidence of her short crying spell. She raised her chin and took a long breath. "I'll be just fine. More tea?"

Ella squinted. Before she could protest, Tori jumped up to make another pot of the warm brew. "Help yourself to some more cookies. I'll be right back."

"Tori..."

"Really, I'll be fine." She injected as much brightness into her voice as possible. "Now, tell me how your garden is coming along."

"My garden?" Ella frowned. "You don't care about gardens."

"Maybe I've found new reason to enjoy them. Or talking about them."

Anything to get her mind off that awful memory. How could she trust a husband to love her when her own father had failed to do so?

～

he council took place Saturday morning at the town hall. Harrison tried not to let nerves take hold as he stood just outside the main room. He peered around the corner, out at the faces in the crowd. Far more than he'd expected showed up—at least a hundred, with more milling in as the meeting time drew closer.

Maybe the number of people was a good sign. Travis said according to town law, two-thirds of a council needed to approve any new business buildings. Harrison didn't like the business distinction, but as hospitals exchanged services for payment, he couldn't argue the title.

Besides, who would object to a hospital?

He turned away from the crowd, coming face-to-face with his wife. She peered up at him, a slight furrow between her brows. "Are you all right, Harrison?"

"I'm fine. Why?"

"You're pale and sweating."

Sweating?

Harrison ran a finger over his forehead. It came away damp. Muttering to himself, he swiped a handkerchief from his pocket and mopped his face. "I don't like public speaking. Apparently to the point my body reacts negatively."

Tori's frown deepened. She stepped closer. "When was the last time you spoke in public?"

"Uhh…" His vision faded for a moment. He blinked hard, passing the handkerchief over his face again. "First year of med school. We had to give a class presentation."

"And?"

Face burning, he shuffled his feet. "I don't want to talk about it."

Tori's eyes narrowed. She plunked a hand on her hip while jamming the index finger of her other hand against his chest. "What happened?"

He pushed her finger away, taking a few steps back. "I need some water."

"Harrison!"

Tori's clipped tone brooked no room for argument. He paused, his head drooping. "I fainted, all right? It wasn't my finest moment."

Her fingers clamped around his upper arm. "You're going to sit down. Now."

"I just need a drink…"

"This isn't up for debate. You look ready to faint again."

She pushed him into a chair. He tumbled down, hitting the hard seat with a thump. "Ow. Was that necessary?"

"Yes."

He sighed, adjusting himself in the chair. "I'm fine."

"I'll be the judge of that. Don't move. I'm going to get your water."

Harrison rested his elbows on his knees and bowed his head. The crowd sounded louder. How was he going to address so many people?

Within a minute, Tori nudged his side. "Here. Drink this."

He accepted the cup and downed the contents in seconds. "Thanks."

"Now, what are you going to do about this anxious feeling?"

"Push through it, I suppose." He got to his feet and promptly began to sway.

Tori shoved him into the chair again. He grunted as his hip connected with the seat. "Would it kill you to be gentle, Victoria?"

"Most likely." She crossed her arms. "It's clear you can't speak to this crowd." Her gaze narrowed, nose scrunched. "You've always been a natural with the patients. I've seen you laugh and joke with them, putting them at ease. Why is this hard for you?"

"One on one is simple. You can get to know the person in

front of you. In groups, it's different. The personal connection isn't there."

"Hmm." Tori tapped a rhythm against her thigh. Her head tilted as she peered around the corner at the gathered masses. "I could address them for you."

His spine went stiff. "You don't have to fight this for me. I'm more than capable…"

"Right now, you're not."

With that blow to his pride, she marched off. Before he could process that exchange, she came back, Travis in tow. Tori gestured at him, eyes flaming. "Talk sense into him, Travis. He thinks he can speak to the crowd when he can't even stand straight. Tell him it's a matter of practicality, not pride."

Harrison shot to his feet. All at once, he felt plenty steady. "This hospital is important to me. I can't risk the people shooting it down because they think I'm not able to speak to them myself."

"We're both doctors. What's the difference if I talk or you do?"

Tori's gaze held a dangerous glint. She knew what he would say, and she wordlessly challenged him to state the obvious.

No backing down.

Harrison straightened to full height. "That crowd is mostly men. Fair or not, my words will hold more weight with them."

A growl escaped his wife's lips. She clamped her mouth shut, crossing her arms in front of her. Her anger emitted in waves—whether at him or the situation in general, he couldn't be sure.

Travis rested a hand on her shoulder. "Harrison is right, Tori. It's not just, but those men will listen to him. The majority wouldn't take you seriously."

The fight suddenly drained from Tori. She sighed, her body slumping against the wall. "I hate that you're right."

Harrison didn't like the defeat in her tone. He took her

hand, cupping it between both of his. "Why don't we talk to them together?"

"You're not just saying that so I keep you from fainting?"

He laughed. Her pluck remained intact. "I told you I just needed some water. The anxiety has passed."

"Only because I distracted you."

Her brown eyes held a spark of sass. Harrison tucked her hand into the crook of his elbow. "Come on, Dr. Blake. We have a crowd to win over."

"Are you sure this isn't just so I won't feel bad?"

He stopped and faced her. "This is so the town trusts us both. Equally."

The light of gratitude in her eyes warmed his heart.

Travis tapped him on the shoulder. "I'll introduce you. It'll just take a moment to quiet them down."

As he headed to the front of the room, Tori tugged on Harrison's arm. "It'll get confusing if we're both 'Dr. Blake' to the townsfolk. How should we differentiate?"

"First names?"

"That doesn't seem terribly professional."

"Maybe not." Harrison paused. Nothing else came to mind. He shrugged. "We'll figure it out."

Travis's voice boomed through the town hall. "Ladies and gentlemen, please take your seats. We're ready to begin."

A scuffle of chairs and lowering of voices accompanied the announcement. Travis motioned for Harrison and Tori to join him. Harrison kept his grip on Tori's hand as they walked to the sheriff.

"Fellow citizens," Travis said, "we're here this evening to vote on whether a hospital may be built on the land purchased by this couple." He smiled, gesturing at them. "Our new town doctors will make their case."

Trickles of sweat slipped down Harrison's back. Even with

the lessening of anxiety, fear clutched him. A sea of faces stared at him, waiting for his speech. He opened his mouth. No words came.

Tori squeezed his hand. "Please excuse my husband," she said, smiling at the crowd. "He gets a little nervous before a big talk. It's because he cares so much about our project." She hugged his side, her voice dropping to a whisper. "You can do this."

Her confidence boosted his own. He lifted his chin and took a deep breath. "Thanks for your time, everyone. I'm Dr. Harrison Blake, and this is my wife, Dr. Victoria Blake. We came west from Boston with the desire to build a hospital here in Montana Territory. It would be a two-story building, with twenty comfortable rooms featuring the latest technological equipment."

"That's an awfully big space," a man called out. "Why d'ya need twenty rooms?"

"I prefer being over-prepared. It's not likely we'll need all the rooms at once, but the possibility exists."

"Yeah," someone else said. "Like that influenza outbreak earlier this year. A hospital would've been real nice then."

Another voice sounded. "But who's gonna fund it? There's no way this project is cheap."

Harrison glanced at Tori. She grimaced with a little shake of her head. They couldn't admit to being the funders. He cleared his throat. "A wealthy, anonymous donor provided the funds to build and run this hospital. It won't cost the town a dime."

People began talking all at once. Excitement brimmed over. Only a few people seemed hesitant. After a couple minutes, Travis called everyone to order. When it quieted down, he raised his hands. "Are there any objections to this hospital being built?"

One burly man in the back stood. "Why's there a lady doctor with him? We don't need no woman in a field best left to men."

Tori bristled. She moved forward in a way Harrison doubted was conscious. He pulled her back gently and spoke under his breath. "Not the time, Tori."

She huffed but gave him a nod. "Fine."

He raised his voice to address the man. "My wife is a fine doctor. She's equal to every male doctor of my acquaintance, and I daresay she's one of the best physicians I've had the pleasure of working with."

A woman in the middle of the crowd called out. "I'm glad there's a female doc. Many of us women would feel more comfortable being seen by a fellow woman."

Another round of chatter broke out, but Harrison's view locked in on his wife. She stared up at him, brown eyes large and unblinking. "Did you mean that?"

Travis addressed the crowd before Harrison could respond. "All right, folks, listen up. All in favor of the hospital, please raise your hand."

"Ayes" chorused throughout the room, hands shooting into the air. A few remained down, but well over two-thirds of the crowd approved.

Travis grinned. "Looks as though we're getting a hospital."

Amidst the cheers, Harrison found Tori's gaze. They shared a smile. Their purpose in coming had been achieved.

Now the work began.

He leaned in for a celebratory hug, but Tori grabbed his hand and pulled him into the hall outside the room. She faced him and drew in a shaky breath. "Harrison...what you said... you meant it?"

He met her gaze, his free hand reaching for hers. "Yes. Every word. You amaze me, Victoria. In so many ways."

Tears filled her eyes. She pressed against him, throwing her arms around his waist. "Thank you."

Jolts of fire rocked his body. He returned the hug, a sudden wish that she held him for reasons other than gratitude filling his mind. Closing his eyes, Harrison lost himself in her embrace.

Who knew how often he'd get the chance to hug his wife?

CHAPTER 9

"Doc, you think this lumber is enough to fulfill the contract?"

Harrison slid a finger over the written proposal as he stood in the small office of the lumber mill at the edge of town. The scent of freshly cut wood filled the air. Men whistled and called out to each other outside as they worked, an easy camaraderie apparent among them. He scanned the numbers, then read them again. "That should be plenty. Thanks, Wyatt." He grinned at the large lumberjack. "I appreciate you getting this together on short notice."

Wyatt Gaines smirked, shaking his blond head as he rolled up the proposal. "With what you're payin', I'm just glad I got the contract."

"When can you start building?"

"I'll get a team together this week. We'll probably begin in a couple days."

"Wonderful. Thanks."

They shook hands, and Harrison left the office. He tilted his face to soak in the sunshine as he walked back to the infirmary.

Everything was coming along without a hitch. He rubbed his hands together and grinned.

He'd never been more grateful to have a large bank account.

When he reached the infirmary door, loud voices spilled from inside, one male, one female—and the male sounded angry. Harrison pushed the door open and strode inside. "What's going on?"

A man stood near the south wall, one hand clutched to his chest, his gaze shooting darts at Tori. "This female thinks she can do your job, Doc."

The female in question looked to scratch the man's eyes out. Tori splayed her hands over her hips. "I'm perfectly capable of practicing medicine."

"Doubt it." The man sneered. "You don't even look like a doc. Why's yer coat white? The other docs we had wore black."

"Times are changing. White coats are being used now, you ignorant buffoon."

The fire sparking from Tori's face could heat the entire town in winter. She'd never used such language before, not in his hearing. How much had the man insulted her before Harrison came in? He stepped between them. "Sir, my wife is a skilled physician. She can take care of your—what's the problem?"

"Got a splinter workin' in my shop."

Harrison stared at the man. "A splinter?" That's what the fuss was about?

"It's deep, and I ain't lettin' no woman touch me with a needle."

Tamping down the rising irritation, Harrison held out his hand. "Let me see, Mr...?"

"Collins." He extended his left hand. A long, jagged splinter ran through his palm. "Tried pushin' an old desk to a corner and was rewarded with this."

The wood didn't require a needle. It was deep but should come out easily. All that fuss over something that would take two seconds. Harrison pinched the end and gave it a quick pull. The splinter slipped from Collins's flesh. "There."

Collins sucked in a breath. "It's bleedin'."

"I'll bandage it."

Harrison reached for his supply basket. As he wrapped Collins's hand, the man grinned. "Thanks, Doc. I appreciate the help. Women docs just ain't as trustworthy, y'know?"

"No, I don't know." Harrison stepped back, crossing his arms. "Dr. Blake is an exemplary doctor. She fought her way to this position and given up a lot to fulfill her dream. She's intelligent and capable. Her skills rival my own. This town is blessed to have her."

With a scoff, Collins shook his head. "You're love-besotted. She ain't even close to you or the previous doc."

As if this imbecile had any proof. Harrison's hands clenched. "You may leave. Now."

Collins ambled out, muttering under his breath. Harrison rubbed two fingers over his forehead. "Tori, I'm sorry you had to..." He paused, glancing around the room. "Tori?"

She'd vanished. His gaze landed on the open door that led to their apartment. Maybe she'd gone upstairs.

He took the steps two at a time. Passing through the door, he saw his wife standing by the window, her gaze on the street below. "Tori..."

She whirled around, brown eyes blazing. She marched across the small room and jabbed a finger into his chest. "How dare you!"

Fury rolled off her in waves. He took a step back, hands up. "Calm down. What's wrong?"

"What's wrong?" Her jaw worked. "You're seriously asking me that?"

"I know you're upset about Collins..."

She scoffed. "Oh, is that his name? I named him something much worse in my mind." A near-maniacal laugh left her lips.

"But back to the fact that you undermined me in front of a patient."

"Undermined? I defended you."

"Ha! You call that defending?" She poked him again, harder this time. "You gave that man what he wanted, without so much as a glance in my direction. He insulted me, refused to let me help him, and then you walk in and bend to his wishes." Hands flying in the air, Tori spun away and stomped back to the window. "I don't know why I bother. You men never listen. If it wasn't you, it'd be my father or Kenneth or…"

Heat surged through Harrison's stomach. Clamping his lips together, he crossed the room in four long strides and gripped Tori's arm. "Do not compare me to those men. I'm nothing like them, which you well know. Don't use your anger to disparage my character."

Tori stilled.

Harrison held her stare, refusing to back down. "I took an oath—as did you—to provide care to those in need. That's why I helped Collins. There was a problem that could be fixed. What would we have gained from more argument?"

"It's the principal of the matter," she said through her teeth.

"Maybe so, but I made it clear that you were just as good a doctor as me. You're facing an uphill battle to win over the residents of this town as a physician. It would be the same anywhere else. Most men haven't accustomed themselves to the idea that women can practice medicine well. You'll have to prove your mettle." He let go of her arm. "I suggest you begin by being polite."

"Polite! That man didn't deserve—"

"No, he didn't. But if you stoop to his level, he'll only dig into his opinion harder. You need to earn people's trust." He moved close enough to feel heat radiating from her body. "Perhaps you could start by learning to trust men."

Tori reared back. "As you just pointed out, trust has to be earned."

"You assume all men fall under the same category as your father. That isn't fair."

Her left eye twitched. "Isn't it? My experience says otherwise."

"You're telling me all the male patients you cared for in Boston during medical school were cunning, manipulative men?"

"Not...necessarily."

She didn't look happy about that. Harrison rested his hands on either side of the window, blocking her in. "What about Travis?"

Tori rolled her eyes. "Obviously, he's a good one."

"Cody?"

"He seems to be as well." She sighed, as if it took a lot to admit the fact.

Harrison leaned forward until he could see the flecks of green in her irises. "And me?"

Her soft intake of breath hitched. Tori pressed herself against the window. Harrison didn't leave her any room for comfort. If this is what it took to get through to her, so be it.

They stayed there in a silent battle of wills. Though the tension made him uncomfortable, if he backed down now, Tori would think him weak. Finally, she released a terse exhale. "Fine. Everything you've done over the past few years told me you're one of the good ones too."

He stepped back, his lips stretching in a wide grin. "There. Was that so hard?"

"You have no idea." She plopped her hands on her hips. "By the way, if you ever corner me like that again, you'll regret it."

He pressed in once more, his hands planting firm against the wall. "Will I?"

Tori's mouth fell open.

Harrison chuckled. He rested his forehead against hers. "I don't know, Tori. This seems pleasant enough."

"Does it?"

Her hands slid behind his neck. Before he could blink, she pulled him down and captured his lips with hers.

Shock coursed through his veins. Tori's kiss demanded a response, but he could only stand there for the first few seconds. Then his eyes drifted shut, his hands moved to her waist, and he kissed her back.

He'd analyze the explosions in his gut later.

Tori pulled back abruptly, placing one hand over his chest. She blinked several times, her eyes clouded over. Her hand curled into the fabric of his shirt. Gaze softening, she gave him a gentle smile.

Was it possible she felt what he did? Harrison leaned closer, intent on kissing her again.

Something flashed in her eyes. Hesitancy? Fear? It was gone before he could analyze it.

Tori stopped him with a push against his chest. She smirked as her gaze roved his face. "Hmm. Flushed cheeks, accelerated pulse, increased respiration. Interesting reaction, Harry."

With a toss of her red curls, she sauntered from the room, leaving Harrison to stare after her in confusion.

⁓

*K*issing her husband was a colossal mistake.

Tori growled as the memory continued to assail her a week later. She'd meant to make a point—catching Harrison off guard enough for her to slip away. It worked, but the unintended consequence had her off kilter.

She'd liked that kiss. Too much.

Another thing she liked? That he challenged her. She'd

been angry when he took charge of Mr. Collins, but part of her also felt relief. Not that she'd admit it. When Harrison came upstairs, she took her anger at Collins out on him.

But he hadn't backed down. He took on her anger and forced her to look inside at the real reason for her rage.

She didn't like what she saw.

If he'd given in to her anger or tried to placate her, she never would have seen it. Instead, she'd spent the past week soul searching—not that she told anyone.

Maybe it was time for a talk with her sister.

She returned to her chore—making the hospital beds. So far, they hadn't seen any use. Tori preferred it remain that way. As she smoothed the cover over one of their patient beds, running feet sounded outside. They rushed toward the infirmary, and moments later, two boys tumbled into the room. They barreled into her with shouts of "Aunt Tori!"

She laughed and hugged her nephews. "Isaiah, Jonah, what are you doing here?"

Isaiah pulled back. His brown eyes twinkled. "Papa and Mama need supplies from the mercantile. They said we could have lunch at the café!"

"And they said we could visit you and Uncle Harrison." Jonah's gaze darted around the infirmary. "Where is he?"

"At the hospital, helping the builders. He should be back soon."

Jonah tugged her skirt. "Can you have lunch with us? Aunt Cassie makes the best food." He lowered his voice. "Just don't tell Mama I said that."

With a chuckle, Tori put a finger over her lips. "Not a word. I like Aunt Cassie's food too. Lunch sounds wonderful."

The boys cheered, little fists pumping in the air. Tori pulled them in for another hug. Ella's children were a source of endless joy. What would it be like to have kids of her own?

Something stirred deep in her heart. Harrison made it clear he wanted children, and she'd agreed to those wishes.

Another feeling stirred, this one bringing a ball of anxiety to her stomach. She'd never been the maternal type. Her focus lay in becoming a doctor and ministering people back to health. When children came, her career would inevitably fall to second. Was she cut out to be a mother?

Thoughts of her own mother invaded. She shuddered and pushed them away.

"What's wrong, Aunt Tori?" Isaiah's brow furrowed as he looked up at her.

Tori smoothed back his sandy hair. "I'm just thinking."

"Are you hungry?" Jonah cocked his head, a strand of hair flopping over his forehead. "Papa says a good meal is good medicine."

"Does he? That's excellent advice." Tori tapped Jonah's nose. "I am hungry. Let me get some of those papers on my desk organized, and then I'll join you at the café."

"Okay!"

The boys scampered off. Tori watched from the window as they skipped down the street toward their parents. Ella and Cody descended the steps of the mercantile, arms laden with purchases. Cody placed them in the nearby wagon, then turned and said something to Ella. She laughed, her hands coming to rest on his chest. They shared a quick kiss before clasping hands and walking toward the café.

She sighed, sinking into her chair. The obvious love Cody and Ella felt for one another surpassed anything Tori had seen before. She was happy for her sister. Cody had proven his mettle time and again. He wouldn't treat her ill like their father and Howard had done. His love for Ella showed itself in all the small, everyday moments of life.

You could have that, too, a small voice whispered inside.

Hope leaped in her chest, but she shoved it back down. "No, I can't."

"Can't what?"

She shrieked, leaping to her feet.

Harrison stood in the doorway. Amusement danced in his eyes. "Everything all right?"

The memory of their kiss flashed through her mind yet again. She spun around and riffled through papers on the desk, praying her cheeks didn't appear as flushed as they felt. "Fine."

His hand clamped down on hers. Tori stilled, her breaths suddenly unsteady. She kept her gaze on the papers. If she looked at him, she might do something crazy.

Like kiss him again.

Her cheeks burned hotter.

Harrison pressed his other hand against her face.

She jerked out of his touch. "What are you doing?"

"You're awfully red, Tori. Are you coming down with something?"

She wrinkled her nose and scooted toward the medicine shelf. "I'm quite fit, thank you. It's hot today, so of course, I'm red."

"August is brutal."

Was he laughing? Tori peeked up to gauge his face and stifled a squeal. He stood right next to her, so close she saw the fine lines around his eyes. She took an automatic step back.

"Hmm—flushed cheeks, increased respiration." He grinned, one brow jutting up. "Interesting symptoms, Victoria."

Throwing her words from the kiss back at her—that was something she'd have done. Crossing her arms, she affected indifference. "As I said, it's hot."

"Right." He winked. "If you say so."

Her mouth fell open. "Harrison Blake, are you flirting?"

"Oh, I wouldn't dare. Unless, of course, you want me to."

Where was this teasing side when they worked together in Boston?

His warm eyes traced her features. When his gaze landed on her lips, her stomach dipped and twirled.

"Hey, are ya coming?"

They jumped apart as Isaiah's voice broke into their moment. Tori's cheeks burned, but her nephew didn't seem to notice. A grin spread over his face when he saw his uncle. "Uncle Harrison, we're having lunch at the café. Wanna come? Aunt Tori said she would."

"I'd love to." Harrison met Tori's gaze, his own still sparking. "Shall we?"

She took his offered arm. As he led her out the door, she tried to ignore the roaring inferno in her gut. This marriage was meant to be one of mutual respect and friendship, yet Harrison provoked far too many conflicting feelings in her.

What was she supposed to do about them?

CHAPTER 10

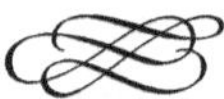

Harrison whistled on his way to the café. His stomach rumbled, a reminder that he had eaten nothing since early that morning. After helping at the hospital for the last six hours, he was ready for a break. Cassie's beef pot pie sounded perfect.

Having his lovely wife on his arm was a happy bonus.

For a second, he imagined they were walking together arm in arm not because it was the gentlemanly thing for him to do, but because they shared a deep closeness, an emotional connection.

He stifled a sigh. That was as likely as a snowstorm in July.

The memory of their kiss haunted him. He wanted nothing more than to repeat the experience—but one look at his wife's face squelched any impulse to act rashly. She was worth more to him than mere satisfaction of his physical desires. Even so, he caught himself daydreaming on occasion about the type of relationship where kisses were freely given and received, and love...

Stop.

No sense wishing for something outside his control. Harrison pushed open the door to the café and extended his hand. "After you."

Tori stepped inside, her face lighting up when she saw the Brooks family. "There they are." She wove her way through the tables faster than he thought possible.

Never had she been that eager to get to him.

Harrison shook his head and shut the door. He made his way, at a more sedate pace, to the table. A chorus of greetings met him. After saying his own hellos, he took the seat beside Cody. No sooner had he sat than three-year-old Addie climbed onto his lap. "Hi, Unca Hawison."

His brother-in-law grinned. "That's a big compliment, Harrison. Addie doesn't go to just anyone."

"I'm honored." Harrison bounced Addie on his knee. "Do you like horsey rides?"

"Yes!"

Cody sipped his coffee, his warm gaze on his daughter. "She'll have you doing that all lunch if you let her."

"You've got a beautiful family, Cody. I imagine it's both wonderful and challenging."

"Sure is." He glanced at his wife, a soft smile on his lips. "We've been talking about having another child. All in God's timing, of course."

"Did you always want a big family?"

"I didn't think I'd have a family of my own. But Ella and our three adopted kids changed that. Now, I'd love a big family." He chuckled. "Though some might say we're already there."

One of the waitresses came to their table. She smiled. "Hi, all. What can I get for you?"

They went around with their orders. As Harrison gave his, he heard his name in hushed tones. He glanced at the other end of the table. Ella and Tori had their heads bent together, whispering. Tori peeked at him for a second, then blushed as her gaze snapped back to Ella.

What in the world were they saying about him?

"Seems our wives are deep in conversation."

Cody's low comment was accompanied by a chuckle, as if he knew exactly what they were talking about.

Harrison leaned closer, dropping his voice too. "Do women ever make sense?"

With a snort, Cody shook his head.

Jonah propped his elbows on the table. He eyed his mother and aunt, then looked at Cody. "Why's everyone whispering?"

"'Cuz they don't want us to hear," Isaiah said, his tone matter-of-fact.

The ladies were so engrossed in their conversation, they didn't seem to hear either child. Harrison didn't know if that was good or bad.

When the food arrived, he tucked into his meal with alacrity. Nothing beat the beef pot pie. Maybe he could cajole Cassie into sharing the recipe...

The door to the café burst open, shaking the walls. Travis rushed inside. His gaze swept the tables before landing on theirs. He ran to them, breaths coming in short gasps. "Harrison, Tori, there was a stagecoach accident just outside town. The passengers are in bad shape. Please hurry."

Hunger forgotten, Harrison leapt to his feet. He barely took in the worried looks on Cody's and Ella's faces before grabbing Tori's hand and hurrying toward the door. "We'll need our bags. How far outside town?"

"A five-minute walk—but I have a better idea. You two take my horse. It'll only be a minute or two of riding double, which won't be comfortable, but it'll get you there. I'll get help and follow on foot." He grabbed the reins of his stallion as they ran for the infirmary. "Head for the train station, then turn east.

Follow the railroad tracks. The stagecoach overturned near the bend outside town."

When they reached the infirmary, Tori snatched up their bags. She peered inside, then looked up at Harrison with wide eyes. "Will this be enough?"

He gathered more bandages, disinfectant, and gauze, stuffing them into the bags. After putting another few items in, he jerked his head toward the door. "Let's go."

Travis helped Tori onto the horse. Harrison handed her the bags, then swung up behind her. The saddle wasn't large enough for two people, so he sat behind it. Definitely not ideal, but it would do. He took the reins and urged the horse into a gallop.

They arrived at the scene in minutes. The stagecoach had turned on its side, splintered into pieces. Three passengers lay on the ground, all appearing unconscious. Harrison's stomach turned as he took in the extent of their injuries. They wouldn't survive the night.

He swung to the ground, then reached up to assist Tori from the horse. Together, they hurried to the stagecoach.

Three more people lay inside, a man and two women. One of the women moaned. Her hands splayed against her belly. Blood poured from a gash at her hairline. She lifted one limp hand toward them. "Help...my baby..."

Harrison's gaze shot to her stomach. It protruded from her body, large and round, and the woman groaned loud, her agony evident.

Tori clutched his arm. "She's in labor."

"Let's get her out first." Harrison took the woman's hand. "Can you climb out?"

"I...don't know." She groaned again, tears streaming down her cheeks. "It hurts."

"Ma'am, we need you to stand, if you can."

She struggled to her feet. Sweat dripped down her forehead, mingling with the blood. Harrison helped her out of the stagecoach. As soon as her feet touched the ground, she went limp. He caught her before she fell, alarm filling him. "Ma'am?"

Another groan ripped through her. He lowered her to the ground, laying her on her back. "Ma'am, can you tell us your name?"

"Amanda."

Tori bent beside her. "How long have you been in labor?"

"Two...days."

Two days? Harrison's heart sank. Labor that long, combined with her head injury, didn't bode well. And what of the babe?

Amanda shuddered, her gaze locked on Tori. "We were trying to get...to the hospital...in Helena for...help." Her words ended with a muted scream as her hands clutched her stomach again.

Tori smoothed back Amanda's hair. "We'll get you to the infirmary. You'll be more comfortable there."

Panic flashed over the young woman's face. "Where's Jimmy?"

Harrison glanced at the men on the ground. Two looked young, the other middle-aged. The man in the stagecoach also seemed young. Any of them could be Jimmy. He took Amanda's hand. "Is he your husband?"

She nodded. "Where is he?"

"He's here." His gaze fell again on the three men, heart sinking. "We'll do our best to help him."

Amanda sucked in a breath. "He insisted on going to the hospital. Said...something must be wrong."

Shouts sounded nearby. He looked up to see Travis and a group of men rushing toward them. He breathed out a short sigh. "Amanda, we're going to help you." His gaze collided with Tori. He looked from her to Amanda, his brow raising. She gave him a quick nod. He squeezed Amanda's hand. "Some men are going to carry you back to town. There's a nice infirmary there. My wife will take good care of you."

"W-wife?" Amanda gasped. Her dull gray eyes landed on Tori. "You're a doctor?"

"I am, and I will do everything I can to make sure you and your child are well."

For the first time since they arrived, Amanda seemed to relax.

Travis dropped to his knees beside them. His gaze swept over the scene, coming to rest on Amanda. "Harrison, Tori, what do you want us to do?"

Harrison stood. "First, we need this woman to go with Tori to the infirmary. From there, we'll assess the others and see who's in most critical condition and whether they can be moved."

As two men gently lifted Amanda, Tori gripped Harrison's arm, pitching her voice low. "This is a losing battle, Harrison. Most of these passengers won't survive."

He covered her hand with his. "But there's a chance we can save some. You have the best chance with Amanda. She'll be in good hands."

"And what about you?" She swallowed as she looked around. "These poor folks are in terrible condition. How will you help them out here with no medical tools?"

Shaking his head, Harrison exhaled. "I'll make do. Travis and the others will help." He released her hand. "I hope all goes well for you with Amanda and her baby."

"See you back at home."

She directed the two men to follow her, and they set off. Harrison drew in a long breath. With a sense of dread, he turned to face the wreckage.

he calm determination that always presented itself in an emergency flowed through Tori as she instructed the men to lay Amanda on one of the hospital beds. Once the young woman was settled, Tori nodded at her helpers. "I appreciate this, gentlemen."

The older one tipped his hat. "Our pleasure, ma'am. We'll head back to the scene now."

"Thank you."

She turned back to the bed. Amanda looked haggard. Her cheekbones were prominent against sallow skin, dark hair plastered against her sweaty forehead. Through a threadbare green dress, her large stomach rose and fell with each breath. Blood streamed down her face, reminding Tori that stitches were in order.

Amanda moaned.

Tori reached for a cloth to dip in cool water. It wouldn't do much, but at least she could clean Amanda's face. As she worked, she asked, "How long has your labor been intense?"

"Since breakfast yesterday."

Tori nearly dropped the cloth. More than a full day of active labor? She wrung out the cloth and placed it on Amanda's brow. "You must be exhausted."

A tear rolled down Amanda's cheek. She sniffed, then groaned in misery, curling into a ball. "Ooooh."

Tori fetched a basket of supplies and placed it next to the bed. She yanked the privacy curtain shut so no one entering the building could see Amanda. The young woman whimpered. "It hurts."

"Take some deep breaths," Tori said, keeping her voice level but firm. Amanda obeyed. While she breathed, Tori took a wad of cotton from the basket. "I need to put this against your head. There's too much bleeding."

Amanda didn't respond. Her face contorted as the contraction built. Tori pressed the cloth to her wound. Amanda yelped.

"Sorry," Tori said. "You might need stitches. That gash is nasty."

"Just get...baby out."

Easier said than done. Two hours later, Amanda's wound had been cleaned and sutured, but her labor continued. Harrison didn't return with more patients. What did that mean for the other passengers? She'd never seen people in such bad shape. She shuddered as the memory of their pain-streaked faces flashed in her mind.

Amanda screamed through her latest contraction. She gripped Tori's hand, but hers slackened before her voice trailed off. Tori checked her, relief flooding her body when she saw the baby's head. "Your child is coming, Amanda. Just a little longer."

Sweat covered Amanda's brow. She shook her head, tears streaming down her cheeks. "I can't do this."

"Yes, you can. On your next contraction, I want you to push hard."

With a little moan, Amanda nodded. The contraction came fast. She bore down and screamed again.

Tori sat on the low stool at the edge of the bed, resting a blanket over her lap to rub the baby when he or she arrived. "You're close, Amanda. A couple more pushes and your child will be here."

Amanda bore down three more times before the baby slipped from her body into Tori's waiting hands. The woman collapsed back against the bed, eyes shut and chest heaving.

"You have a son, Amanda."

Her only response was a tiny, whispered sigh.

Tori cleaned the boy and wrapped him in a blanket. "Would you like to hold him?"

No response.

She held the squirming infant against her chest and peered at his mother. "Amanda?"

The baby fussed. She gently placed him on Amanda's chest.

The young woman's eyes slitted open. She smiled softly. "He's here." Her words slurred together, but she rested both hands on her son's back. "We decided if it was a boy to name him David after my pa."

"That's a good name."

Amanda sighed. "I'm tired."

"You've had a trying few days. And I'm afraid you're not quite done yet. The afterbirth still must pass…"

A soft knock at the door drew her gaze. "Cassie?"

Her friend stepped into the infirmary, lips set in a grim line. "Can I speak with you?"

"Of course."

Tori bent to Amanda, smoothing back some of her damp hair. "I'll be right back." She strode to Cassie, heart thumping out a warning. "What's wrong?"

"Harrison sent me. He's on the train to Helena now with one of the passengers from the stagecoach accident. They managed to get her stabilized, but her leg needs amputation, and Harrison wasn't comfortable performing that here."

Tori bit her lip. "That poor woman." She glanced at the curtain hiding Amanda and David from view. "What about the others?"

Shaking her head, Cassie swallowed. "They didn't make it. Harrison and the others tried hard to save them, but all four of them died."

Grief crashed into Tori. She might not have met any of the other passengers, but she knew Harrison would take their deaths hard. No doubt he was reviewing anything he could have done differently as he rode to Helena. Her arms itched to embrace him, her lips to tell him it wasn't his fault.

Cassie gasped. Her eyes widened as she pointed to the curtained area. "Is that blood?"

Tori whirled around. Dark-red blood dripped in a steady stream to the floor. She rushed to Amanda. The baby wailed suddenly against her chest, but the young woman didn't move. Blood soaked the bedsheets like a red river.

Tori lifted David and called to Cassie. "Can you take the baby?"

Cassie came to her side and accepted the tiny bundle. Her face went white when she saw Amanada. "What's happening to her?"

"She's hemorrhaging." Tori grabbed a handful of cloth bandages and balled them together. "I need to try stop the bleeding. Can you care for David until I get her stable?"

"Yes. Shall I take him to the café?"

"That's a good idea. I don't know how long this will take."

Once Cassie left, Tori worked to slow Amanada's bleeding. The bandages soaked faster than anything she'd seen before.

Amanda's face contorted. Her eyes slitted open and focused on Tori. "Take care of him for me."

"There's no need for that. I'm going to help you."

"Please, Doctor. I don't want my boy growing up in an orphanage." Tears rolled down her cheeks. "I heard that woman say the other passengers didn't survive. Jimmy is gone. David has no one."

Not wanting to give her false hope, Tori instead took her hand. "I'm doing everything I can to make sure you mother that little boy yourself."

Amanda's breathing slowed. Her eyes grew glazed. "Promise me...he won't go...to an orphanage."

Before Tori could answer, Amanda went limp against the bed.

"No," Tori murmured, her throat tightening. She firmly

patted Amanda's cheeks. "Please wake up. Your little boy needs you."

She remained with Amanda through the night, hoping and praying the young woman would turn a corner. The bleeding slowed but never fully stopped. At midnight, a fever ravaged Amanda's already weak body. Tori tried to keep her cool with wet cloths. She urged her to drink water in the fleeting moments that she woke.

But by morning, all her efforts were for naught.

Amanda was gone.

CHAPTER 11

Tori sat in one of the infirmary chairs, staring at the wall, Amanda's son wailing in her arms. He'd been crying for hours. Cassie had brought him by shortly after Amanda passed, concerned about his incessant fussing. Tori fed him infant formula mixed with cow's milk, put a diaper on him, and wrapped him in a fresh blanket.

Nothing worked.

She checked him multiple times for any known infant illness, but she couldn't find a problem. He simply kept crying.

Maybe I'm not a good doctor, after all.

First, she failed his mother. Now, she was failing him.

"It's okay, David," she murmured.

He screamed in response.

How could one so small keep up such a racket?

Someone knocked on the door. A moment later, it opened to reveal Ella.

Tears sprang to Tori's eyes. She jumped up, clutching David to her chest. "Oh, thank God. I don't know what I'm doing wrong. You're a mother. Please, you have to get him quiet."

Ella's eyes blinked wide. "Oh, my word. It looks as though we came at just the right time."

We?

Another woman came through the door. Her black hair hung in a loose braid. Warm hazel eyes landed on Tori with a smile. "Hello, Tori. It's good to see you again."

"You remember Lydia?" Ella asked, plucking the squalling baby from Tori's arms.

Relief sluiced through her as her sister took over. "Of course. How are you, Lydia?"

Lydia smiled, one hand going to her belly. "I am well. Samuel and I are expecting a baby by the end of the year."

Children were certainly plentiful in this town. Tori managed a smile, pushing back an errant curl. "Congratulations."

"Thank you. My husband and I got back from a trip yesterday. When Ella said you came, I wanted to welcome you to town." Her gaze landed on David. "Where's his mother?"

Through the lump in her throat, Tori whispered, "Over there."

Ella gasped while Lydia's hands went to her throat. Tori fought tears, Amanda's pain-stricken face burning in her mind. As if he sensed her thoughts, David's wails intensified.

"I'll get Travis," Ella said, handing the baby back to Tori. "Lydia, you should get Samuel."

"Samuel?" Tori echoed.

"Lydia's husband, our pastor. He and Travis will give his mother a proper burial." Ella placed a hand on Tori's arm. "What are their names?"

"The woman's name is Amanda. She named her baby David before she…"

Unable to get the word out, Tori blinked hard.

Ella squeezed her arm, then headed for the door. "We'll be back soon."

Why was this death affecting her like this? Patients had died on her watch before—though none had been her sole responsibility. Harrison had trusted her to care for Amanda. She'd failed him, Amanda, and David.

Heaviness pulsed in her chest. Tori sank onto one of the hospital beds as she lost the battle with her tears. They flowed down her cheeks in torrents. She choked on a sob, her tears falling on David's blanket.

So much for being a capable physician.

She cradled David as she lay back on the bed. His face, red from screaming, looked miserable. She laid a hand on his stomach, then frowned. "Why is your belly so hard?"

Carefully, she massaged the area. David's frantic cries lessened. He gulped in air even as tremors shook his little body.

Understanding flashed over her. Tori laid him on his back and sat up. She continued her massage. "You can't handle regular milk, can you? And that's what I mixed with your formula."

When had she last fed him? Tori consulted to clock to calculate the time. She groaned. "Six hours. That's far too long. Let me make you a bottle. With water, this time."

David's cries lasted until she'd heated some water, mixed in the formula, and brought him the bottle. When he latched onto the sustenance, blessed silence filled the room. She exhaled and closed her eyes.

Minutes later, as David was halfway through his bottle, Ella and Lydia returned with the men. Travis removed his hat. "Howdy, Tori." He set the hat on a desk. "Where's Amanda?"

"On the bed behind that curtain." Tori pointed to the left. "Thanks for coming."

"No problem. This here's Pastor Samuel Allen, Lydia's husband."

Pastor Allen held out a hand. His blue-green eyes shone

with compassion. "It's nice to meet you, ma'am, though these circumstances are not ideal."

"Likewise, Pastor."

"Please, call me Samuel. Everyone does."

"Samuel, then. I appreciate you doing this."

"Everyone deserves a proper burial."

The men went to the bed where Amanda lay. Tori kept her gaze averted, focusing instead on David. Lydia and Ella sat on either side of her. "He's calmed down," Ella said.

"For now. We'll see what happens when I take away the bottle."

Lydia traced a finger down his cheek. "He's about to fall asleep."

"Is he?" Tori peered closer. David's eyelids sank downward, his mouth moving slower. Within a few seconds, his eyes closed completely.

Travis and Samuel walked past, Amanda's body wrapped in a white sheet. Tori shuddered as her gaze snagged on the blood-soaked sheets still on the floor. She'd have to wash those soon. Or burn them.

"What are you going to do with David?" Lydia asked.

Tori's gaze returned to the sleeping boy. "I don't know."

"There's an orphanage a couple towns over," Ella said quietly. "Infants are more likely to be adopted than older children. That might be his best chance."

I don't want my boy growing up in an orphanage.

Amanda's desperate plea locked into Tori's brain. She hadn't promised anything, but if she couldn't save the young woman, shouldn't she honor her last wish? Not that she planned to raise David herself, but surely, someone in Harmony Springs could take him?

"Is there anyone in town who wants a baby?"

Ella tipped her head, brows drawn together. "Not that I can think of. Most folks around here are busy with their own families and not looking for the responsibility that comes with adopting an infant. But I could be wrong." She looked at Lydia. "Do you know of anyone?"

"I'd be open to it if we weren't expecting a baby of our own soon." Lydia sighed. "As much as I hate to say it, Ella's right. An orphanage is probably the best option."

A surge of protectiveness shot through Tori. "He could end up with anyone. How would we know he got a good home?"

Ella took her hand. "Unfortunately, there's no guarantee. All we can do is pray he ends up where God wants him to be."

The weight in Tori's chest grew heavier. For the second time, tears welled in her eyes and slipped down her cheeks.

"Oh, honey." Ella pulled her into an embrace. "You've been through a lot since yesterday. It's normal to feel overwhelmed."

"Is it?" Tori wiped away the tears. Her cheeks heated. What a time for a display of emotion. "I prefer being in control of my feelings."

"Don't we all? But you're human. Let yourself feel."

Squaring her shoulders, Tori dried the remaining tears on her dress sleeve. "Maybe later. Right now, David needs me." She picked him up, resting him against her chest. "I'll be in my apartment. We both need sleep."

"You were up all night?"

"Yes."

Ella grimaced. "A newborn isn't going to let you get the sleep you need. Just keep that in mind."

"He'll be up every few hours wanting to eat," Lydia said. "Babies are hungry all the time."

Despite her exhaustion, Tori chuckled. "You both sound like mothers."

"You'll join us one day." Lydia smiled. "Won't it be fun for our children to grow up together?"

The thought of children brought Harrison to mind. A blush

heated Tori's cheeks. "We'll see. I want to be established as a doctor before having children."

"These things have a way of happening outside our time-line," Ella said. "Maybe you'll be a mother before you know it."

Tori glanced down at David. His face had returned to a normal color, and he rested against her in total trust. Warmth bloomed inside as an idea took hold. Amanda had asked, after all.

"Maybe I will."

~

Harrison stepped off the train in a daze. His mind felt numb, his limbs heavy. He'd performed amputations before, and doctors at the Helena hospital had asked him to take the lead because of his experience. While the operation saved the woman's life, her horror-stricken expression when she'd woken tore at him.

Then there were the four passengers who'd died at the accident scene. He'd done his best, unable to move them because of the severity of their injuries, but none made it. Hopefully, Tori had better success than him.

As he approached the infirmary, an infant's cries came from within. The pregnant woman, Amanda, must have had her baby. He released a small sigh, relief blooming inside. At least someone survived that wreck unscathed.

He opened the door and walked in. Setting down his bag, he looked around the room. "Tori?"

The cries continued. His gaze swung to the stairs. Were they coming from the apartment? He trudged up the steps and pushed open the door, then stopped in his tracks.

Tori stood in the kitchen, a bundle in her arms. She bounced it up and down as she paced.

He moved into their home. "Hi."

"Harrison."

The weariness in her voice had him moving toward her at a rapid pace. "What's wrong?"

To his surprise, she burrowed into him, one arm wrapping around his waist. His arms automatically lifted to hold her. And...the baby?

He rubbed her back. "Are you okay?"

Tori pulled back with a sniff. She laughed, but no humor lurked in it. "I'm just finding out what a terrible mother I'll be."

"What do you mean?" He took in the red-faced infant. "Where's his mother?"

"In the graveyard."

His gaze snapped to her face. "The graveyard?" A sick feeling twisted his stomach. "Amanda died?"

"Yes. Now David has no one."

She said the words with a fierce look on her face, as if she expected him to argue.

About what?

He raked a hand through his hair. "I'm sorry to hear that. Is David healthy?"

"As far as I can tell. He just cries a lot." Her expression fell. "It's constant. I can't get him to stop unless he's eating or sleeping."

"Do you have any guesses why?"

"I think his stomach can't handle milk. He had some yesterday." She resumed pacing. "How long can that affect a child?"

"Anywhere from a few hours to a few days."

Tori groaned. "I can't take days of this."

Harrison rubbed his forehead. "Maybe tomorrow I can take drop him off at the nearest orphanage. I'm sure Travis can tell me where..."

"No."

He lowered his hand back to his side. "No? Is someone in town going to take him?"

Tori lifted her chin, her mouth setting into a determined line. "We are."

"I beg your pardon?" He blinked several times, his brain reduced to mush. "What do you mean, *we* are?"

"Amanda asked me to take care of him. She doesn't want him going to an orphanage." Her eyes flashed fire. "I couldn't save her, but I can honor her last request."

"Tori." He reached out, halting her steps with his hands on her shoulders. "You can't take in a child out of guilt."

She jerked away. "Yes, I can. I'm responsible for her death." Her lips trembled and tears welled in her eyes, a sudden change coming over her expression as she looked at David. "I can't let her down in this."

"Was there some neglect on your part that led to her death?"

"I'd never neglect a patient."

"Did you purposefully let her die?"

She rolled her eyes. "Of course not."

"Then I fail to see why her death is your responsibility." He crossed his arms. "Which means this child isn't either."

David's cries slowly stopped. Tori grunted. "Good. He's asleep." Her chin lifted once more, and she pinned Harrison with a glare. "If he's put in an orphanage, there's no telling what kind of home he'd end up in. I'm not about to let him go to a bad one. Not when we can care for him and provide a good life."

"Victoria, be reasonable. You and I just moved here. We're trying to start our own practice, and we're building a hospital that we'll have to staff and run. How are we going to care for a newborn? Are you planning on giving up your dream?" He pointed at David. "Because that baby is going to need constant care for months. He'll be up at all hours night and day. It'll be near impossible for you to mother him *and* care for patients."

The mulish set of her mouth didn't bode well. She hugged

the baby close. "We'll figure it out. He's not going to an orphanage."

He sighed. "This is an emotional response. You're not thinking clearly."

"I'm thinking just fine."

Drawing in a deep breath, Harrison shook his head. "Can we at least take some time to think the situation through? I'm not ready to commit to fatherhood on a whim. We need to pray about this."

Tori opened her mouth but shut it before anything came out. She looked at David again, her throat bobbing with a swallow. "Why can't we just decide now?"

"You know decisions made in the heat of a moment can turn out bad. We can't just adopt a baby. We need to consider what's best for him—and that it might not be us."

She sighed. Shoulders slumped, she walked to the living room and sank onto the sofa. "I proposed to you on a whim. That turned out fine."

His lips turned up. "If you recall, I asked for time to pray and think it over."

"You did." Tori tipped her head, giving him a self-deprecating smile. "I suppose it's a good thing we're not both hot-headed emotional wrecks."

He sat beside her. "You're passionate, not hot-headed."

"Semantics."

"Your heart is pure, Tori, and you want to do the right thing. That will serve us well in determining what to do about David."

She extended her arms. "Do you want to hold him?"

He accepted the tiny bundle. David moved in his sleep before settling once more. Harrison leaned back against the sofa, releasing a long breath. It had been years since he held an infant.

Tori touched his arm. Harrison met her gaze. She smiled and motioned to the baby. "You're a natural."

He chuckled, the hope in her tone impossible to miss. "We'll see, Tori. No decision for at least a week."

She bit her lip. "So long?"

"This is a life-altering choice. Yes, so long. At least."

"Fine." She leaned closer. "Now, tell me what happened in Helena."

"It's not a pretty story. Are you sure you want to hear it?"

She stayed quiet a moment. "We both had a rough couple of days. I think it would be good to share how we're coping."

"Sounds like something an old married couple would do."

Her lips twitched. "Then I guess we're an old married couple now."

CHAPTER 12

$\mathcal{A}$ few days later, Harrison walked the length of the hospital's stone foundation. The crew had an excellent work ethic. Not only was the foundation complete, but construction had begun on the frame. The outline of four walls were up, logs having been transformed into long beams. Wooden planks lay in a large pile close by, ready to be affixed to the frame.

A hot breeze blew, giving mild relief from the burning sun in a cloudless sky. Several of Wyatt's crew milled about, on their midday break, finding shade where they could.

Harrison shook a beam. It didn't move. He grinned and held his hand out to Wyatt. "You're doing great. There'll be a bonus for all your workers if this keeps up."

Wyatt chuckled, slapping his hat against his thigh. "You're already paying us a high fee. This operation's gonna keep me afloat for at least a year, thanks to your generosity."

"It's worth it for the quality you produce." Harrison stood back, taking in the entire structure. "At this rate, you'll be done by autumn."

"That's the goal."

"Did the glass for windows come in yet?"

"Nah. Mr. Peterson said it could be another week."

"That reminds me, I need to talk to Mr. Peterson." Harrison clapped Wyatt's shoulder. "I'll see you in a few days."

"Sure thing, Doc."

Harrison strode to the mercantile. He needed to put in an order for more infant formula. Feeding David multiple times a day would quickly put a dent in their supply.

When he walked through the door, Mr. Peterson greeted him from the counter. "Good afternoon, Dr. Blake. I'll be with you in just a moment."

"Take your time."

Harrison wandered the aisles. A package of lemon drops caught his eye. Tori loved lemon drops. This was the first time he'd seen them in Harmony Springs. He picked up the package and smiled. What would her reaction be?

The memory of their kiss flashed through his mind. It still had the power to make his cheeks flush. She hadn't kissed him out of affection—that much was clear. Even so, he couldn't help but wish to repeat that moment.

He'd married a feisty, passionate woman, and though their marriage had been strictly convenient, his heart wanted more. So much more. She grew dearer to him with each passing day.

Was it selfish to wish for love when his wife had no desire for it?

"Harrison."

Her voice sounded close by. Gracious, was he hallucinating? He shook himself. "Get it together, Blake."

"While I don't disagree, what is it you need to get together?"

He whirled, meeting Tori's amused gaze. "Tori? What are you doing here?"

She swayed gently, nodding down at an alert David in her arms. "We're going to need more infant formula. A lot more. He'll be drinking it for months."

Even if they didn't adopt him, having formula to give to his new family would be ideal. He smiled. "I came here to order more."

She blinked, her brown eyes going wide. "Really?"

"Is that so hard to believe?"

"I suppose not." Her gaze fell to the lemon drops. "What are those for?"

"You."

Tori's eyes grew even larger. "Really?"

"You like them, so I thought I'd purchase them."

She swallowed. "I...appreciate that. Thank you."

David began to fuss. Tori bounced him from side to side. "I should probably take a walk. He seems to like that. I'd like to see how the hospital is progressing."

"I'll join you once the order is in."

She nodded, and as she left, Mr. Peterson walked up to him. "Dr. Blake. How can I help you?"

He placed the lemon drops on the counter. "I'll take these, and I'd like to order infant formula from Boston."

"Follow me, and we'll get that ready."

Five minutes later, Harrison left the mercantile. He retraced his steps to the hospital. Once he arrived, he surveyed the field, searching for Tori. She wove through a grove of trees a stone's throw from the building. He strode toward her.

She caught sight of him long before he reached her. With a little wave, she paused under the shade of a large pine tree. Harrison stopped beside her and peered at David. "He's sleeping."

"The walk tuckered him out."

She began walking again, and Harrison fell into step with her. "What do you think of the hospital?" he asked.

"It looks better than I imagined. How long until it's complete?"

"Wyatt thinks they'll have it done by summer's end. His

crew will install the doors and windows as well. After that, we'll be in charge of furnishing it and stocking it with supplies."

"I can't believe we really did this." Tori sighed. The content sound sent a rush of butterflies through his stomach. She smiled at him, and the butterflies swarmed. "Isn't it amazing that we're here and accomplishing our goals? This marriage was an excellent answer to our problems."

The butterflies fell along with his heart. "Right. A good business transaction."

His wife gave him a long look, a strange expression crossing her face. "Exactly."

So much for wishing for love. He'd be happy if they remained friends. Especially if the issue of adopting David or giving him to another family came between them.

"I was thinking," Tori said. "Cow's milk upsets David's stomach, but what if we tried goat's milk? That worked for another child I cared for once in Boston."

"It's worth a try. Though if it doesn't work, he'll be fussy for another few days."

A slight wince hunched her body. "I don't like that thought, but if he can stomach goat's milk, he'll get more nutrients than he would from water alone." She barked a small laugh. "Besides, it's not as though we're getting lots of sleep, anyway. If he cries a lot after drinking it, we'll know what the problem is."

"Maybe we can stop by the café and see if Cassie has any goat's milk." His stomach rumbled. "We should get some lunch too. Did you eat this morning?"

"Uh..." Tori squinted. Her lips pursed, drawing his gaze. He forced it away and fought the memory of their kiss to the recesses of his mind.

"I don't think I did."

Blast. That had become common since David's arrival. "Tori, you won't be able to care for him or our patients if you're not getting enough food yourself." He took her free hand. "Come on. We're going to eat."

She chuckled, shaking her head. "If I wasn't so hungry, I'd protest your assumption that I wanted to eat."

"It's a fact, not an assumption. You haven't eaten anything since supper last night." He led her toward town. "Someone needs to take care of you."

"And you think that's your job?"

"You're my wife, so yes, it is my job. One I'm happy to fulfill."

She paused, pulling him to a stop. "Harrison…"

When she didn't continue, he came closer. "Yes?"

Her breath hitched. The sound did something to his insides. He cupped her cheek, rubbing his thumb against her soft skin. Her eyes glowed amber in the sunlight. They drew him in, and he leaned toward her, his gaze falling to her lips.

David jerked with a soft cry. Tori's attention dropped to the baby. She rocked him and made quiet shushing sounds.

The moment was gone.

Harrison stepped back and cleared his throat. "Let's go get you some food."

Maybe the walk would help him make sense of the jumbled emotions swirling inside.

~

The next day, Tori sat on Ella's front porch, watching her sister's four children play in the yard. David slept on a blanket beside her. So far, the goat's milk they'd gotten from Cassie seemed to be working. He ate ravenously and showed no signs of discomfort.

Thank God.

"Jonah, don't trip Addie," Ella called.

Tori chuckled. "They can be a handful, huh?"

"You have no idea." Ella took a sip of her lemonade. "Sometimes I wonder what I got myself into."

"But you love being their mother."

A smile softened Ella's face. "I wouldn't trade it for the world. My family is everything to me." She glanced at Tori. "Speaking of family, how are things with Harrison?"

Harrison.

Tori shifted. In the aftermath of Amanda's death, she'd never had a chance to process her confused feelings for her husband, not with Ella. Since caring for David, she'd shoved those feelings away to examine later. But yesterday in that field, after he'd purchased those lemon drops and stood so close, so focused on caring for her, everything stirred up again.

Now Ella gave her the perfect opportunity to share. With a deep breath, Tori willed her voice to remain steady. "I kissed him last week."

Her sister's brows shot up. "Oh?"

"And I think he almost kissed me yesterday, when we were checking on the hospital."

"That's progress, isn't it?" Ella's eyes sparkled, no doubt pleased with the prospect of another love match in the world.

Tori shrugged. "Is it progress? Or is it just fickle feelings?"

Forehead scrunching, Ella tilted her head. "Fickle feelings?"

"A kiss is universally considered pleasant. The fact that I enjoyed kissing Harrison doesn't necessarily mean anything, right?"

A smile crept over Ella's face. "You enjoyed it?"

"Focus, Ella."

Her sister chuckled. "Fine. Tell me—have you ever kissed another man?"

Kenneth's face flashed through her mind. "Yes."

"Was it pleasant?"

Tori scrunched her nose. "Absolutely not."

"But you enjoyed Harrison's kiss?" Ella grinned. "Would you kiss him again?"

Heat burned Tori's cheeks. Did she have to answer that?

Ella sat back with a satisfied look. "I'll take that as a yes."

"I don't want to fall in love."

"Why? What's the worst that could happen? You're already tied to Harrison for life. Would it be so awful to love him?"

Pain speared Tori's heart. She rubbed her chest, tears stinging her eyes as old fears rose. "It might be. What if he never loved me back?"

"Impossible."

"It's not impossible. Father never loved me. He said I was unlovable."

Ella froze. Her green eyes burned with fury. "He what?"

"When I was little. He said it many different ways, but I got the message. And he wasn't the only one."

"What do you mean?"

"I allowed a few men to court me over the years. When I broke it off, they all said the same thing—that I was a shrew, incapable of love or being in love."

Anger pulsed from Ella's face. "Of all the ridiculous—"

"Is it?"

The quiet question hung in the air. Ella sucked in a sharp breath. "You don't truly believe them?"

"I'm opinionated, stubborn, and prickly. No one—other than you—has expressed love for me. What am I supposed to think?"

Tears welled in Ella's eyes. She reached for Tori's hand. "Anyone who knows you well knows you are lovable. I'm sure Harrison will see it too." Her lips set in a tight line. "Unless he's entirely dimwitted."

Tori threw her arms around Ella. "What would I do without you?" She squeezed her sister tight, then drew back. "Now, can we move on from love talk?"

"If you like."

Little cries came from the blanket. Tori rose, but they stopped as quickly as they started. She sank back onto the step. "Is that common for babies?"

"Yes. Rosie made noises all the time in her sleep, or she'd start to wake but fall back asleep in seconds."

Tori rested her chin in her hands, elbows digging into her thighs. "The longer I have David, the more I realize I know almost nothing about babies."

"That's common, Tori. Women have been figuring it out as they go from the very beginning."

"Most women have nine months to prepare." She shook her head. "I don't know how you handled becoming an instant mother to three children."

"I did what I had to, and so will you. If you choose to keep David." Ella peered at her. "Do you think you will?"

"I don't know, Ella. This little boy needs a home and a family. No one here is a likely candidate. Amanda asked me to take care of him. He needs me. I wanted to adopt him on the spot, but Harrison said we should take time to think it over."

"And?"

She sighed. "And he was right. It's been five days. I haven't slept. I'm exhausted. Harrison has been seeing all our patients because I'm caring for the baby." Her throat felt tight. "I fear I'll have to choose between being a doctor and being a mother."

"And you've wanted to be a doctor your whole life."

Tori swallowed hard. "I've worked hard to get here. It's the whole reason I'm in Harmony Springs. But...I can't let David go to an orphanage. I just can't."

"What if you could find a good home for him? One where you knew he'd be treated well?"

"That'd be a blessed relief." Though a small part of her heart twinged at the thought of giving him up.

Her sister's teeth sank into her lower lip. Dead giveaway she had something to say.

"What's on your mind, Ella?" Tori asked.

Ella chuckled quietly. "You've always been able to read me." She fell silent for a moment. Finally, she spoke. "I haven't been able to get David's situation off my mind. You don't want him going to an orphanage, and I understand. Cody grew up in one —and it scarred him in ways he had to fight to overcome. We talked it over last night, and we'd like to adopt him."

Hope sprang through Tori. "Really?"

"There's just one caveat."

"Oh?"

"Cody is driving some of our cattle to Helena next week. He'll be gone at least seven days. It would be a struggle to care for five children on my own…"

"If it comes to that, I can stay with you."

Ella studied her. A small smile crossed her lips. "I believe you would. But what about the infirmary?"

Tori bit her lip. "I don't know. We can figure that out."

Another cry came from the blanket. This time, it didn't stop. Tori started to rise, but Ella put a hand on her arm. "Let me."

Tori watched the children play a game of tag as Ella got David. When she sat again, Tori smiled at the baby. "Hey, little guy. How would you feel about Ella as a mama?"

He gurgled, one hand waving in the air.

Tori let him grasp her finger. "I think he likes you."

Ella snuggled him close. The smile on her face lit her features. "I love babies." Her gaze lifted, meeting Tori's. "Are you sure you're okay with him coming to us?"

"I think so. This way, he's still part of the family. He'll just be my nephew instead of my son." She ran a finger down his soft cheek. "Though it might be an adjustment. As tired as I am, I've gotten used to him being around."

"Will Harrison be all right with this plan?"

"I imagine so. He seemed hesitant to adopt while we're settling in town and having the hospital built. I think he was also concerned about me—because he knows how long I've worked to become a doctor." She huffed a laugh. "He married me to make sure that dream lived on."

"You married a good man." Ella nudged her. "One you should consider loving."

"That wasn't our agreement."

"Agreements change."

Standing, Tori shook her head. "You focus on loving that little baby and integrating him into the family. I'll bring by formula and show you how to use it."

"Thanks, Tori." Ella hugged her new son, then shot Tori a pointed look. "Can you promise me you'll at least keep an open mind about love?"

Her sister wouldn't let up unless she agreed. Tori plunked her hands on her hips. "I'll think about it."

"Good. I'll see you later."

Tori embraced each niece and nephew before heading back to town. Ella's words raced through her mind on repeat. *Keep an open mind about love.*

She sighed. Easier said than done.

CHAPTER 13

That evening, after getting back from Ella's, Tori paced nervously in the infirmary as she waited for Harrison to get home. Would he be relieved that David was with the Brooks? Upset? Something else?

She crossed her arms. Despite the July heat, chills pricked her skin. Had she made the right decision in letting Ella adopt David? Should she have discussed it with Harrison first?

And why did she care so much what he thought?

"Tori."

With a squeal, she jumped back. Harrison stood nearby, a wry smile on his lips. "You didn't hear me come in?"

"No, I—" She gasped. "Harrison, what happened?"

His torn, blood-stained shirt clung to his stomach. He chuckled quietly, then winced. "I was helping Wyatt fell some trees for more hospital lumber. One of the branches nicked me when I didn't get back fast enough."

"'Nicked'?" She stared at his shirt. "That's no nick." She took his arm and led him to one of the beds. "We need to get you cleaned and bandaged. Take that shirt off."

"Yes, ma'am."

At least he sounded amused. He couldn't have lost too much blood, then. Even so...

He struggled with the buttons. Tori fought a wave of nausea seeing his hands bloodied. She'd never had a problem with blood before. But seeing his blood?

She shoved the queasiness aside and rested her hands over his. "Let me."

He stilled, gaze locked on her as she began working the buttons apart. "You know, some would consider this improper."

"Then it's a good thing we're married, so there will be no hint of impropriety," she retorted, slipping the shirt from his torso. Another bout of nausea assailed her. So much blood.

"It's not as bad as it looks," Harrison said.

She gulped. "I hope you're right. Let's get you cleaned up and see what we're dealing with."

After washing the six-inch gash stretching from his chest to abdomen, she breathed a small sigh of relief. "It needs sutures, but otherwise, you should be fine."

"Stitch me up, Dr. Blake."

"I'm glad you haven't lost your sense of humor." She walked to the shelf with materials for sutures. "Hopefully, this won't hurt too much."

"I have faith in you."

Her hand trembled as she threaded the needle. A lump clogged her throat. "That makes one of us."

Silence descended as she worked to close his wound. She felt his gaze on her, but she refused to make eye contact. A few minutes later, she placed a clean bandage over the area. "Now, let's get your other scratches cleaned...oh!"

In her focus to patch up Harrison's gash, she'd not noticed the raised white patches along his chest and shoulders. The scars were old—and there were several. She traced the largest one just under his collarbone. "Harrison, what happened?"

He caught her hand. "I'm more interested in why you suddenly doubt yourself. That's not the Victoria I know."

Her fingers moved to another scar on his upper arm. "Maybe we can trade stories. You first."

"Not here. Let's go upstairs."

He turned for the steps. Tori's mouth dropped open when she saw his back. More scars marred his skin.

Burns, all of them.

She followed him silently to their apartment, questions rising with each step.

Harrison shut the door behind them and rubbed his neck. "I'll get another shirt, then we can talk."

Tori lowered herself onto the sofa. A heart-to-heart with her husband hadn't been the plan, but it looked as though they were about to spend their evening that way.

He came back into the room, buttoning a blue shirt. "Where's David?"

"Umm...that's something we need to talk about as well."

Harrison sat beside her and stretched his arm along the back of the sofa. "Oh?"

"My sister said she and Cody would like to adopt him. He's with them. I brought Ella some formula to feed him. She said she will need help next week when Cody is on a cattle drive, and I told her I'd stay at her place. You can, too, if you'd like, but you don't have to. Someone needs to keep the infirmary open. I'd still help, of course, but Ella will need me. I probably should have talked to you first..."

Harrison put a finger over her lips. "Tori."

She met his gaze.

He dropped his hand, rubbing it over his beard before taking a deep breath. "For your sake, I'm glad Ella and Cody decided to adopt David."

"My sake?"

"Being a doctor is your dream. Caring for an infant would

have made that difficult. Someday, once our practice is established, we'll have children of our own, and we'll figure things out then."

Iron claws gripped her stomach. Tori swallowed. "I don't think I'll be a good mother, Harrison. After caring for David, I do want children—but I'm afraid I don't have what it takes. And how would I be able to practice medicine with an infant? It's not practical."

Something shone in Harrison's eyes. "The fact that you want children is enough. When it happens, perhaps we can hire someone to help with the baby so you can be a mother and a doctor."

She blinked. "You'd be okay with that?"

"Why wouldn't I be?"

"So many people told me I should give up my dream to be a society wife and mother. None of them would consider anything else. But you...you keep surprising me."

"Your dreams are important to me because they're important to you." He gently nudged her chin. "I happen to like having you as a partner. Which brings us back to why you doubted yourself earlier."

"I thought you were going first."

He leaned back, a smile curling his lips. "You're already baring your heart, my dear. Might as well continue."

Her heart skipped a beat. "'My dear'?"

"Do you not like it?"

"It's not that. It's just such a..."

"Married person thing to say?"

"Yes."

He winked. "We are married."

"Did that tree whack your head?"

The smile on his face grew. "Nope." He sobered quickly. "If you don't like it—"

"It's fine."

Taking her hand, he smiled again. "Good. Now, why were you doubting yourself? Is this about Amanda?"

"I can't let go of the guilt. Logically, I know there was nothing more I could have done. But what if there was something I missed? Some sign, some hint? Maybe I shouldn't have walked away to talk to Cassie before the afterbirth passed. Anything."

"You did what you could. It was out of your hands." Sadness seeped into his expression. "Sometimes, that will happen. Amanda won't be the last patient you lose. This is the dark side of our job." He tugged her a little closer, arm coming to rest across her shoulders. "Did I ever tell you about the first patient I lost?"

"No."

"He was a teenager, barely sixteen years old. There was a terrible logging accident, and he was bleeding internally. I'd never had a patient with that level of trauma, but there were no other doctors available. He died before I finished readying him for surgery." His grip tightened on her hand. "I blamed myself for months, wondering if I could have done something different. It took a wiser physician telling me—repeatedly—it wasn't my fault for me to finally believe it. So, Victoria Blake, hear me when I tell you, Amanda's death wasn't your fault."

"Thank you for telling me that story. It does help, a little." She sighed. "I can't just stop blaming myself."

"It's hard, but you'll get there."

She rested her head on his shoulder. "I hope you're right."

Her eyelids grew heavy. Snuggled against Harrison, she felt warm and safe. She rested a hand against his chest. His heartbeat thumped strong, stable. Just like the man himself.

How fortunate she'd been to marry such a man.

His chest rose and fell with each breath. Though she couldn't see them, Tori imagined her fingers rested over one of his puffy scars.

"How'd you get those scars?" she whispered.

He tensed, but a moment later let out a breath. "It was a fire. A few days before I turned seven, a friend and I were playing in the kitchen. The cook warned us to stay away from the open flames in the hearth.. We heeded her for a time, but when we started wrestling, we rolled too close. My shirt caught fire. The cook managed to get the flames out, but I'd been burned pretty bad. I was in the hospital for a week after that. Thankfully, I healed, though these burn scars will be with me the rest of my life—as will a fear of fire. Flames terrify me to this day."

Understanding flickered. She lifted her head. "That's why you couldn't go into that burning building. The one with the immigrant workers."

Pain flashed in his eyes. "Yes." He exhaled slowly. "I still wish I could change my actions that day."

"That's not your fault either. You might have died along with them."

"Or I could have saved them."

She framed his face in her hands. "Harrison, we can't change the past, can't worry about what might have been."

His lips twitched. "Oh?"

The meaning of her words hit. She shook her head. "All right, fine, I can apply that to my life too."

He gripped her hands, pulling them from his cheeks. "Maybe we can work on this together, hmm? Giving ourselves some grace and leaving it all in God's hands?"

She smiled, laying her head on his shoulder once more. "I think that's a good plan."

 few days later, Harrison pulled off the bandage covering his wound. He turned to Tori. "How does it look?"

She hummed, eyes narrowing. "There's some oozing. It needs to be cleaned again."

His least favorite part of recovery. He braced himself for the sting of carbolic acid. When Tori pressed the soaked cloth against his skin, he hissed.

"Sorry." A small smile played on her lips.

He eyed her, shaking his head as her smile grew. "You're enjoying this."

"It's amusing that a seasoned doctor is a baby over his own injury."

"I don't think anyone would appreciate the feel of phenol over a stitched wound."

"Excuses." She applied a thick honey ointment to his skin, then a new bandage. "There. Feel better?"

"It still stings."

"Of course it does. It'll start itching soon too."

He groaned.

Tori shook her head. "A big baby."

She cleaned up the medical supplies she'd used while Harrison rebuttoned his shirt and slipped a gray vest over it. He reached for his doctor's coat. "I saw we got several requests for house visits today."

"Yes. It was a good idea to allow folks to make those requests. Today's are mostly from some elderly residents who want relief from aches and pains. But there's another from the Kopper family. It seems their daughter has been fighting a cold for weeks. Mrs. Kopper requested we come early. We should probably see her first."

"'We'? You don't want to split up? We'd get done faster."

She let out a mirthless laugh. "I'm a woman, Harrison, as the people of this town keep reminding me. Until they trust me, I'd rather have you around."

He grabbed her arm as she passed and waited until she

looked at him. "As much as I wish folks trusted you already, I'm not sorry we'll be working side by side for now."

She stared at his hand before slowly lifting her gaze to his. Something electric crackled in the air between them. Harrison's gaze fell to her lips. The desire to kiss her pulsed through him, so strong he leaned toward her before he realized what he did.

No. That's not what she needs.

He jerked back, his hand falling to his side. Clearing his throat, he grabbed his doctor bag. "I'll meet you out front."

It was all too easy to lose control around his beguiling wife.

Stepping outside, he took a deep breath of the hot August air. Partners. He needed to remember that Tori was his partner. She wasn't looking for romance. Though...what would she do if he tried to win her over?

Probably smack him.

Harrison chuckled under his breath. Maybe he'd run it by Ella's husband. It couldn't hurt to bond with his brother-in-law, and if Cody could give him advice, so much the better.

His wife exited the building a minute later, shutting the door behind her. Her cheeks looked a tad pink as she met his eyes. "Where is the Kopper place?"

"A little ways out of town. It's a ten-minute walk. Would you prefer a buggy?"

"No. Walking is fine."

As they set out, her face definitely looked flushed. Was it from their near-kiss moments before?

The walk passed in silence—a comfortable silence. He looked forward to being with her today, taking care of patients together.

The Kopper home was small, built of logs and roofed with thatch. A large vegetable garden sat to the left of the house. A brown-haired woman met them at the door, wringing her hands. "Thank God you've come. My little Cynthia is not gettin' any better. Can you help her?"

Harrison gave her a nod. "Mrs. Kopper?"

"That's me. Come in."

Mrs. Kopper led them into the one-room dark house, to a cot along the far wall. A little girl around six lay there, pale and still. The stuffy interior was far too hot. Harrison knelt beside the child. "Why is everything shut up?"

"My husband said that's what his ma did when they were sick. It's supposed to help."

Tori began sliding open curtains and throwing open the windows. "That's not the case, ma'am. Stuffy, hot air will make her worse. She needs the fresh breeze."

Already, the room felt better. Harrison opened his bag. "What are her symptoms?"

"Cough, wheezing breath, sometimes a fever, and a sore throat. The cough's the worst. It's been persistent."

Harrison pulled out his stethoscope. "Let's see…"

"Before ya go on, Doc, I should tell you we don't have any money to pay. I can trade ya some vegetables from our garden, though."

"That's fine. Dr. Blake and I love vegetables. Don't we, my dear?" He shot a smile at Tori.

She smiled back and knelt beside him. "We do. Especially zucchini."

Mrs. Kopper straightened, a glimmer of hope in her eyes. "We have plenty of those. I'll go pick some and clean 'em for ya." She slipped out the front door.

"You hate zucchini," Harrison said under his breath.

"But I could see that was the most plentiful vegetable in her garden. They'll still have some left over." Tori shrugged. "We can give them to Cassie. She'll know what to do with zucchini."

"You're a good woman, Victoria."

Her face flushed again. He hid a smile, pleased that he could provoke such a reaction. She felt Cynthia's forehead. "No fever."

Cynthia burst into a coughing fit. Harrison lifted her to allow for easier breathing. When the fit passed, he laid her back. "We need to elevate this pallet."

"I saw some wood in the yard. Perhaps we could use that?"

"Excellent. I'll be right back."

He went to the yard and examined the wood pile. After finding a few pieces he liked, he returned to the house. Tori lifted the pallet while he arranged the wood beneath. "There. That should do."

Cynthia pulled at her blanket. "Am I gonna die?"

"Not if we can help it." Tori smiled at the girl. "Dr. Blake is going to listen to your lungs now with his stethoscope."

He extended it to her. "Why don't you do it?"

She startled, staring at the stethoscope. "Maybe you should—"

He pressed the instrument into her hands. Bending close, he whispered, "You're a good doctor, Victoria. I believe in you."

She inhaled softly, her brown eyes wide and uncertain. Amanda's death had taken a heavy toll on her, but the best way to overcome her doubts would be to keep practicing. He nodded at Cynthia. With shaky hands, Tori put the earpieces in her ears and pressed the bell to the child's lungs. "Breathe deeply, please."

Cynthia obeyed. Air wheezed in and out. Tori listened for a few moments, then put the stethoscope back in the bag. "Based on the symptoms her mother listed and the sound of her lungs, I think she has bronchitis."

A gasp came from the door. Mrs. Kopper stood there, holding a basket of zucchini, one hand at her heart. "Bronchitis? That sounds bad."

"It can be, but we have some remedies." Harrison pulled a small bottle from his bag. "This is garlic syrup. It's not pleasant to the taste, but it helps soothe the lungs. I also recommend pepper tea and honey, along with lots of rest. Keep the bed elevated like it is now. We'll come by in a couple days to check on her."

"Thanks, Doc." Mrs. Kopper exchanged the basket for the bottle. "Both of ya."

"No trouble, ma'am. Thanks for the zucchini." Harrison extended his arm to Tori. "Shall we?"

Before they got to the door, a burly man walked in. Harrison recognized him at once—the man who'd protested having a lady doctor at the town hall meeting.

The man's gaze narrowed on Tori. "What's she doin' here?"

Mrs. Kopper clutched the bottle in her hands. "Gerard, the docs were here to see Cynthia. She's got bronchitis. We have a remedy—"

"I don't want no lady doc in my house." The man—Mr. Kopper—glared at Tori. "You can leave."

"That's no way to treat the doctor who just diagnosed your daughter," Harrison said, pulling Tori closer to him. "You should be thanking her."

"No reason to. Ain't it enough that they're buildin' that silly hospital?" He huffed out a laugh. "It won't last more than a month."

Tori bristled. "What are you saying, sir?"

Mr. Kopper hung his hat on its hook, never taking his eyes off Tori. "All I'm sayin' is, some folk here might not accept a lady doc. If I was you, I'd be careful."

The words felt more threat than caution. Harrison took a step forward, putting himself between Tori and Mr. Kopper. "Folk like you?"

Mrs. Kopper looked between the three of them uneasily. "Gerard, we should let the docs get back to town. They've other patients to see."

"Bah." He slashed his hand through the air and went to the table, turning his back on Harrison and Tori.

Mrs. Kopper ushered them out. "I'm so sorry you had to see

that." She glanced back at her husband. "He hasn't always been like this. Times are hard, and he can't find work. It's gratin' on him somethin' fierce."

"He shouldn't take it out on my wife." Harrison crossed his arms.

"I know. I'm sorry." She held up the bottle. "Thanks for comin'."

As they made their way back to town, Harrison put a hand over Tori's. "How are you feeling?"

Her gaze lifted to his, delight sparkling in her eyes. "Good. Very good."

Not the reaction he'd expected.

"Oh?"

She laughed. "I have no control over the fact that Mr. Kopper is a cad. So I'm not going to let him upset me." Tori's smile grew. "I'm happy because you believe in me. What you did in there, making me take the lead, knowing I struggled after Amanda's death—it restored my confidence." Lifting onto her toes, she pressed a kiss to his cheek. "Thank you, Harrison."

His tongue seemed incapable of speech, not with her kiss branded on his skin. Finally, he managed to croak two words. "You're welcome."

CHAPTER 14

The evening before Cody left on his cattle drive, Harrison and Tori came for supper with the Brooks. They'd intended on settling Tori in for the duration of Cody's trip, but Lydia had volunteered to stay with Ella instead, since she had Samuel to watch their two girls.

Harrison didn't admit it to his wife, but he was relieved. The thought of being alone in their apartment depressed him. He could have stayed at the Brooks ranch as well, but they'd agreed that having one of them in town in case of an overnight emergency was important. The fact that he felt such happiness at not being left alone gave him pause.

When they arrived, Tori headed straight for Ella in the kitchen, and Cody offered to give Harrison a tour of the house, which he accepted.

Cody led him to a corridor with several bedrooms. "It's a good thing we built this addition," he said, hands splayed on his hips. "When Ella and I first married, there were only two bedrooms. Now we have five."

Harrison laughed. "How many kids you planning on?"

"As many as the good Lord gives us." Cody grinned. "We certainly have plenty. Five now, thanks to you."

A sliver of guilt slid over Harrison. "Are you sure you're okay with that? I know it's a big responsibility to adopt a child."

"David already feels like part of the family. The kids love him, and Ella and I do too."

"I'm glad. He deserves to have a good life."

"We'll do our best." Cody motioned out one of the bedroom windows. "Ever seen a barn before?"

"No. Barns were in short supply in Boston."

Cody chuckled. "I imagine so. C'mon. The boys will probably tag along."

As soon as they left the hall, Isaiah and Jonah raced up. "Uncle Harrison," Jonah said, "we have a barn cat now, and she had kittens. Wanna see?"

"Sure. I love kittens."

"Maybe you and Aunt Tori can have one," Isaiah said as he ran for the front door.

"I don't think we have time for a kitten right now, buddy, but thanks for the thought."

He and Cody followed the boys to the barn. Jonah scurried to one of the cow stalls. "Here, Uncle Harrison. Look."

Peering into the stall, Harrison smiled at the three balls of orange fluff. They moved about in halting movements, their meows light and shrill.

Isaiah picked up one of the kittens. "Aren't they cute?"

Harrison entered the stall and sat beside his nephew.

Isaiah plopped the kitten on his lap. "You pet this one."

Doing as he was bid, Harrison smiled. "What soft fur you have," he said to the kitten. The tiny animal meowed and curled up, purring.

Jonah moved closer, a kitten nestled in his arms. "I think he likes you."

Cody rested his arms on the stall wall. "Boys, I'm gonna

show your uncle the barn now. Can you keep the kittens entertained?"

"Yeah, Papa," they chorused.

Harrison handed the kitten to Jonah. "Have fun." He left the stall and looked around. "So you built this?"

"Yep. Took me a few months, but it turned out pretty good." He motioned for Harrison to follow. "I'll show you the loft first."

They came to a staircase. Cody started up. "There used to be a ladder leading up here, but after a fire, I decided to put in stairs instead."

"The fire started by Howard Archambeau's hired man?"

"Yeah." Cody glanced his way. "How much of the story do you know?"

"All of it. Tori told me after Ella gave permission."

"Hmm." Cody regarded him a moment, then chuckled. "Tori must trust you."

Harrison sighed. He dropped onto a hay bale. "I hope she does."

Cody sat opposite him, head cocked. "Want to talk about it?"

Despite not knowing his brother-in-law well, Harrison liked Cody. Could he open up to a near stranger who happened to be family?

Cody chuckled. "I see the struggle in your eyes. No pressure —I just happen to know a thing or two about being married to a Mountbatten woman."

Harrison drew in a deep breath. Time to leap. "I think I'm falling for Tori."

"I'm not surprised."

"You're not?"

"Nope."

No one could accuse Cody of being verbose. Harrison spread his arms. "Please expound on that."

"Are you a romantic?"

Blinking at the unexpected question, he stammered. "Uh... not really."

"You never wanted to fall in love?"

"Of course I did."

Cody hiked a brow. "And you gave that up when you married Tori?"

"She and I were friends. I thought we'd have a comfortable life together, maybe even affection."

"You didn't answer my question."

He huffed. "Fine, I suppose I believed I was giving it up."

"But now you think you're falling for her."

Where was Cody going with this? Harrison shrugged. "Yeah. I think so. Maybe?"

Cody laughed. He rested his elbows on his knees. "If you always hoped to find love, maybe knowing Tori is your only option has you seeing her in a new light. Were you attracted to her before getting married?"

"Uhh...no. I never thought of her in that way. We worked together, and it wouldn't have been professional to develop feelings for her."

"But now you have?"

He thought of the way Tori looked in the mornings, hair wild, eyes sleepy. The way she cared for the patients that came to their infirmary. Her passion, vivaciousness, heart. Her kiss.

"Yeah, I'm attracted to her. But it's more than that. This isn't just some surface feeling. I want to know her more, understand her. I want..." He paused, the weight of his desire pressing in. "I think I want to love her."

"Then love her."

Harrison drummed his fingers against his thigh. "It's not that easy."

"Why not?"

"She's got walls around her heart, Cody. I don't know if I can breach them."

Cody crossed his legs at the ankles. He looked out a large, open window that gave a perfect view of the pastures. "Ella had walls too. It took some time, but once we trusted each other, love grew. I fell before she did, and it sounds as though that might be the case for you as well. You have to be patient with Tori, Harrison. She's been beat down by that awful father of hers. The men in her life haven't been reliable."

"What do I do?"

"Be reliable. Be trustworthy. Show her every day that you choose her. Love her in all the little things, whether she reciprocates or not." Cody leaned forward. "She needs to know she can count on you no matter what."

Harrison stood and began to pace. "I've been reliable for the last several years we've worked together. She knows me."

"That was before you married her. It's different between spouses. She knows you admire and value her work. But do you admire and value *her*?"

"Yes."

"Show her." Cody got to his feet as well. "Keep being her friend, Harrison. That's what marriage largely is—you're building a life-long friendship that happens to have romance as well."

Harrison nodded slowly. "Thanks, Cody. I'll consider your advice."

He and Tori were friends already. Was it truly a matter of adding romance? If his brother-in-law was right, it could change so much. They had everything to gain and nothing to lose.

*T*ori woke exhausted a few days after dinner with the Brooks. She and Harrison had a steady stream of patients late into the night, and after she fell into bed, she couldn't seem to sleep. Three days of late nights and sleep deprivation had her off kilter.

She felt like a horse had trampled her. Tori rolled to her side with a groan. It was going to be a long day.

A splash of purple, blue, and yellow caught her gaze. She pushed herself up, staring at the bouquet of wildflowers on the bedside table. Beside the crystal vase sat a small note.

Victoria, I hope these flowers bring a little joy to your day. See you downstairs. -H

She blinked. The note fell to her lap. Though small, the flowers brightened the room with vivid color and sweet perfume. No man brought her wildflowers before. Every bouquet in the past had been large, ostentation—meant to buy her affection.

It never worked.

Yet this simple arrangement of flowers from the fields around town—and the one who'd taken time to pick them— made a flutter parade through her stomach.

She got out of bed, washed up, then donned a checkered brown skirt and white waist shirt. After pinning up her hair, she headed down to the infirmary.

Harrison sat at the desk, his back to her. Uncertainty paused her steps. How should she greet him? Should she bring up the flowers with a simple thank you? Why had he picked them in the first place?

He peered over his shoulder. A smile lit his face. "Good morning, my dear. How did you sleep?"

My dear should not cause her heart to increase its pace. Plenty of men had called her that over the years, her father included—in derision, of course. None ever affected her beyond causing disgust. But when Harrison said it?

All the butterflies.

He rose. "Tori?"

Right. He'd asked a question. She cleared her throat and forced her feet to move. "Sorry. I didn't sleep well. It's affecting me more than I'd like."

"This is the third night you've not had good sleep." He lifted a cup from the desk and brought it to her. "Here, drink this. I made the coffee strong today."

She sipped the dark brew. The hot, bitter liquid sent a shot of strength to her weary limbs. With a smile, she sat in his vacated chair. "Thanks, Harrison."

He crouched in front of her, dark gaze searching her face. "Three nights, Tori. That's not good. Maybe we need to set firm closing hours—"

"No." She took another sip from the mug, then placed it on the desk. "We already have closing time, but the cases the past few nights were emergencies. We can't turn people away."

His eyes didn't waver as he stood tall. "Then maybe we should rotate who takes on emergency cases. If both of us are needed, fine, but that wasn't the case the last two evenings."

"That's a good idea." Her lips tugged upward. "You can have tonight." She studied him, taking in the well-rested look on his face. "You don't struggle with sleep?"

"No. Never have. I can sleep anywhere, anytime."

Tori grunted and took up her coffee again. "Must be nice."

"Is this common for you?"

"Just when I get to bed too late. For some reason, that means I don't sleep well—if at all." She shrugged. "It'll pass."

"Are you sure? You don't want to go rest a bit longer? I can handle the patients if you want to try sleeping."

"That's kind, but I'm fine. Once the day gets going, I'll wake up."

"If you're sure."

He didn't look convinced. Tori drained the remainder of her coffee and stood. "This happened all the time in medical school. A little coffee, a little food, and I can get through the day."

"Speaking of food, I got breakfast from the café." He pointed to a plate sitting on the desk. "Cassie had muffins that looked good. There's lemon blueberry and cranberry almond. Take your pick."

Her tastebuds tingled with excitement. She selected the cranberry almond and took a large bite. "Oh, this is good." It didn't take long to polish off the rest.

Harrison smirked. He slid the second muffin her way. She shook her head. "That's yours."

"I already had mine."

She eyed him.

His smirk disappeared, replaced with a genuine smile. "Truly, Tori. I got two of each when I went to the café." He headed for the coffeepot. "You want more coffee?"

"Yes, please."

She made herself slow down with the second muffin, taking time to chew each bite slowly and let the flavors dissolve on her tongue. Harrison deposited the new, steaming mug of coffee beside her plate and rested his hand on her shoulder. "We've only got one house call today, no other appointments. Why don't we go for a walk after you eat? Maybe the fresh air will help you feel better."

"That sounds good."

He smiled. "Great."

His hand slid from her shoulder. Before he could turn, Tori reached out and caught it. "Harrison, wait."

Gaze going from her hand to her eyes, he tilted his head. "Yes?"

Words stuck in her throat. Tori blinked away sudden moisture blurring her vision. "Th-thank you. For the flowers. That was a nice surprise."

His lips curved in a soft smile. "You're welcome." He brought her hand to his lips, pressing a gentle kiss on her skin before releasing it. "I'm going to finish some paperwork. Let me know when you're ready to walk."

Her gaze followed him. Somehow, she'd been fortunate enough to marry a kind man. The man brought her muffins, coffee, and flowers because he could, and asked nothing in return. They'd both gotten what they needed by marrying, but Tori felt she got the better deal.

When she finished her breakfast, she called out, "I'm ready to walk."

Harrison stacked some papers and placed them under a paperweight. "Where would you like to go?"

"I'd like to see the progress at the hospital."

"Then that's our destination."

He held out his arm. Tori accepted it, and they stepped outside. The warm air blew against her face. Taking a deep breath, she closed her eyes. Sweet scents perfumed the air, reminding her of the flowers on her nightstand.

They started down the boardwalk. A train whistle sounded, the blast signaling a new batch of passengers about to disembark.

Someone raced past them. His sudden movement jostled Tori. She stumbled, prevented from falling only by Harrison's strong grip. He pulled her closer and stared after the offender. "How rude!" He turned his gaze on Tori. "Are you all right?"

Other than being so close to him she could smell the soap he used each morning? "Fine."

Grumbling under his breath, Harrison continued down the

boardwalk. The silence between them broke as they walked onto the street. "I received some news this morning from my parents. They plan on visiting in September with Temperance."

"Did they say when in September?"

"No. My father's business requires a lot of attention. I imagine he'll want everything well settled with his associates before they travel so far. They said they'll be staying a whole month."

"Are you excited to see them?"

"Of course." He paused a moment, his jaw flexing. "I didn't expect to miss them this much."

She squeezed his arm. "Perhaps we can arrange for a photographer to capture a family portrait. Then we could hang it in our home. Maybe that would help."

He stopped walking and turned to fully face her. The smile brightening his eyes made her breath catch. He opened his mouth, but before he spoke, another voice broke into their moment.

"Mr. and Mrs. Blake. Imagine running into you here."

The smooth, arrogant timbre of the speaker, combined with the Bostonian accent, made Tori freeze. *No. It can't be.* She clutched Harrison's arm. Her gaze swung to the newcomer, who stared them down with a sneer. Her blood turned to ice.

Kenneth.

CHAPTER 15

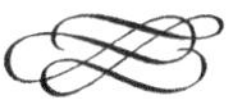

Tori's body stiffened beside Harrison. He followed her gaze and frowned. The last person he expected to see stood mere feet away. "Mr. Williamson. What are you doing in Harmony Springs?"

Kenneth twirled his walking stick. "A business venture, my good man. Did you know the purchase of a saloon in the west can be extremely profitable? Pennies for the sale itself, with rich dividends. I've come to make an offer on your fine establishment here."

Harrison snorted. "Fine establishment? The saloon attracts ruffians and drunks. We've had many folks wander to our infirmary because of injuries sustained in bar fights."

"And yet, the profits remain."

Kenneth's slick smile reminded Harrison of a snake, especially when his gaze roamed over Tori. Harrison stepped in front of his wife. "Why this town?"

"The connections, of course. I've known the two of you for years." His eyes locked onto Tori. "Especially your lovely wife. I couldn't pass up the opportunity to see you again."

Tori shrank against Harrison. Her fingers dug into his arm in a clear *get me out of here* message.

More than happy to oblige, Harrison gave Kenneth a short nod. "Enjoy your stay. We're going to check progress on the hospital."

"Ah, yes." Kenneth's tone dripped with disdain. "The filthy rich benefactors providing charity for the town. Tell me, do people here know you could buy this little hamlet several times over?"

Several people stopped and stared at his words. Harrison clenched his teeth. "That is no one's business," he growled quietly.

"So they don't know?" Kenneth chuckled. "More's the pity. You could finance the finest hospitals in Boston, but you choose to come here."

Whispers drowned out Kenneth's words. People gaped at Harrison, their eyes wide. A few men watched him openly, their expressions ranging from disbelief to calculation.

Chills raced down his spine. Travis hadn't wanted word to get out. With Kenneth's rash declaration, the entire town would know before long. Gossip burned like wildfire in Harmony Springs. Already, some women scurried to others and whispered behind their handkerchiefs or fans, presumably about his wealth.

Heat flared in his stomach. "My affairs are none of your business, and I'll thank you to keep them to yourself," he bit out.

Kenneth laughed. "Why you care what some provincial, backwoods townspeople think is beyond me."

Tori tugged Harrison's arm. "Let's go," she whispered. "It's not worth arguing with him."

He covered her hand with his and nodded curtly. "Good day, Mr. Williamson." He set off at a rapid pace. Tori kept up at his side. They didn't speak until they reached the outskirts of town and the hospital came in sight.

Tori released a long breath. She let go of his arm and plunked her hands on her hips. "The nerve of that man! He's only here to torment me. Buying a saloon, indeed. He's never shown interest in business ventures. His father built the family empire. Kenneth benefited from the wealth but cares too much about leisure. What a viper. I have half a mind to—"

Harrison pulled her into his arms, cutting off her rant. Her body felt like a board—straight and rigid. He ran one hand along her back and leaned down to whisper near her ear. "You're safe with me, Victoria."

She stared up at him. Her chest heaved as moisture welled in her eyes. Gripping his shoulders, she swallowed several times in succession. Was she avoiding tears?

He continued his gentle back rub. "It's okay to cry. If you want."

"I don't want." Steely determination etched itself over her face. "He doesn't deserve any tears. It would feel like he won."

Remaining quiet, Harrison allowed her to process whatever thoughts went through her mind. If she wanted to talk, she would. Until then, he'd be her rock—if she'd let him.

After a while, her body slowly relaxed into him. She rested her head on his chest. A long, shuddering breath shook her. Her hands moved from his shoulders to his waist, enveloping him in an embrace.

He waited, quiet and still.

A small moan escaped his wife. She buried her face into his shirt, her words muffled. "He makes me feel dirty, cheap. That kiss he forced on me—" She shuddered again. "It haunts my dreams. I hate that he has that kind of power."

Everything in Harrison wanted to march back into town and pummel Kenneth Williamson to a pulp. His grip on Tori tightened. "He can't do anything to you now. Not on my watch."

She pulled back enough to look into his eyes. A tiny smile tugged at her lips. "Are you assigning yourself my hero, Harry?"

Even with the teasing expression, he saw the pain behind her mask. He cupped her cheek and leaned closer. "Since we're married, protecting you is my duty. It's an honor I take seriously."

Her gaze dulled. She broke away, crossing her arms. Her body faced the hospital instead of him. "Until you grow tired of me."

What in the world?

He reached for her hand. "Where'd that come from?"

She avoided his touch, darting a few steps forward. No answer came. He slipped his hands into his pockets, confusion swirling inside. What did he do wrong?

You have to be patient with Tori. She needs to know she can count on you no matter what.

Cody's words from their barn talk whispered through his mind. He closed his eyes and breathed a silent prayer. *Lord, show me what to do. I'm at a loss.*

With his eyes still closed, he heard a small sniff. He opened them to see Tori swipe a finger over her cheek. Her arms crossed tighter over her chest.

His heart squeezed in response. How badly had she been hurt that she couldn't trust the love and friendship he offered?

Just love her.

He walked beside her, hands still in his pockets, gaze on the hospital as Wyatt's crew worked inside. "I'm not going anywhere, Tori."

She didn't respond, but another tear slid down her cheek. He let his words hang in the air between them. She might struggle to believe it, but he'd never meant anything more.

The silence almost became unbearable as it stretched into minutes. Finally, Tori sighed softly. "Looks as though they're making good progress. I didn't realize the outside was finished."

So she didn't want to address his comments. But trust took time to develop. He wouldn't push her, no matter how much he wanted to. *Just love her.*

He looked at the wooden structure standing tall against the blue sky—strong and inviting, a place of refuge. He shook his head with a wry smile. Exactly what he wanted to be for his wife. "Wyatt is a hard worker, and the men respond to his leadership. They're far ahead of schedule with construction. He thinks the interior will take longer to complete since there are so many rooms."

"Can we look inside?"

Gone were her tears. To look at her, one wouldn't know she'd been struggling moments before. Her walls were once again in place.

Harrison stifled his disappointment. "Let's see if Wyatt will give us a tour."

Maybe someday, she'd see him as a confidant. Until then, he'd try to remain patient.

~

Tori managed to avoid Kenneth over the next week. She knew he was still in town, thanks to the chain of gossip, which was also how she knew he'd been successful in his bid to buy the saloon. Throw enough money around, and people capitulated all too easily.

She rolled her eyes. Why were people so obsessed with money?

Her hands stilled in the middle of restocking the medicine shelf. The rumor mill had also spread word that she and Harrison had incredible wealth. While they tried to downplay it when asked, the gossip persisted, to the point that Travis recommended they pull some of their money from the bank to put in safes. He remained uneasy over the reports of gang activity in the surrounding areas. Multiple train robberies in the territory were attributed to the Otterson brothers within a span of three weeks.

While she didn't think they had anything to worry about, Harrison took Travis's advice seriously. They now had a safe stuffed with cash in their apartment, and another at Ella's house for safekeeping.

"Uh...excuse me, Mrs. Blake. Is Dr. Blake in?"

Tori pressed her lips together. She spun around, lifting her chin as she faced the man in the doorway. He appeared to be in his fifties, with a thatch of graying blond hair and pain-filled brown eyes. Tori crossed her arms. "I am Dr. Blake. How can I help you?"

He shuffled forward, wincing with each step. "I'd prefer the mister doc, ma'am."

She bit back a retort. Taking a deep breath, she willed herself to remain calm. "My husband is helping at the hospital. He won't be back for a few hours. If you want medical attention, you'll have to settle for me."

The man fiddled with his hat. Indecision warred on his face.

Tori shook her head and went back to stocking medicine. "Let me know when you've made your decision."

Maybe she shouldn't be so curt, but for goodness' sake, hadn't she proven herself to the people of this town yet?

"Um...I suppose you'll do."

Swallowing a sarcastic reply, Tori faced him again. "All right, Mr...?

"Tolson. Henry Tolson."

She waved at one of the hospital beds. "Please have a seat." He complied while she grabbed a clipboard. She sat in the chair beside his bed. "Now, what seems to be the problem?"

"I've been the saloon manager for about twenty years. The

new owner wants the place updated. Fresh paint, a few more game rooms—that sort of thing. We started construction, but the crew he hired is messy." Mr. Tolson grimaced. "They leave their wood and nails all over the place. It's not been good for business, I'll tell you that."

"I imagine not."

"Well, they went and left a stack of wood right beside my bar. I didn't see it and tripped over the darned thing." He twisted his leg to show her the back. "A sharp piece of wood lodged in my calf like an arrow."

Tori frowned at the wet blood stain covering his pant leg. "Where's the wood?"

"I took it out."

Her eyes widened. "You took it out?" No wonder it bled so much.

Mr. Tolson grunted as he straightened his leg again. "Should I have left it in?"

"Yes."

"Oh." A sheepish look crossed his face. "Sorry, ma'am."

"It's not me who's lost a lot of blood from your mistake."

He blanched. "Too much blood?"

"Enough that you'll be dizzy for a bit." She placed the clipboard on his bedside table. "I'm going to cut away the pant leg to your knee, and we'll see what we're dealing with."

He stayed quiet while she gathered a few supplies, then cut away the fabric covering his wound. "Please turn onto your side."

He complied without argument. Tori washed away the blood as best she could. It continued to seep out in a steady stream. The cut was deep and would require stitches. Splinters framed his wound. Tori reached for her tweezers. "I need to pull some excess wood from your skin. This might sting."

It only took a few minutes to remove the splinters. Tori

wrapped a bandage around his leg to staunch the flow of blood. "We'll let that do its work for a couple minutes, then I'll stitch up your wound and clean it again."

"Will it get infected?" Mr. Tolson peered over his shoulder as he tried to see his leg.

"Not if you keep it properly cleaned and bandaged."

After five minutes, she unwrapped his leg. The blood didn't flow as much, giving her room to work. She threaded the needle and began stitching. When she finished, she dabbed carbolic acid over the area and finished it off with a fresh bandage. As she put away her supplies, she instructed him on proper care of the wound. "And I want you to stay here for about half an hour to rest after that blood loss. I'll make you a cup of coffee."

"Thanks, Missus Doc. For the coffee and for fixing me up."

The new moniker made her smile. "You're welcome. Now, get some rest."

After giving him the coffee, she pulled a curtain around his bed to block out some of the light streaming through the windows. Now to finish stocking the medicine.

She'd almost finished when footsteps came through the infirmary door. She smoothed her doctor coat and turned to welcome the next patient.

Words died on her lips when she saw Kenneth standing far too close for comfort, smug grin firmly in place. He held out a bouquet of flowers. "Good afternoon, Victoria."

She ignored the offering and stepped back. "It's Mrs. Blake to you."

Dr. Blake would be more accurate, but emphasizing that she belonged to another man felt safer in the moment. Especially considering the predatory light in Kenneth's eyes.

Her gaze snapped to the door, hoping Harrison would walk through. With a start, she realized Kenneth had shut it when he arrived.

Cold fear sliced through her. She backed away even as Kenneth advanced, her gaze snapping about for anything to use as a weapon.

He grabbed her arm. "Oh, no you don't. We have unfinished business, Victoria. And this time, I won't be caught off guard by your tricks."

"Let me go!"

He pressed her against the wall. She fought panic at being trapped once again and unable to free herself. She let out a shrill scream.

Kenneth slammed his hand over her lips, muffling the sound. He leaned close as she struggled to escape. The smirk on his face made Tori's skin crawl. "No one's going to help you this time."

"You sure about that?"

The male voice, hard and sharp, was accompanied by a distinctive click. Mr. Tolson stood behind Kenneth, eyes lit with fury. He pointed a gun at her attacker. "Let the lady go."

Kenneth all but jumped away from Tori, hands in the air. "Hold on, Henry, this isn't what it looks like. Mrs. Blake and I have an understanding."

"Is that what you call it?" Mr. Tolson's hand didn't waver. "Something you should know about me, Mr. Williamson—I have three daughters, one of whom is around the doc's age. Between that and working at the saloon, unwanted male attention is something I recognize easily." His tone became steel. "You have ten seconds to get out of this building before I blow you to kingdom come. One...two..."

A wild expression crossed Kenneth's face. "You wouldn't dare!"

"Three...four..."

"All right, all right." Kenneth bolted to the door and opened it. He sneered at Tori. "Your reputation is already ruined."

"Five...six..."

"You're fired, Henry."

Mr. Tolson shrugged. "Better to be fired than work for a snake. Seven…"

Kenneth growled and turned to go. He grunted as he walked into someone. "Watch where you're going, you imbecile."

"Imbecile, am I?"

Tori knew that voice. She hurried to the door in time to see Travis eyeing Kenneth with raised brows. His gaze swung to Tori. "Someone came to my office, said they heard a scream from the infirmary. Do you know this man?"

"Unfortunately."

Mr. Tolson slipped his gun into its holster. "Sheriff, you should arrest him. He accosted Dr. Blake, not realizing I was in the room."

Travis's expression hardened. His hand went to his own gun. "Is that so?"

Kenneth sputtered. "Hardly. I was simply reacquainting myself with Victoria. Nothing untoward."

"Tori? Did he do what Mr. Tolson said?" Travis asked, not taking his eyes off Kenneth.

She wrapped her arms around herself. "Yes."

"Why you little…"

Kenneth lunged at Tori. She launched to the side just as Travis took hold of his collar and dragged him back. "You just tried to assault a woman in the presence of a law enforcement officer. Can't say I've ever seen anything so stupid in my years as sheriff. You're under arrest."

Kenneth screeched curses as Travis hauled him away. Her friend looked back for a brief moment. "I'll come by later to get your statement."

She nodded, heart pumping furiously. It galled that she hadn't been able to protect herself. If Mr. Tolson hadn't been there…

She turned to him, looking for any signs of stress. "Are you all right? Any dizziness or pain?"

"I'm fine, Missus Doc. Are *you* okay?"

His concerned look reminded her of Harrison. Thoughts of her husband sent a strange yearning in her heart for his presence. She pushed it away, running shaky hands down her lab coat. "I'm fine." She exhaled hard. "I misjudged you."

"And I you."

At her raised brow, he shook his head. "Mr. Williamson spread rumors that you were a woman of…loose virtue. I'm sorry to say I believed him. It was part of my hesitation in letting you treat me." He grabbed his hat from the bed. "Forgive me for judging without proof. What I just witnessed proves otherwise."

Her ire rose, aimed at Kenneth. "He's been a thorn in my side for some time now. Hopefully, his arrest puts those rumors down."

"I'll do my part to stop them, ma'am."

She managed a small smile. "I appreciate that. Sorry you lost your job."

"I doubt it's gone."

"What do you mean?"

He chuckled. "The sale of the saloon wasn't finalized yet. When the owner finds out about Mr. Williamson, I'm sure he'll pull out of the contract." He frowned. "Abuse of women is not looked on kindly in these parts, even amongst the riffraff of town."

Relief pulsed through her. "Then we're well rid of him."

"Seems so." He plunked his hat on. "Am I cleared to go?"

"Yes. Please come back in a few days so I can check the sutures. Otherwise, follow the instructions for keeping your injury clean."

"Yes, ma'am. Thanks again."

She impulsively took his hand. "No, thank you. I'm afraid to think of what would have happened if you weren't here."

He patted her shoulder. "As I said, I have daughters. Just doing what any father would."

A lump lodged in her throat as he left the building. She stood frozen, tears welling in her eyes.

Not all fathers.

CHAPTER 16

Travis sent Kenneth packing back to Boston, with a warning that if he ever showed his face again in town, he'd be locked up and the key tossed. Tori had a feeling they'd never see him again.

Good riddance.

Harrison had been livid when he discovered what happened. She suspected he blamed himself for not being there when Kenneth tried to finish what he started in Boston. Her husband had not left her side in the last week. He also insisted on taking over any night emergencies, saying she needed the rest.

He wasn't wrong. Tori couldn't remember ever being so exhausted. In the days since Kenneth accosted her, she'd not been able to sleep thanks to recurring nightmares. She tried to hide her sleep deprivation from Harrison, but he noticed, anyway.

It unnerved her how easily he could read her.

She also got the impression he was attempting to woo her. Flowers continued to show up on her nightstand each morning.

He brought her scones and muffins from the café. When they walked through town, he kept her close to his side. Once or twice, she thought she saw affection in his gaze.

Was her husband falling for her? Did she want him to?

Tori stuffed the questions down. She had a job to do, as did he. Ever since Mr. Tolson spread word that she'd fixed him up right—and that the rumors about her were wrong—people seemed more inclined to trust her. She'd only heard a couple protests about her gender over the last week. Things were finally looking up.

Now if she could just sleep through the night.

Thunder boomed in the distance, making her jump. She stared out the apartment window and watched rain pour down in sheets. It looked cool and refreshing. The early-August heat vanished with the storm.

An impulse seized her. Tori bit her lip. The longer she watched the rain, the more she wanted to be in it, let it wash away her cares and worries.

Why not?

She crept down the stairs to the infirmary. Harrison sat at their desk, working on a list of necessary supplies. She slipped out the back door without alerting him to her presence.

Rain pounded her skin, soaking her hair and clothes in a matter of seconds. She laughed, spreading her arms wide and twirling in the cool torrent of water. When she stopped, she closed her eyes and lifted her face to the sky, letting rain pour in rivulets down her cheeks.

"Tori?"

Harrison's shout had her eyes flying open. She turned her head to the door. The bewildered look on his face made her grin. He cupped his hands over his mouth and hollered, "What are you doing?"

Giggles shook her, giggles she'd not experienced since she

was a small girl. "Playing in the rain, of course." She extended her hands to him and wiggled her fingers. "Come join me."

He frowned. His expression said he wondered if she'd lost her mind.

Maybe she had.

To her surprise, he descended the porch steps and loomed over her, hands on his hips. "All right, you win. Now what?"

Whether it was sleep deprivation making her reckless, or something deeper she didn't dare analyze, Tori stepped closer, putting her hands on his chest. "Dance with me."

His eyes sparked with amusement. "You called me out here to dance in the rain?"

"Why not?" She pushed away and began twirling again. "It's fun. We need some fun in our lives, don't we?"

He grabbed her hand. Tori giggled again, letting him turn her in circles until she felt dizzy. Laughing, she fell against his chest, her hand resting right over his heart.

His rapidly beating heart.

Time slowed as they stared at one another. His gaze flicked to her lips but just as quickly snapped back up to her eyes. He slid one hand behind her, resting it on her upper back, and took her other hand in his. They began to sway, dancing to the rhythm of the rain.

Harrison pulled her a little closer, until she could feel the heat emanating from his body. Her breath hitched. Her own heartbeat pounded out a too-fast rhythm. Unable to hold his dark gaze any longer, she let her head fall against his chest.

Her stomach swooped as he pressed her close, leaving no room between them, and rested his head against hers. Guiding her hand to his heart, he held it there, completing the intimate embrace. Tori closed her eyes. For once, she chose not to fight these feelings. Just this once, she wanted to feel the emotions he provoked in her.

Emotions that felt an awful lot like affection. Fondness. Maybe even...love?

She remained in his arms as he turned them in a slow circle. Never had she danced with someone like this. Harrison's embrace was safe, warm. Everything she'd thought impossible with a man. But him—he was a protector, a fighter. He didn't do things by halves. When they said their vows, he meant them. Deep down, she knew he'd love her if given the chance.

And that frightened her. The thought of being so vulnerable made her shiver.

Harrison pulled back. His deep brown gaze searched hers. "You're cold."

"N-no."

His brow quirked, a small smile playing on his lips. "And stuttering. Let's get you inside. I'll make some tea while you change into dry clothes."

Considerate. Another word that described him well.

Harrison had always been a friend, but she'd started to believe he could be something more.

Tori wondered at the subtle shift in her feelings. She wondered at it while she drank the tea her husband provided. She wondered at it when they made house calls that afternoon. And she wondered at it when meeting her sister for a late lunch after church the next day.

"Tori? Is something on your mind?"

Snapping out of her reverie, Tori smiled at her sister brightly and cuddled little David closer. Her gaze bounced around the Brooks' kitchen before landing back on Ella. "Everything's fine."

Ella's lips twitched as she took a sip of tea. "That's not what I asked. I can tell when you're avoiding something—and right now, that's exactly what you're doing."

Tori lowered her gaze to the baby. She lifted him to her

shoulder, letting his head rest more comfortably. "Because I know what you'll say if I tell you what's on my mind."

"Like how you should keep yourself open to love?" Ella's eyes brightened. She plopped her teacup on its saucer and leaned forward. "Is that it? Are you falling for Harrison?"

"You sound far too excited about the possibility."

"Because you two are perfect together. He treats you well, and I'd swear I see attraction and admiration in his eyes when he looks at you." She took Tori's free hand. "I just want you to be happy."

"I am happy."

Ella raised her brows.

Tori sighed. She did want to confide in Ella. The problem was, she wasn't sure of her own feelings. "There's something there, on my part, at least. Some feelings...feelings I can't label."

"You find Harrison attractive?"

She thought of his dark hair, twinkling eyes, and neatly trimmed facial hair. Her stomach fluttered. "Yes."

"And you've been friends for a while."

"Yes."

"Do you like him?"

"Of course."

"What about respect? Admiration? Trust? Are those part of your relationship?"

"They are."

Ella sat back. "Then what's the problem? Sounds like you're on your way to love."

Tori shook her head. "It's not that simple." *Is it?*

"Honey, we complicate things too often in life. This doesn't have to be one of those times. Learn from my mistakes—I pushed Cody away for a while because of fear. I think you're doing the same with Harrison."

Tori wanted to deny it but couldn't. She sighed. "Maybe so."

She stood, rubbing David's back as she did. "Thanks for lunch. I think I'm going to stop by the hospital on my way home. Harrison said the workers set up one of the rooms to make sure everything we need would fit. I'd like to see it."

"Are you sure? You look tired. Maybe you should try to rest."

Tori kissed David's soft cheek, then handed him to his mother. Ella didn't need to know about her lack of sleep over the past month. "I'll rest after. I promise."

Ella hugged her. "I love you, Tori."

"I love you too."

She urged her horse into a gallop on the way back to town. The wind felt good against her face, reviving her from her near-constant exhaustion. She returned the horse to the stables, then made her way on foot to the hospital.

It being Sunday, no one worked on the structure today. Tomorrow, Wyatt and his crew would be back, hammering and building away. For now, she felt grateful for the quiet.

She wandered the various half-finished rooms, searching for the one set up with a bed and medical equipment. At the last room, near the back door, she found it.

"What a lovely set up," she murmured. The bed sat in the middle of the room, a bedside table on either side. To the right of the bed was a wooden chair. A closet held medical supplies, towels, and bandages. The window looked out over the meadow.

It was better than she'd imagined.

"Your dream is coming true, Harrison," she whispered.

Out of nowhere, a large yawn overtook her. Her eyelids drooped. She sighed. "I should get home."

She eyed the bed. It looked comfortable and inviting. *Maybe I should try it out, just to see if it'll do.*

As soon as she laid down, she breathed a small sigh of relief. Comfortable, indeed, rivaling the bed at home. She closed her eyes and relaxed into the mattress.

Just five minutes...

~

Harrison paced on the boardwalk in front of the infirmary. Afternoon had given way to dusk, and still no sign of his wife. She'd gone for lunch with Ella after church and should have been home by now.

His worry grew as stars began dotting the sky. Without another thought, he rushed to the stables and selected a horse to take him to the Brooks ranch. He rode at a gallop and arrived within ten minutes. Vaulting off the horse, he landed hard on his feet, then ran up the porch steps.

Cody answered, surprise on his face. "Harrison. What brings you here?"

"Where's Tori?"

"Tori?" His brother-in-law frowned. "She's not been here for hours."

The blood drained from Harrison's face. He gripped the doorframe. "Are you sure?"

Worry reflected in Cody's eyes. "I'm sure. She left around two."

It was now seven. Harrison fought the rising fear.

"Cody? Who's here so late?" Ella appeared soon after her words. She blinked at Harrison. "Is everything all right? Did Tori get home okay?"

"No," he rasped. "She never came home."

"What?" Ella latched onto Cody's arm. "We need to find her. She said she was going to the hospital—"

The hospital! Why hadn't he thought to look there? Harrison spun around and hurried down the steps. "I'll check it out."

"I'll be right behind you," Cody called.

"Thanks."

He shouted the word over his shoulder as he mounted the horse. The animal flew over the miles to town. As they got closer, an acrid scent hit his nostrils. His stomach turned for another reason.

Smoke.

Something was on fire. People shouted and rushed for the source of the flames. An eerie light flared just outside of town. His heart dropped to his stomach. Only one structure stood in that area.

The hospital.

Tori!

When he arrived at the scene, all the breath whooshed from his lungs. Flames engulfed the hospital, red and angry against the night sky. The crackling fire sent involuntary shudders through him. His experience with previous fires marched across his mind. The scars on his skin seemed to come to life, throbbing with painful memory. The cries of the workers he couldn't save.

Harrison doubled over, hands clapped over his ears. The heat from the fire licked against his skin. He wanted to run away. But he couldn't.

He had to find Tori.

Forcing himself up, he searched the crowd. Men formed a line, passing bucket after bucket of water along from a nearby well in a desperate attempt to quench the flames.

They fought a losing battle.

The fire roared while the building shuddered. Harrison ran along the crowd, hoping to see Tori.

"Doc!" The call came from Wyatt. He hurried up to Harrison, wringing his hands. "We don't know what happened, Doc. This fire came out of nowhere." He watched his work go up in flames, orange reflected against his face. "It's a good thing no one was working today. I saw your missus go in earlier today, but that was hours ago."

Dread consumed Harrison. His wife was in that building. For what reason, he couldn't say, but he knew without a doubt she'd never left.

He rushed to the door. The heat singed his clothes and gave him pause. Memories flooded him again, but he shoved them back. His wife needed him. He shrugged off his jacket, held the fabric over his face, and ran into the building, ignoring calls for him to stop.

The heat nearly brought him to his knees. Flames licked up the walls and consumed the ceiling. He prayed she'd stayed on the first level as he passed the stairs. They were riddled with fire, making passage impossible. Fighting the sick feeling in his gut, Harrison ran on, calling Tori's name.

A new sound rose above the crackling fire. Someone coughed, deep and hoarse.

Tori!

He followed the sound. In the room at the end of the hall, his wife lay on the bed, surrounded by flames.

Panic flared. He rushed to the closet, taking out a blanket that the inferno hadn't yet claimed. He threw it over Tori, gathering her in his arms even as fire torched his clothes. He dropped to the floor and rolled them both, praying it smothered the flames. Getting up, he clutched Tori to his chest and ran for the back door and freedom.

The cool night air filled his parched lungs. It burned his sore throat, but he thanked God they made it outside.

Tori groaned. Her eyes opened briefly before closing again. She lay limp in his arms as people raced toward them. He took in her soot-lined face and scorched clothes, her still form. The dread from earlier rose once more. Cupping her cheek, he pressed his lips to her forehead, tears falling onto her darkened skin. "Please don't leave me."

Cody reached them first. He reached down and took Tori

from Harrison. "Come on," he said. "We need to get you both to the infirmary."

Someone helped Harrison to his feet, but he only saw his wife's unmoving body as Cody carried her back to town. Tears ran uncontrollably down his face, and he pressed a hand to his lips to keep the sobs at bay.

Please, God—please let her be all right.

CHAPTER 17

*H*arrison sat at his wife's bedside. He dipped his fingers into a pot of honey and smoothed it over her left arm. The angry red burns against her pale skin made his stomach revolt, but he continued his ministrations.

A deep cough racked his body. He'd inhaled far too much smoke in the few minutes he'd been in the burning hospital. His throat and lungs hurt with every breath. He could only imagine the pain Tori would be in when she woke.

If she woke.

His heart thumped heavily. He closed his eyes and took Tori's hand. If he'd been just a few minutes later, she'd have been badly burned, or worse. Though her left arm had been licked by flames and would likely scar, the rest of her had escaped burns. Her red face looked as if she'd been in the sun too long, but that would fade.

The unknown state of her lungs from smoke inhalation concerned him. She'd coughed often overnight, the deep sound pricking him with fear each time. Twice she opened her eyes, and Harrison coaxed water down her throat, but she barely drank an ounce or two before falling back into unconscious sleep.

"Come back to me," he whispered, running his hand over her unruly curls.

The door opened. Cody and Ella came inside, wearing identical looks of concern.

Harrison attempted a smile. "Hi."

"How're you doing?" Cody asked, seating his wife in the chair across from Harrison.

He shrugged, his throat tightening as he fought to control his emotions. "I need her to wake up."

Ella clutched Tori's hand. Tears welled in her eyes. "She's always been strong. She'll get through this."

"You were brave to run into that building," Cody said. "Wyatt told me it collapsed minutes after you got out."

Harrison could almost feel the heat against his skin once more. He shook the feeling away. "Do we know what happened?"

Cody's mouth set into a firm line. He glanced at Ella before releasing a sigh. "Looks like arson."

"Arson?" Harrison stared at Cody. "How do you know?"

"We found three discarded containers of kerosene in the rubble. Whoever did this set the fire on purpose and made sure it wouldn't be put out."

"Why would someone deliberately destroy a hospital?"

Cody shrugged. "Beats me."

"Arson is a serious crime," Ella said, gaze on her sister. "Why would someone risk years of jail time to burn down an unfinished hospital?"

Cody set a hand on his wife's shoulder. "People aren't always logical. Though whoever did this probably didn't mean for anyone to get hurt. They chose a Sunday, when the workers were off."

Harrison's teeth clenched. "But someone did get hurt."

"Which turns the crime into a potentially capital offense."

Nausea worked its way through Harrison's stomach. It would only be capital if Tori died—and that option was unthinkable. Tears burned his eyes. He pulled her hand to his heart, watching her for any sign of wakefulness.

"Cody," Ella said softly, "can you get some food from the café? I think Harrison needs sustenance."

He didn't need sustenance. He needed his wife.

"Anything specific you want to eat, Harrison?" Cody asked.

Harrison shook his head. Words suddenly seemed impossible.

Ella went to the door with her husband. They whispered together while Harrison held onto Tori as if his grip were enough to keep her on this side of heaven. He leaned close and pressed his lips to her knuckles. "Wake up, Victoria. Please wake up."

No response.

Ella closed the door behind Cody and returned to her chair. Harrison felt her gaze but couldn't tear his own from his wife.

"How long have you been in love with my sister?"

He jerked. He straightened in his seat, heart pounding. "What?"

A soft smile graced Ella's face. "It's a simple question, Harrison."

Simple? Not in the least. He scrubbed a hand over his beard.

"Let me ask you another question."

His gaze lifted.

"Why are you sitting here?"

His sister-in-law asked strange questions. Harrison scrunched his nose. "Because my wife almost died. She still could. I want to be here when she wakes up."

"Why?"

"Because...she's important to me."

Ella returned her gaze to Tori. "Let me tell you something about my sister. When we were young, she loved going to the hospital with me and our mother. Mother didn't do charitable works out of the goodness of her heart. She did it for the visibility. But Tori took an interest in the patients. She'd sit with them for hours if Mother let her." Her eyes glazed a little, as if lost in the memory. "One day, we sat with an elderly woman who was dying. She asked Tori to come back the next day. Tori promised she would. When the time came to visit, Mother refused to allow her to go. There was some society event that she claimed we couldn't miss. Do you know what Tori did?"

As if there was any doubt. "She went, anyway."

"Yes. She ignored Mother's anger, left the house without a chaperone, and marched the three miles to the hospital on foot." Tears misted Ella's eyes. "Two hours later, the woman died. If Tori hadn't gone, she would have been alone in her final hours. But because my sister honored her promise, she was able to provide comfort to that woman as she lay dying and when she passed from this world." She looked back up at him. "That's when she knew she wanted to be a doctor. She hoped to provide that same comfort no matter what situation patients found themselves in."

"She has a beautiful heart."

"She does." Ella pierced him with her eyes, gaze direct and unwavering. "And that heart of hers is capable of a fierce love. When she decides someone is worthy of it, she gives it unreserved—loyal for life. But she is cautious about who she chooses. She needs to know that person will be there no matter what, that there are no conditions attached to the relationship. I think she wants to be loved for who she is but fears it's impossible, at least where men are concerned. Now, she only has one option for being loved romantically." Ella bit her lip, breaking their stare. "You think she has a beautiful heart. Can you love it?"

That question felt weighted. "You believe I'm already in love with her."

"Yes."

He stared at his wife, throat working. "Even if I am, she doesn't feel the same."

"Maybe not, but proving that you'll be there will go a long way to winning her heart."

His lips twitched. "Cody said something similar."

Ella sat back, a smile spreading across her face. "He's a wise man." She appraised him a moment, then clenched her hands in her lap. "Let me ask you something. What will you do if Tori dies?"

His stomach turned to stone. He shook his head, his grip on Tori's hand tightening. "She can't die."

"Why not? If she does, you're free. You don't have to share your practice, your home, or anything else. You could do whatever you want."

"I don't want to do whatever I want," he burst out. "I want Tori."

"Why?"

Her pointed question hung in the air, sucking the breath from his lungs. He clutched her hand to his heart. Tears welled in his eyes and fell to his cheeks as he pictured a life without her. In a short time, she'd become vital to him—not just in their practice as doctors, but as his wife. He'd told Cody he thought he could love her, wanted to woo her. But now, thinking he could lose her, facing Ella's knowing questions, the truth smacked him in the heart.

"I love her."

Ella nodded. "I'm glad you admitted it. We've watched the two of you together. It felt inevitable that you'd fall in love. Cody and I both thought you would fall first, but I wouldn't be surprised if Tori falls soon. Perhaps she has already."

"Doubtful. We're friends, but she hasn't indicated she wants more."

Then again, that dance they shared the other night...maybe she did have some kind of feelings for him.

Ella rose. "I think I'll see if Cody needs any help getting food from the café." She gave him a soft smile. "You can take some time to process."

"Thanks, Ella." He stood and hugged his sister-in-law. "For everything."

With a nod, she left the infirmary.

Harrison sat beside Tori once more. He claimed her hand. "What do I do with this information, Victoria?" He kissed her fingers before resting them once more over his heart. "And is there a chance you'll ever feel the same?"

~

*I*t hurt to breathe.

Tori moaned. Her left arm hurt too. What happened? And why couldn't she open her eyes?

"Tori?"

Harrison's voice sounded close to her ear. She tried to move her head, but it felt like a lead weight. Her lungs burned.

Sleep.

She drifted on the brink of unconsciousness, but Harrison's broken words pierced through her. "Please, Lord, please let her live," he whispered. "I love her."

Tori didn't register the rest of his prayer. Was her life in danger? The pain radiating through her indicated something bad had happened. Bad enough to kill her? The thought should be frightening, but a strange peace came to rest in her heart.

Then her mind latched onto his declaration.

He loved her?

Tori fought the sleep dragging her under. She needed to talk to Harrison. Why did he love her? She was unlovable. Her father said so. Nothing she did ever changed his mind.

Something tickled the back of her hand, accompanied by a warm pressure against her skin. With monumental effort, she opened her eyes enough to see her hand pressed to Harrison's lips, his head bowed low. His shoulders sagged and his beard looked fuller, as if he'd not trimmed it. She opened her eyes a little wider and stared at his clothing.

Disheveled and dirty. Harrison never let himself look so unkempt. He lifted his head, and she gasped. What were those streaks all over his face?

He stared at her a moment, disbelief and hope warring in his eyes. "Tori?"

"Harris—"

A deep cough racked her body. If she'd thought her lungs burned before, they did doubly so now. Her throat felt raw. She groaned and closed her eyes. "That hurts."

"No, don't sleep, love. You need water." He propped a pillow behind her, then pressed a cup to her lips. "Drink this."

The lukewarm water slipped down her throat. Instead of relief, it made the pain worse. She pushed the cup away, but her husband brought it back. "I know it doesn't feel good, but you need this. You're dehydrated."

She'd insist the same if she had a dehydrated patient. Opening her mouth once more, she drank the water in small sips until it was gone. As Harrison put the cup on the table, she asked, "What happened?"

His face tightened. "You don't remember?"

"No."

He opened his mouth, but the door opening interrupted him. Ella and Cody entered the room. They both stopped when they saw her. A choked sob left Ella, and she flew to Tori's bedside, grabbing her hands. "You're awake."

"Was I asleep long?"

"Almost a full day," Harrison said.

Tori blinked. "So long? Why?"

"You were caught in the fire," Ella said. "We were worried sick."

"The Lord had His hand on you," Cody said, setting bags of savory-scented food on the table. "If Harrison had run into that building just a minute later, you wouldn't be here."

Her gaze shot to her husband. The pieces fell into place. She'd gone to the hospital and fell asleep in the new bed. When she woke, she'd been surrounded by the roar of flames. Coughing, she tried to get out of the bed, but she felt weak—likely from lack of sleep. Then her world had gone dark.

Smoke inhalation. She'd gone unconscious from breathing in too much of the toxic fumes. She shuddered. Thank God Harrison had found her in time...

Wait. *Harrison* had found her?

She struggled to sit up fully, gaze locked on her husband. He helped her into a comfortable position. When she rested upright against the pillows, he started to pull back, but she stopped him with a hand to his cheek. "You saved my life."

He shifted, gaze somewhere on the blanket. "I couldn't let you die."

"You went into a burning building."

The words hung in the air, heavy with meaning. Harrison wouldn't meet her gaze, but his sooty cheeks turned pink.

Ella glanced between them. Her brow furrowed. "Are we missing something?"

"Yes." Tori smiled at her sister. "Can Harrison and I have a moment, please?"

"Of course." Ella kissed Tori's forehead. "I'm so glad you're awake." She threaded her arm through Cody's. "Shall we head back to the café? Cassie said she had caramel cake today."

Cody's eyes lit up. He nodded, and the two of them headed off.

Tori returned her attention to Harrison. Why wasn't he looking at her? "So—about you running into a burning building..."

"I couldn't do anything less, Tori." His voice broke, and his gaze finally lifted, connecting with hers. She inhaled a sharp breath at the intensity in it. He captured her hands. "When I realized you were in that hospital, my heart stopped. I had to get you out. You mean...everything...to me."

Everything?

His quiet declaration of love repeated in her mind. She questioned it then, but now she wondered. Harrison had made it clear he hoped for something more than friendship between them. He'd flirted, pushed, encouraged—all with a kindness she'd never experienced before. The flowers he left on her bedside table each morning bore witness to his feelings. Why do that for someone he didn't care about?

She drew in a shuddering breath. Pain sliced through her throat, but she ignored it. If she let herself love him, he'd have the power to break her. Was love worth that risk?

Her gaze dropped. "You could have asked someone else to get me out."

"There was no thinking. Just action."

"But fire is your greatest fear. You shouldn't have risked—"

"I'd risk it again for you." His eyes snapped as he stood. Raking his hands through his hair, he paced beside the bed. "You don't see it, do you?"

"See...what?" she whispered, heart lodging in her throat.

He dropped into the chair once more. His head fell into his hands, his voice muffled. "It's so obvious. I can't believe I didn't make the connection sooner. Ella had to force it out of me, but now that she has, I can see just how long I've been in love with you. I've been falling since the day we married." He raised his head, and the torment in his eyes lanced her heart. "Do I have any chance of winning your love, Tori?"

All coherent thought vanished, leaving her staring at her husband, mouth gaping open, not knowing how to respond.

When the silence stretched a full minute, Harrison heaved a sigh. "I suppose it was too much to hope. Forget I said anything."

What? No. She just needed time to think about this…

The door opened. Travis strode in, a frown on his face and hat in hand. He nodded at them both. "Afternoon. I wanted to come in person with the news. I'm afraid there's no good way to say this." He shuffled his feet, the frown deepening. "The bank's been robbed. Your money is gone."

CHAPTER 18

Gone?

Harrison gripped the arms of his chair. His head hurt. The emotional turmoil of the past day, Tori's silent shock that spoke volumes when he asked if she could ever love him, and now this.

There was only so much a man could take before he broke, and Harrison felt himself teetering over the edge of the precipice.

"How?" he rasped.

Travis tossed his hat into an empty chair. "The Otterson brothers left their calling card at the bank and the hospital. They always carve their initials into a tree or the dirt near their heists. I believe they started the fire to distract the entire town, then robbed the bank." His gaze bored into Harrison's. "It was only your money. They targeted the safe we brought that held your fortune."

Tori groaned, then coughed. Her fit lasted long enough that Harrison refilled her water cup and pushed it into her hands. "Drink."

She drained the cup even though she winced with each

swallow. When she finished, she slapped it against the bed. "I knew Kenneth's blabbing would get us in trouble."

"You said no one knows what these men look like?" Harrison asked.

"No, but there were three strangers about town this past week. They looked so much alike, they must be brothers. I'd put my money on them being the Ottersons. My guess is, they heard about your wealth from someone here and decided to go for it. It's not often you come across that kind of money. They likely couldn't resist."

"Good thing we pulled some money, then." Tori's gaze met his. "Right, Harrison?"

A sense of despair smothered him. He clenched his hands. "It's enough to get us by for a time, Tori, but what about the hospital? We promised this town excellent medical care. How are we supposed to provide that now?"

"The same way doctors have for generations before us. We provide care and receive payment." She shrugged. "The infirmary is set up and well stocked. We have money in those safes. Everything will be fine."

Something snapped inside. Harrison's jaw set. "Everything is *not* fine, Victoria. I'm going to look like a man who can't keep his word. The hospital is gone. I can't finish paying Wyatt's crew. Our whole reason for coming here has been shattered." He threw up his hands. "So don't tell me it's going to be fine!"

He'd never yelled at her before. The stunned expression on her face almost made him apologize, but his anger still burned hot. He turned and stormed out of the infirmary.

Blind to his surroundings, he ruminated on the events of the last twenty-four hours. They rolled through his mind one after the other, again and again, taunting him with his failures. What did he have left to give? Without his aunt's money, he had no way to rebuild the hospital.

And now his reason for marrying Tori had gone up in smoke. Literally.

What kind of life could he give her now? He would someday inherit wealth from his parents, but that wouldn't be for years.

The fast clip at which he walked had his lungs screaming for air. Probably not the best idea to speed walk after inhaling lots of smoke. He came to an abrupt stop when he paused to see where he was.

He'd gone straight to the burned-out remains of the hospital.

Blackened wood rose up in jagged peaks, surrounded by piles of ash and debris. He stared at the wreckage. Once more, he felt the heat of the flames. He saw the raging inferno. He heard the crackling thunder. His fear at knowing his wife was somewhere inside, strong enough to overcome his fear of fire.

His anger faded away. In its place, despair crashed in.

Harrison sank to his knees. He covered his face with his hands. *Why, Lord? Why did this have to happen?*

"Tori's worried about you."

Travis's voice made him startle. Harrison dropped his hands, bringing the dismal view into sight once more. "Is she alone?"

"No. Ella and Cody came back." Travis sat on the ground beside him. "She asked me to find you and make sure everything's all right."

Barking out a short laugh, Harrison flung his hand toward the burned-out remains of his dream. "Does that look all right?"

"Not the hospital. She wanted me to check on you." After a short pause, Travis continued, his voice low. "It's clear she cares about you."

The lump in Harrison's throat grew large. He blinked to

clear away the gathering moisture in his eyes. Shoulders slumping, he sighed. "Just not enough."

Travis eyed him but didn't speak. Silence stretched between them. Harrison pictured his wife as she'd looked just before he left the infirmary—brown eyes wide, mouth hanging open, shock in her gaze.

She'd just been trying to help. He shouldn't have taken his anger out on her.

Guilt slithered through his belly. Tori didn't deserve his volatile reaction. It wouldn't make things different, and he might have strained their relationship by losing his temper.

Though his declaration of love may have done that as well.

He sighed again. Shifting, he sat on the hard ground. Dust sprang up and settled once more before Travis spoke.

"What's this really about?"

"I don't know what you mean."

"I think you do." Travis crossed his arms. "You said 'just not enough' a moment ago in response to Tori's care for you. Why don't we start there?"

Harrison had a sudden, childish urge to squirm. "I don't see how that will help—"

"Let me tell you something." Travis turned his hazel gaze on Harrison, eyes serious and direct. "Relationships are about honesty. There's always some give and take. Nothing is going to be perfect. You have to decide what's worth fighting for and what can be given up. This hospital?" He waved his hand at the ruins. "It's a temporal thing. Your relationship with Tori? That's something that can last."

Harrison shut his eyes. "What if she doesn't want it to last?"

"You won't know if—"

"I told her I love her."

He opened his eyes in time to see Travis's brows shoot up. "You did?" Understanding flashed over his face. "Oh. It didn't go as you hoped."

188

"No. I bared my heart, asked her if she could ever feel the same. She just looked at me." He ran both hands over his cheeks, palms scratched by his rough beard. "Her silence was answer enough."

"That's a big declaration, especially considering her past." Travis laid a hand on Harrison's shoulder. "Give it time. She may surprise you."

"What if she doesn't? What if this working relationship is all we have?"

Travis exhaled long and slow. He shook his head, looking out over the field. "Then I guess you have to decide if it's worth it."

Harrison rested his head in his hands. He loved his wife and wanted nothing more than her love in return. But if she couldn't give it, was it fair to keep her trapped in this marriage? Especially now that he had nothing to offer?

~

*T*ori grew restless waiting for Harrison to return. Dressed in a clean nightgown—thanks to Ella—she felt a little more herself, even if her sooty hair remained in desperate need of a wash. Ella sat with her and tried to engage in conversation, but Tori didn't want to talk. She wanted her husband to return.

Her shock at his display of emotion had long worn off. She hadn't thought him capable of such an outburst, but she understood. His dream had crumbled to ash. If she'd been forced out of being a doctor, her reaction would have been ten times worse—and then some.

"You should eat some soup," Ella said, breaking the quiet.

Tori lifted a hand to her throat. "It hurts to swallow. Food doesn't sound appealing."

"At least the broth, then. You need to build up your strength."

"Fine."

Tori let Ella feed her broth from Cassie's chicken soup. Her sister eyed her before speaking. "What is the significance of Harrison going into a burning building?"

"He's deathly afraid of fire."

A twinkle lit in Ella's eyes. "Is that so?"

Tori gulped down some more broth. "Please don't make more of this than it is."

"What am I making of it?"

"That...that he..."

Drat. She couldn't come up with anything but the truth. With a sigh, she continued. "That he loves me."

"Does he?"

Ella's gaze bored into hers. Tori cleared her throat, then winced. She massaged the area while the burning sensation lessened. "I'm tired. It would probably be good to rest."

"Avoidance is a temporary fix, Tori." Ella leaned forward. "What happened to being open to love?"

Tori fiddled with the sheets. "Not much scares me, Ella, but love does. It would be opening myself to the potential for serious pain."

"It also opens the door to a joy greater than anything you've known before. Isn't that worth the risk?"

"I don't know."

"You've been hurt." Ella covered Tori's hand with hers. "It takes time to trust that another person won't let you down when all you've known is disappointment and rejection."

"You're not upset that I can't return his love yet?"

Her sister blinked. "He told you he loved you?"

"Yes."

A smile bloomed on Ella's face. "Good. He's been keeping it

to himself for far too long." She squeezed Tori's hand. "And no, I'm not upset."

Tori straightened. "What do you mean, he's been keeping it to himself?"

"I had to pry a confession out of him while you were unconscious, even though it's clear he's loved you for a while. I don't think he could fully admit it to himself until last night."

"I wish…" Tori sighed. She smoothed the covers over her lap, then folded her hands. "I wish I could freely give him my love. But I'm just…not ready."

"And that's all right."

Ella offered her more broth. Tori accepted the nourishment, but her mind churned over every detail of their conversation. As she forced down the last painful swallow, Harrison shuffled through the door.

He moved to her side. Dark bags hung under his eyes. He sank into the seat beside her. "I'm sorry for losing my temper, Tori. It was wrong to take out my anger and frustration on you."

"I understand."

His gaze flitted to hers before dropping again. "You're not upset?"

"No."

Ella stood and gathered up the soup dishes. "I'll return these to Cassie. Cody and I need to get back to the children." She pressed a gentle kiss to Tori's forehead. "Get some rest."

"Thanks, Ella."

Once her sister left, Tori turned to see Harrison arranging papers on the desk. He stacked them in perfect order, then moved the pens into a straight line. When he opened the drawer to begin organizing, Tori called him. "You can get the desk together another time."

Harrison stopped. He didn't turn, keeping his back to her. "Did you need something?"

She searched for something to distract him. If she didn't, he would reorganize the entire infirmary in his stress. She pushed a curl out of her face. All at once, the answer appeared. "Yes, actually. Would you mind washing my hair?"

He dropped the paperweight he'd been holding. It clattered against the desk. He turned, blinking rapidly. "You want me to wash your hair?"

"Please." She lifted a handful from her shoulder. "It's full of soot and ash."

Rubbing his neck, he gave a slow nod. "All right."

He pumped water into a large pitcher.

Tori slid out of bed and wrapped herself in a blanket. She shuffled over to a large basin near the pump.

"What are you doing?"

Tori raised her brow. "You can't wash it while I'm lying in bed." She pointed to the basin. "That will make things much easier."

He pulled a chair up beside her.

She smiled. "Thank you."

As he placed a bar of soap beside the pitcher, he glanced at her. "I've never done this for a woman."

"Really?" She situated herself in the chair. "It's not difficult. It might take more time than washing a man's hair, but it's the same process. Wet, wash, rinse."

He eyed her mass of curls. "If you say so."

She bent over the basin. "I'm ready."

As he poured cool water over her hair, Tori moved one hand to shield her face. No one had washed her hair before. She wouldn't trust anyone else to do it, but with Harrison— even in his mood—she felt safe.

His hands dug into her hair. She smelled lavender and smiled. He'd used the calming soap. Moments later, he began massaging her scalp. Tori nearly gasped. Her eyes slid shut, and a gurgle of pleasure slipped from her lips.

He paused. "Are you all right?"

More than all right. Who knew having one's hair washed could be so heavenly? "Yes."

He resumed his ministrations. Tori relaxed under his touch, letting the pain of the last few hours wash away with the soot and grime.

"You have a lot of hair," he said, rubbing a spot just above her forehead.

"Mm-hmm. Mother always called it untamable. I think she resented how curly and thick it is."

"It's beautiful."

She sucked in a breath. No one other than Ella thought her hair pretty. More often than not, Tori found the unmanageable locks tiresome to pin up. But Harrison called them beautiful. Her stomach swooped with delight.

"Thank you," she said quietly.

She bit back a groan when he stopped the massage and rinsed out her hair. It took several refills from the pitcher before all the soap washed out. Harrison gathered her curls in hand and squeezed the water from them. He rubbed her hair with a towel, removing excess moisture.

"Would you like me to comb it as well?"

Now why did that send more butterflies dancing through her gut? Tori put a hand over her stomach and nodded. "If it's not too much trouble."

He fetched a brush from the shelf and set to work. Harrison moved the comb in short, methodical pulls as he made his way through her curls. Once more, Tori found herself surprised at how good it felt. It never felt like this when she combed it.

All too soon, he finished. Tori stood and waited until he'd returned the brush to its place. She moved forward and hugged him. "Thank you, Harrison. For saving my life and for taking care of me."

He inhaled a sharp breath, but his arms circled her in return for just a moment. "My pleasure."

When he released her, Tori felt cold. She stepped back and wrapped her arms around herself.

Harrison's gaze swept over her. "You should get back in bed. You need rest."

She shuddered, eying the hospital bed. "Not there. I want my own bed."

Crossing his arms, he hiked his brow. "You think you can climb those stairs?"

"Why not?"

She walked to them and started up. Five steps in, she realized her mistake. Her lungs burned with the effort. She stopped, leaning against the wall.

Harrison muttered something under his breath as he came up behind her. In one swoop, he lifted her into his arms, holding her like a baby. His display of strength stole the little air remaining in her lungs. He carried her to the apartment, his face set in stone. Tori couldn't read his expression.

He made his way to her room and pulled back the covers on the bed before laying her on it. "Try to sleep," he said, covering her with the blankets. "I'll check on you later."

She rolled to her side and snuggled against the pillow. "Thanks."

For a single heartbeat, his hand rested on her head. Then it was gone.

CHAPTER 19

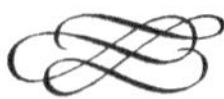

A week after the fire, Harrison tried to focus on the patient reports in front of him, failing miserably. He tapped his pen against the desk and downed his coffee. No change. After a minute, he stood.

It might not yet be daybreak, but he needed a breather. Sleep hadn't come easily the past few nights.

He went upstairs and tiptoed into Tori's room. She slept with both hands under her cheek, turned on her side, hair spread like a veil over the pillow. Her body had healed well. The only remnant of her ordeal lay in her pink skin.

His heart ached watching her. Once he'd admitted he was in love, that seemed to be all he could think about.

And he desired her love in return. He physically hurt with the desire to earn her love—and the fear it would never happen.

Suppressing a sigh, he tucked the covers closer about her chin. She murmured something, her lips curving into a sweet smile. His chest tightened. Without thinking, he leaned down and pressed a soft kiss to her forehead.

She made a tiny sound of contentment, sending a curl of yearning through his heart.

Time to go.

He slipped from the room and left the infirmary. Dawn's first light spread over the town. The sky lit with yellows and pinks. He stuffed his hands in his pockets, grateful for the morning breeze cooling his face.

A heavy sensation settled in his gut. He didn't like the constant feeling of worry he'd picked up.

Lord, help me.

He turned at the end of the street. The church came into view beyond the last building. He stared at it before determined steps took him to the sacred place.

The doors were unlocked, so he let himself in. The floorboards creaked under his boots. Light filtered in through the windows, still dim. He sank into a front row pew. At the front of the church, a large cross hung on the wall. He stared at it, a deep sigh rattling his lungs.

"I know I've had an easy life. My family never wanted for anything. Even my dream seemed to fall into place when I married Tori. I don't want to sound ungrateful, Lord. But with everything that happened last week...why?"

"That's everyone's favorite question."

Harrison shot to his feet and whipped around.

Pastor Samuel Allen stood in the doorway, mug in hand. "Good morning, Harrison. I didn't expect to see anyone here this early."

"Pastor Allen. I'm sorry to be here unexpectedly. I can leave..."

The pastor waved his hand. "It's Samuel." He walked down the aisle and took a seat. "Please stay. I assume there's something on your mind?"

Harrison lowered himself onto the pew again. "You could say that."

"You've been through a lot, in a short amount of time. Most people would be asking 'why' in your situation." Samuel sipped his coffee. "Has Travis found any information on the gang that stole your money?"

"Not that I know of."

"Do you want to talk about it?"

Harrison let out a short laugh. "If you're here at this hour, you probably had things you wanted to get done."

"Not particularly." Samuel leaned back against the pew. "One of my girls had a nightmare and needed comforting. When I finally got her back to sleep, I figured I'd come here to work on my sermon. But that isn't as important as lending a listening ear. So…" He raised his mug. "I'm listening."

Harrison massaged his temples. "It's not so much the loss of my money. That stings, but despite my upbringing, I've never been materialistic. It's the fact that I can't keep my promise to this town. I told them I'd build a hospital, which would not only bring good medical care to the residents, but would attract people from other towns, stimulating the economy here." He dug his hands into his hair. "This is all I ever wanted to do—help people. I could do that here in Harmony Springs in a way I never could in Boston. Now that dream is impossible."

"Hmm." Samuel regarded him as he took another sip of coffee. "So it's the loss of your dream that hurts more."

"Yes."

Samuel put his mug on the pew. "Harrison, may I be honest?"

"I'd expect nothing less."

"Good." Samuel leaned toward him. "Don't take this the wrong way, but there was an awful lot of 'I' in your words."

Harrison blinked.

Samuel continued. "The people of this town never asked for a hospital. They just wanted a doctor. Your announcement to build a hospital certainly got folks excited, but they were happy to have a health professional here once more. So your hospital went up in flames." He arched his brow. "You can still practice medicine. The infirmary is well stocked, far better than anything Harmony Springs has seen before. Isn't that what matters?"

It sounded so simple when Samuel put it like that. Harrison closed his eyes with a shake of his head. He scrubbed a hand over his jaw. "I've been rather selfish, it seems."

"Selfish may not be the right word. Your heart was in the right place. If this was your dream, you're not going to feel better about it being gone just like that. Sometimes, though, we have to let things go. There's wisdom in discerning when to hold on and when to release." Samuel chuckled. "The hard part is figuring out which is best."

Tori's face flashed through Harrison's mind. "Is it ever good to release a person?"

Samuel tilted his head. "That depends on what you mean."

"What if you entered into a bargain with someone, then couldn't uphold your end? Would it be best to end the agreement?"

"Possibly." Something passed over Samuel's face. Regret? Grief? Before Harrison could analyze it, the pastor spoke again. "The important thing is to have an honest conversation with the person. Misunderstandings can ruin a relationship." He shook his head. "If I'd learned that when I was young, I could have prevented a lot of heartache for both Lydia and myself."

"What do you mean?"

"Because of a big misunderstanding, I lost her for seven years. It was only by God's grace that we reconciled and reconnected." Samuel clapped him on the shoulder. "Whatever you do, make sure any decisions made with a person are made *with* that person."

Harrison nodded. "Thanks, Samuel. I'll keep that in mind."

The pastor stood. "I'll let you have some time to think. Holler if you need anything."

"I will."

His gaze found the cross again. Sacrifice. Something all followers of Christ were called to.

Was he being selfish holding onto Tori? If she couldn't love him, should he release her from their vows? When she agreed to marry him, she hadn't known they'd lose everything. If she were free, she could find someone else, someone she could love.

It certainly wouldn't be him.

Heart aching, Harrison let tears fall for the first time in years. He knew what he needed to do. It would break him, but for Tori's sake, he'd let her go.

~

Tori didn't like the depression that had taken hold of her husband. Though he remained kind and dedicated to his work, she saw the shift. His smile had vanished along with the twinkle in his eyes. He walked with his shoulders hanging low and his chin bent toward his chest.

Seeing him like that hurt her heart. His dream had been crushed, and it had affected him more than either of them thought possible. This morning, he'd left before she woke, and she hadn't seen him all day, as he was on house calls while she tended those who came to the infirmary.

If only she could take away the pain, but how?

Maybe a good meal would help. She ordered his favorite dish from the café, along with one of Cassie's delicious cakes. When she brought it up to their apartment, she readied the food on their small dining table. Moments later, Harrison's footsteps trudged up the stairs, echoing through the enclosed hall.

Her stomach flipped when she saw him. It'd been doing that regularly these days. Did it have to do with the fact that he'd been her hero, facing his own fears to rescue her?

She still couldn't believe he'd done that.

He hung his hat on its hook as soon as he came through the door. His gaze met hers before flitting to the table. "Is that pot roast?"

"Yes. I thought it'd be nice to eat together at home."

"It smells good." He shrugged out of his jacket and hung it beside his hat. "Thanks."

As he approached the table, Tori reached for his hand. His fingers flexed against hers before relaxing. He glanced at their joined hands. Something flickered on his face. Just as quickly, his expression evened. He squeezed her hand once before releasing it, then pulled out her chair and waited for her to sit. Once she did, he went to his seat.

They prayed over the meal and began to eat. He did not attempt to start a conversation. When the silence became unbearable, Tori broke it.

"Your parents are coming soon."

"Three days."

"Are you looking forward to seeing them?"

"No."

Tori blinked, her fork suspended between the plate and her lips. "No?" She set the fork down. "Why not?"

He copied her movement while leaning back in his chair. "I'm not looking forward to them finding out their son is a failure."

"You are not a failure."

His gaze dropped to the table. "The very thing I set out here to accomplish is lost. I've even lost myself. Yelling at you last week—"

"Harrison. You've apologized multiple times. It's fine. You were stressed."

"And you were vulnerable and injured. I shouldn't have taken it out on you. Or anybody." He shoved a hand through his hair, shaking his head. "And right after I claimed to love you," he muttered.

Judging from the widening of his eyes and the pink in his cheeks as he glanced up, he must not have meant for her to hear the last part. Tori's own cheeks flushed. She picked up her fork and dug into the mashed potatoes.

He'd not mentioned love since that first instance after the fire. The reality of his feelings hung over them like a heavy cloud, ready to burst at any moment. At some point, she'd have to face them, but for now it felt safest to pretend he'd never said those words.

She froze as she speared a string bean. Was it possible his depression stemmed from more than losing his inheritance and the hospital? She emitted a silent groan. Of course it was. What a fool she'd been, thinking more time was needed. Harrison deserved answers, even if she couldn't tell him what he wanted to hear. She'd left him in limbo for a week after his heartfelt confession.

Her gaze flew up to find his already on her. They stared at each other for a moment. Determination soon lit his face. He folded his hands and let out a long breath. "Tori, I've come to a decision."

She arched her brow.

"We should have our marriage annulled."

Her mouth fell open. Indignation sparked a fire in her gut. "I beg your pardon?"

"You married me to get away from your family and become a doctor. Now that we're established in town, you don't need my name. We can keep practicing medicine together, but we don't have to be married. I can move to another apartment—"

"Harrison, stop talking."

His throat bobbed, but he obeyed. Tori stood, palms

pressed against the table as she leaned toward him. "I don't want an annulment. We made promises to each other on our wedding day, promises that last until death. I have no intention of breaking the vows we made before God and man."

Even the promise to love?

Harrison pressed his lips together. He stood as well, towering over her. "You deserve someone you can love. That's obviously not me. I want what's best for you, Tori, and if that means letting you go so you can find a different man—"

"No."

She rounded the table. Slipping her arms around his waist, she pulled him close. "I don't want another man. I want you."

He tensed. "Don't say that unless you mean it."

"I do mean it." She tilted her head to meet his gaze. The heat smoldering there sent a swarm of butterflies careening through her stomach. "I can't say the words back yet. But you've softened my heart, Harrison, just by being you. Your kindness and humor, gentleness, wisdom—it's all helped me see that you're a trustworthy man. I enjoy being around you. I look forward to our conversations, to working together each day. When I think of a life without you..." She shuddered, shaking her head. Her hands curled around the outside of his vest. "It makes me cold. You matter to me, and even if I can't say I'm in love right now, I think I will get there. So please, no more talk of annulments."

He crushed her against him. Great, heaving breaths pulsed against her chest. His lips pressed against her hair, and a few drops of water landed on her cheeks. She pushed back enough to look up at him. The tears raining from his eyes tore at her heart, but his smile radiated with joy. She lifted her hands to his cheeks, wiping away the moisture with her fingers. He captured her right hand in his. Pressing his lips there, he left a lingering kiss against her knuckles. Their gazes met, and his smile grew.

"Thank you, Victoria."

She blinked. "For what?"

"For giving me hope. I took your silence in the infirmary as confirmation that you could never feel love for me. It's been eating at my very soul."

She traced the lines of his jaw. "Is that why you've been so sad?"

"That's a large part, yes." He sighed. "I am disappointed about the hospital, though. And the fact that we can't rebuild it."

"So it's not that the money's gone? It's that you can't use it for good?"

"Yes. It hurts knowing I can't fulfill my promise to the town."

"They'll understand." She pressed closer, resting her head on his chest. "We'll get through this together, Harrison."

He held her close and shut his eyes. Hopefully, she was right.

CHAPTER 20

Three days after his talk with Tori, Harrison strode down the street. A late-summer breeze brought a slight relief from the heat. Children's laughter brightened the air as they played in a meadow on the other side of the shops.

What a beautiful afternoon.

"Harrison, do you have a minute?"

Travis's voice halted Harrison's steps. He waved at his friend standing on the steps in front of the sheriff's office, then checked his pocket watch. "My family is due on the noon train. I'm headed there now."

"I'll be quick."

Harrison took in the grim expression on Travis's face. Whatever he had to say must be serious. "All right."

He entered the office behind Travis, who crossed his arms and turned to face Harrison. "Federal marshals nabbed the Otterson gang. They were caught red-handed robbing a train outside Helena."

"I'd have thought they'd lay low after getting my money." Harrison tried to ignore the twinge in his gut. "Why would they rob again so soon?"

"Greed, arrogance—the thrill of the chase." Travis shrugged. "Who knows? They did, and it cost them their freedom."

"That's good news, isn't it?" Harrison eyed Travis. "Why do you look upset?"

"Because one of them escaped. And your money is still missing."

"Oh."

"I'm sorry, man." Travis sighed. "The marshals will try to find out where they stashed the money, but it might be gone for good."

"I've accepted that." Harrison slid his hands into his pockets. "It's not an easy reality to swallow, but this is life now. Tori and I will simply have to earn our living like everyone else in town."

And he'd have to tell his parents he failed to build the hospital he promised. That still stung.

"If something comes up, I'll let you know," Travis said.

"I appreciate that."

He shook Travis's hand, then left the office and turned toward the station. Before he'd taken three steps, someone called him.

"Dr. Blake!"

He swung his head to the left. Wyatt hurried toward him, a smile etched on his face. "Glad I caught you. Got a minute?"

The station remained quiet. The train hadn't yet arrived, and no whistle sounded to announce its incoming. "Sure."

"What I have to say isn't up for debate."

"Okay..."

"We're going to rebuild the hospital."

Harrison's brow furrowed. "Wyatt, there's no money to rebuild."

"Yes, there is."

"I don't understand."

"You paid me generously, Dr. Blake. Some would say too generously. It was double what other people charge. I talked with my team, and we agreed to fulfill the contract at no further cost to you."

At no further cost?

Harrison shook his head. "I can't let you do that, Wyatt. That's your livelihood."

"We ran the numbers, and we'll still turn a profit once it's all said and done. You're not talking us out of this, Doc." Wyatt grinned. "Besides, we had some help."

Head spinning, Harrison blinked a couple times. "Help?"

"The townsfolk took up a collection after church on Sunday. They wanted to help you and the Missus Doc out. We know how important this hospital is for you two. The money Pastor Allen handed us will cover a good deal of hospital supplies and the like."

Sunday. The day he and Tori hadn't been at church because a child was brought into the infirmary with a broken leg.

If enough money had been taken up to purchase supplies... that wasn't a small number.

He gripped a nearby hitching post. "How...why...?"

"That's just what neighbors do. We're happy to help. It wasn't just the church either. Mr. Tolson at the saloon took up his own collection and raised a substantial amount as well. He donated that money yesterday." Wyatt slapped his back. "That's all I wanted to say. We'll need a new site for the build, since the other is burned out. I was thinking we could build closer to the pond. It's still peaceful and quiet, but just as close to town."

"It's too much," Harrison blurted.

Wyatt chuckled. "I remember saying something like that when you insisted on paying me far more than I charged."

"Wyatt, I appreciate your support, but..."

"Don't say anything about not accepting, Doc. This hospital is getting built, and that's that." He arched a brow. "I'm headed to stake out the spot we want to use before digging the foundation. Come on by tomorrow and let me know if you approve."

He began walking away. Harrison shook himself and leapt after him. "Wyatt."

"Yeah?"

"Thank you."

Wyatt smiled, the skin around his eyes crinkling slightly. "Happy to help." Whistling, he sauntered down the street.

Such sharp turns of circumstances in a short time had Harrison's feet rooted to the ground. The mix of emotions he'd experienced in the last week were more than he'd felt over his entire life. From utter fear to despair to hope...and now joy. A town coming together to save the hospital? He shouldn't be surprised. That spoke to the character of the residents of Harmony Springs. Doubtful something like this would have happened in Boston.

The shrill blast of a train horn brought him back to his task. Overcome with gratitude, he whispered a prayer of thanks, then hurried toward the station. He reached it just as the train screeched to a halt.

Passengers flowed out. He peered over the crowd. A smile broke across his face when his sister stepped onto the platform. "Temperance!"

She laughed and ran toward him. Launching herself into his arms, she laughed again. "It's wonderful to see you, Harrison." When they broke apart, she hiked a brow. "Can you come home now? I don't like you living so far away."

He chuckled, tapping her chin. "Or you could move here."

Her nose wrinkled as her gaze darted over his shoulder. "And leave behind all the conveniences of Boston? I don't think so."

"It grows on you."

The look she threw him spoke of her doubt. Before she could say anything, their parents approached.

Mother's eyes gleamed with tears. She hugged him tight with a little sigh. "My boy."

"Hello, Mother."

She pulled back. Her gaze searched his face. "You look tired."

Good thing she hadn't seen him a few days ago. He mustered a smile. "A lot has happened recently. You'll hear all about it soon."

Father clasped his hand. "If it's ever too much, just say the word and we'll help you get situated back in Boston. You could have your own clinic."

"I have my own clinic here."

"Yes." Father appraised him. "Are you still set on that hospital?"

"Well...yes..."

All three of his family members squinted in unison. "That didn't sound certain," Temperance said.

He didn't want to get into details here. "Why don't we get you settled at the hotel and then head to the café for lunch? Tori will meet us once she finishes with a patient. We can talk there."

At the mention of Tori, his parents glanced at each other. Harrison's gaze swung between them. "What is it?"

Mother grimaced. She bit her lip, looking at Father once more.

His father's mouth set into a thin line. He released a short sigh. "We hate to be the bearers of bad news, but there's been a development involving your wife."

Harrison's stomach sank. "Is this about her family in Boston?"

"It is."

He sighed. "Let's go to the café. We can talk there."

Whatever it was, he prayed Tori handled the news well.

~

ori finished wrapping her little patient's leg. "No running for you anytime soon," she said, smiling at six-year-old Harold White.

He frowned. "But I like to run."

"That's what got you into this scrape in the first place." His mother frowned at him and held a hand out to Tori. "Thanks for fixing him up."

Tori shook Mrs. White's hand. "Pleasure to help. Try to have him stay off that foot for two or three days."

"Tell a little boy to sit still?" Mrs. White winced. "That's a tough order, but we'll do our best."

Tori chuckled. "Bring him in a few days from now. We'll check on the sprain then."

"Thanks, ma'am."

After the Whites left, Tori hung up her doctor's coat and checked her hair in the wall mirror. Curls hung in disarray around her face. She pulled out the pins and smoothed the locks into place, pinning them secure. It wouldn't do to meet Harrison's parents and sister with untamed hair.

She checked the time. They should be at the café by now. She closed up the infirmary and walked down the steps.

"Tori!" Her brother-in-law's voice cut through the street, loud and frantic.

She spun around to see him galloping toward her on his horse. Her heart dropped to her feet. She raced to meet him. "What's wrong? Is it Ella? The children?"

"Our neighbor," he gasped, dismounting. "Miss Hattie. She was visiting us and had a bad fall. Ella's with her now."

Tori remembered the elderly woman from her previous visit. If she'd taken a fall at her age, she may have broken a bone. "I'll come at once." She rushed back into the infirmary and grabbed her doctor bag. Going outside once more, she found Cody pacing.

"Take Preston." Cody thrust the reins into her hands. "I'll get a horse from the livery and follow."

Tori mounted the horse, and at her command, he leapt forward. They flew past building after building, quickly approaching the edge of town. She let Preston have his head. When they reached the ranch, she hopped off and hurried into the house.

She found her sister with Hattie in the parlor. The older woman lay on the sofa, a mutinous expression on her face, her arms crossed tight over her chest. When she caught sight of Tori, her mouth relaxed into a smile. "Hello, dear. How lovely to see you again."

"Hello, Miss Hattie. What's this I hear about a fall?"

Hattie rolled her eyes. "I love Cody, but that boy worries far too easily. I'm fine. Took a tumble down the porch steps, and he overreacted."

Ella shook her head, lips pressed together. "Miss Hattie, you were unconscious for a full minute. Cody was right to worry." Her gaze slid to Tori. "Wasn't he?"

"Certainly." Tori reached into the bag for her stethoscope. "Let me check your vitals, Miss Hattie." She pressed the instrument to Hattie's heart. "Your heartrate is slightly elevated, but nothing to worry about."

"I'm fine," Hattie insisted. "A little sore, perhaps, but fine."

"Let me check for bruising."

She examined Hattie's legs and arms, moving them about. "Your mobility is good. Nothing's broken."

"As I said..."

Cody burst into the room. His blue gaze darted around the room. "How is she? Is everything all right?" He dropped to his knees beside Hattie, gripping her hands. "Does anything hurt?"

She patted his cheek. "I'm right as rain, young man. Thanks for your concern, but I just needed a moment to rest."

"Are you sure?"

He glanced up at Tori as if to confirm. She gave him a nod. "I can't find anything problematic. She might need some rest after such a fall, though."

Cody nodded. "We'll make sure she gets it."

Hattie chuckled. "Oh, *we* will, will we?"

Their good-natured bickering continued as Tori said goodbye and headed for the door. Ella trailed after her. "Thanks for coming, Tori. Miss Hattie is like a mother to Cody. I don't know what he'd do if anything happened to her."

"He did seem panicked when he got to the infirmary."

"I hope this didn't interrupt anything important."

"Just lunch with Harrison's family."

Ella's eyes widened. "I forgot they were coming. Oh my goodness, you need to get back to town."

"They'll understand." Tori embraced Ella. "We'll see you for supper tomorrow."

"I look forward to it. Mr. and Mrs. Blake always seemed kind, and Temperance had spunk. I like her."

"So do I."

Tori descended the porch steps. She halted, looking between the two horses in the yard.

Cody called from the window. "Would you mind taking the chestnut back to town?"

"Of course."

She patted the horse's neck. "Hi, girl. Ready to go home?"

The animal nickered. Tori gave her another pat, then climbed on. She cantered back to the livery. After getting the horse into her stall and feeding her a sugar cube, Tori walked to the café. She entered and looked around for Harrison and his family.

They sat at a table in the center of the room. She made her way to the table.

Mrs. Blake saw her first. Rising from her chair, she held her arms out to Tori. "Hello, Victoria."

"Mrs. Blake. It's good to see you."

Something in the woman's brown eyes shifted. She smiled, but it didn't spread wide. "Please, sit."

Harrison stood and slid out her chair. She smiled to thank him. His fingers squeezed her neck gently before he sank into the seat beside her. A look that matched his mother's flashed over his face.

Tori glanced between them, but Mr. Blake greeted her before she could ask anything. "How's the territory treating you, young lady?"

"Well, sir. I love Harmony Springs."

Temperance rounded the table. She threw her arms around Tori, hugging her tight. "I still can't believe my only sister-in-law is so far away. We had no time to get to know one another."

"We'll have to remedy that while you're in town."

Harrison flashed his sister a grin. "Or you could move here."

She rolled her eyes. "We've already established that's not happening."

Tori laughed. She looked at Harrison's parents, ready to ask about their journey, and caught them exchanging anxious looks. A shiver of dread sliced down her spine. "Mr. and Mrs. Blake, is everything all right?"

"Fine, dear." Mrs. Blake smiled, again without it reaching her eyes. "Though there is something we need to tell you." She patted Tori's hand. "After lunch."

Tori's gaze whipped to Harrison. His grimace told her the news wouldn't be welcome. She bit her lip, torn between wanting the news immediately or allowing the Blakes to have a nice lunch before imparting bad news.

Cassie came by with a notepad. "What can I get you folks?"

"Surprise me." Temperance beamed as she handed over her menu.

"Yes, ma'am." Cassie accepted the menu. She smiled at Tori and Harrison. "We have fried chicken on special today."

Tori's mouth watered. "I'll have that, please."

Harrison rubbed his hands. "Me, too."

Mrs. Blake squinted at the menu. "Fried chicken? That sounds interesting. What does it come with?"

"Mashed potatoes and string beans." Cassie collected the menus. "It's one of our best-selling dishes."

"I'll give it a try. Thank you, ma'am."

Cassie looked at Mr. Blake. "And for you, sir?"

"Beef pot pie, please."

Tori smiled. She slipped her hand over Harrison's. "Is that where you get your love for that dish?"

He returned her smile with a warm one. His free hand covered their joined ones. "It is."

Her stomach flipped. Oh, gracious. She felt no desire to remove her hand from his. Their gazes remained locked as a delicious warmth spread through her heart.

"A-hem." Temperance cleared her throat loudly.

Tori blushed and straightened.

Harrison kept his grip on her hand. "Something on your mind, sister?"

She gave their hands a pointed look.

He grinned. "What can I say? Married life agrees with me."

Tori noted his careful phrasing. He didn't say *us*...giving her the freedom to confirm or reject the statement herself. She drew in a quick breath. "With me as well."

Harrison blinked at her, then a slow smile tipped his lips.

Tori's cheeks heated. She looked down, aware of everyone's eyes on her.

Mr. Blake tapped the table. "It's good seeing you two happy together. I wasn't sure moving to the wilds of Montana so soon after your marriage would be good, but it seems to have strengthened your relationship."

Tori lifted her head. "It has. Your son is an excellent husband."

"We'd expect nothing less." Mrs. Blake sent a fond grin to Harrison.

The chitchat continued. The Blakes were pleasant, good conversationalists, but Tori grew restless. Her leg bounced and her fingers tapped against her thigh. Whatever news Harrison's parents brought weighed on her mind. How did it connect to her? Had Kenneth spread more rumors and lies when he went back to Boston?

She fell silent during the meal. Harrison noticed and nudged her. "You all right?"

"I'm a little nervous." She let out a small chuckle. "Sorry, Mr. and Mrs. Blake. I'm afraid the anticipation of your news has me anxious."

Mr. Blake clenched his fork in hand. He blew out a long breath. "We're sorry, Victoria. It was not our intention to frighten you. But I'm afraid the news we bring isn't good—and it directly impacts you."

She sipped her water. Biting her lip, she considered the best way to phrase her question.

Harrison beat her to it. "Father, maybe you should tell her now." His hand found hers again, squeezing gently.

Mr. Blake released a short breath. He shook his head. "There's no good way to say this." His gaze met Tori's. "Your father has been arrested."

CHAPTER 21

Father's pronouncement hung in the air like a cloud. Harrison ran his thumb along Tori's hand, providing what comfort he could. Silence reigned as she sat processing the news. How would she react?

Of all the possibilities going through his mind, laughter was not one of them.

Tori put a napkin over her mouth, but her shaking shoulders and amused eyes confirmed that she indeed laughed.

His parents stared. They'd been prepared for shock, sadness, or even anger—but this? Harrison knew her relationship with her father was rocky. Her reaction confirmed that in stark reality.

Tori recovered and lowered the napkin. She adjusted it on her lap before picking up her fork once more. "I thought you brought bad news. What a relief to find otherwise."

She began eating again while his family members looked at him with open mouths. He shrugged. Torn between relief that Tori wasn't affected and concern that emotion might hit her later, he also resumed his meal.

After swallowing a few bites of chicken, Tori waved her fork in the air. "Let me guess. Father was finally caught swindling, blackmailing, and otherwise cheating his clients, and he couldn't talk his way out of it."

"Well...yes." Father leaned forward. "How did you know?"

"He's been doing this for years. Part of the reason he tried to force my sister to marry Howard Archambeau is because the man knew about his shady dealings. No one could ever stop him, though." She sat back, a satisfied light in her eyes. "Until now. So, who did he cross?"

"Mayor Hart."

Tori whistled low. "I didn't think he'd go after politicians. He's never tried that before."

"Apparently, he convinced the mayor to invest in a nonexistent company." Temperance winced. "Mayor Hart's assistant was the one to question the deal after a contract had been signed. He looked into the company and found no evidence of its existence. Your father was arrested for fraud. After that, others came forward with testimonies of how he'd swindled them out of thousands of dollars."

"That sounds like Father." Tori's voice went bitter. "He never did anything if he couldn't gain more wealth or power. When I think of the people he's harmed, it makes me sick." Her eyes flashed. "I hope he's in prison a long time."

"From what I've heard, restitution is being made to those he wronged." Father rubbed the back of his neck. "Unfortunately, it means you and your sister no longer have an inheritance."

Tori laughed again. "Father disowned us both. There wasn't going to be an inheritance."

Mother fiddled with her napkin. "What about your mother?"

"What about her?"

"She's left in disgrace. She isn't destitute, but she won't be able to continue the life she's always known. Society will disown her. Who will she turn to?"

Tori shrugged. "Mother is resourceful. She'll figure something out."

Harrison's mother grasped her pearls. She gaped at Tori.

Harrison reached out to pat Mother's hand. "Tori doesn't have a close relationship with her parents. What do you expect her to do?"

"I...I don't suppose anything specific." Her gaze turned pleading. "Won't you visit her? I'm sure seeing you and Ariella would bring her comfort."

Tori jerked in her seat. She barked out a harsh laugh. "Ella and I, comfort Mother? She'd likely turn us away out of arrogance."

Mother looked as though she'd been slapped. "Crystalline and I have been friends for years. She's always seemed a sweet woman, if maybe a bit driven."

"Appearances are everything to my parents," Tori muttered. "At home, she was a hard, exacting person. Nothing my sister or I did was enough. Believe me, she wouldn't want us there now. She can derive comfort from her friends, not her daughters."

The rest of dinner passed in strange, stilted conversation. Tori remained silent while she finished her meal. As soon as she took her last bite, she pushed the plate aside and gave a tight smile. "This has been lovely, but I should probably get back to the infirmary."

Father waved a hand. "Stay a bit, Victoria." He smiled, understanding in his expression. "It's not as though you need to work for money. If there's an emergency, I'm sure someone will find you."

Tori blinked. She gripped Harrison's arm. "You didn't tell them?" she whispered.

"Not yet."

She sank back into her chair. "Then I'll stay."

"Are you sure? We can both head back..."

Her brows shot up. "This is a small town. Do you want to risk someone else telling them?"

"Telling us what?" Mother asked, glancing between them. The shock hadn't quite faded from her expression, but it was less pronounced as the promise of different news presented itself.

Harrison tugged his collar. Tori slipped her hand into his—her turn now to support him. Funny how quickly the tables turned.

He drew in a long breath and closed his eyes. "We lost Aunt Lucille's inheritance." His free hand clenched. "And the hospital."

His parents stared at him. Temperance's jaw dropped before snapping shut again. Her eyes went wide. "What happened?"

Harrison related the events as succinctly as possible. When he finished, his family members sat stunned. He clung to Tori's hand.

She gave him a soft smile and leaned close. "It's fine—not as though our lives are crumbling to pieces or anything."

He chuckled, briefly resting his head against hers. "You are my sunshine, Tori," he murmured.

They were so close, he could see flecks of green in her brown eyes, could smell her jasmine scent. For a moment, everything around them faded. He got lost in her gaze, lost in her smile. Even with receiving and then imparting hard news, she found a way to smile.

One of the many things he loved about her.

"Well." Father's voice brought their attention back to the present. He crossed his arms, head tilted. "That's a lot to process."

"Tell me about it." Harrison snorted.

"You should have seen him," Tori said, reaching for her water. She smirked at him over the rim of the cup. "He moped for a week."

That had more to do with her perceived rejection of his love, but he wasn't about to air that in front of his family.

Temperance huffed, disbelief written on her face. "Only a week? I'd have been out of sorts for months."

Mother wrung her hands. "Oh, darling, I'm so sorry. This is horrible. How will you manage?"

"We had some funds hidden in safes. We're not destitute. We'll have to earn our keep here, like the other residents of town, but it's not a hopeless situation. There are others in far worse circumstances than us."

"But the hospital?" Temperance said. "I thought that's why you moved here."

"It was." He swallowed his pride, gaze on his parents. "I'm sorry to be a disappointment."

His father's brows lowered. "You're not a disappointment, Harrison."

"I failed, Father."

"Failure almost always occurs in the pursuit of one's dreams." Father chuckled. "Do you know how many times I've failed in my life? Too many to count."

Mother reached for Harrison's free hand. "Darling, you could never be a disappointment. We love you and want you to be happy. I'm just sad that your hospital was destroyed."

"Well...we can't build the hospital anymore, but the towns-folk can."

Tori's head whipped toward him. "What?"

"Turns out generosity is a hallmark of this town. Wyatt insisted on providing the materials for building a new hospital, and both Samuel and Mr. Tolson took up collections that will fund most of the equipment we need."

Joy shone from his wife's eyes. She laughed, throwing her arms around his neck.

His mother clasped her hands to her heart. "We were worried when you left, Harrison." Her gaze flitted between him and Tori as they pulled back. A smile pulled at her lips. "But I think you're exactly where you need to be."

~

Tori paced in her bedroom, hands splayed on her hips. Despite the good news about another hospital, she couldn't dispel the disappointment she'd seen in Mrs. Blake's eyes when she said she wouldn't visit Mother.

She huffed, hands on her hips. It was past her bedtime, but sleep remained elusive. Her white nightgown billowed around her legs as she spun at the window. Her curls bounced against her cheeks. She gathered her hair up, dividing it into three sections and weaving a quick braid. "That should keep it out of my face," she muttered.

Maybe some tea would help calm her. Tori opened her door with more force than necessary. Before she took two steps, she paused in front of Harrison's door. Light filtered beneath it. He was still awake?

She pushed the door open. Harrison sat in bed, a book in hand. His eyes widened when he saw her. "Tori?" He laid the book on his nightstand. "Is everything all right?"

Uncertainty assailed her. Tori chewed on her lower lip. "Um...not really. But it's late. We can talk in the morning."

"You won't sleep if you don't get this off your mind."

Tori's lips twitched. He knew her well.

A sudden, pulsing need for comfort swept over her. She wanted to be near him. Never before had she experienced such a desire. Not stopping to analyze the feeling, she let her heart lead.

Approaching the bed, she pointed to the spot beside him and drew in a deep breath. "May I?"

Surprise flashed over his face, but he nodded. "Of course."

She crawled in next to him. Despite the warmth from his body, she shivered. "Don't get any ideas. We're just talking."

He chuckled. "Don't worry, I have no intention of taking advantage of you. Though if you'd be more comfortable in the parlor…"

"This is fine." She twisted the covers in her hands. "Harrison, am I an awful person?"

"Not at all. Why would you think that?"

"Because I don't want to see my mother."

He turned his body to face her. "Tori, from what you've told me, your parents were not loving or kind. That makes it difficult to find sympathy in their misfortune."

"The virtuous thing to do is forgive."

The words tasted bitter.

He studied her, head tilted to the side. "Have you?"

Her stomach pulled tight. Her hands clenched into fists as she pictured her parents. She wasn't sorry for their turn of circumstances. If anything, she felt vindicated. "They got what they deserved," she said through gritted teeth.

Harrison took her hand. The regularity with which he'd been doing that brought calm to Tori's heart. Some of her anger melted away at his touch.

"They did get what they deserved. Justice is important, Tori. But there is something more important than justice."

"What?"

He clasped her hand to his chest. "Love."

She recoiled. "*Love*? My parents beat me and my sister down every day of our lives. They didn't care for us, didn't love us. They only cared about money and their standing in society." She ripped her hand from his. "Are you telling me I should love them after what they've done?"

He didn't respond, just looked at her with those deep brown eyes and held her gaze.

She shook her head in jerky motions. "No. I can't."

"Love doesn't mean you like them. It means willing the best for them, for their souls."

"And forgiving, I suppose," she said, bitterness piercing each word.

"It's what our faith teaches. That doesn't mean it's easy." He smoothed a loose curl from her forehead. "Who's most affected by your unforgiveness? Your parents?"

Her jaw set. Remaining quiet, she crossed her arms over her chest and glared at her husband.

He didn't seem fazed. Their stare off continued until Tori finally dropped her gaze. His thumb inched her chin up. "Who, Tori?"

"Me. Is that what you want me to say?" She shoved his hand away. "I can't help it, Harrison. They hurt me. Sorry if I don't feel like running home to help them now."

Hot tears burned her eyes. Dismay welled up inside. The last thing she wanted was to cry in front of her husband. She willed the tears away, but they refused to cooperate. One fell, then another. A sob caught in her throat. The tears fell faster, and uncontrollable sobs shook her.

Harrison wrapped his arms around her. She resisted for a moment, then sank into the comfort he offered. The shoulder of his nightshirt grew wet with her tears. He didn't say anything, but the gentle movement of his thumb against her back spoke volumes.

She dug her fingers into his shirt, clutching fistfuls of the white fabric. Anger fueled her tears, along with hurt from years of emotional pain. Time passed in a blur. When her tears finally subsided, she felt like a mess.

Harrison pressed a handkerchief into her hands. She mumbled her thanks, wiping her eyes and then blowing her nose. He continued to rub her back. "Better?"

"Not really." She swiped her nose again. "I need to talk to Ella. She's the level-headed one. She'll know what to do."

"I think you know what to do, Tori. You just don't want to do it."

She stiffened. "What does that mean?"

"You know your own mind. You know what is right. The hard part is doing it."

"I don't want to." She crossed her arms, feeling like a petulant toddler.

Harrison pulled her close again. "You don't have to make any decisions tonight. Maybe a good rest will help you see more clearly in the morning."

She sighed. Her head fell against his shoulder. "I'm not sure a week's worth of rest would help in this situation."

"You're strong, Tori. You'll get through this. And you don't have to do it alone."

She glanced up at him, and her lips tipped up. "I'm glad you're here."

He kissed her forehead. Tori's breath hitched. He started to pull away. "It's late. We should turn in."

She gripped his arm. "Harrison..."

"Yes?"

For the second time that night, she gathered her courage. "Can I stay with you?"

He blinked. For several heartbeats, he stared at her. "You want to stay?"

"If you don't mind."

He still stared. Oh dear. She'd made a muddle of things.

Tori swung her legs toward the edge of the bed. "On second thought, maybe I'll just go back to my room."

He laced their hands together before she got far. "You can stay, Tori. I don't mind."

Heat curdled in her stomach as his chocolate eyes remained on her. "Are you sure?"

"Of course." He smirked, nudging her shoulder. "Just don't get any ideas."

CHAPTER 22

Tori rummaged through her drawers, muttering. "Where did that comb get to?"

"Looking for this?"

She glanced up. Harrison stood in the doorway, her sturdy comb in his hand. Her stomach fluttered when their gazes met. When she woke up this morning curled up beside him, she felt safe, even happy. He had that effect.

She wasn't sure what to make of it.

Holding out her hand, she approached him. "Yes, thank you."

He lifted it over his head, just out of her reach.

Tori raised her brows. "Harry."

"Victoria."

She plunked her hands on her hips and cocked her head. His lips remained in a straight line, but the twinkle in his eyes belied his humor. She lunged, hands extended for the comb. He lifted it farther beyond her reach.

Tori landed against his chest with a thud. His free arm snaked around her waist, drawing her flush to him. He grinned. "Isn't this cozy?"

Fire flooded her cheeks._When had her husband turned into a flirt? Not that she minded...

But two could play that game.

Pushing against his chest, she looked into his eyes. She gave him a little pout and batted her lashes. "You're going to keep my comb from me?"

He waved it over her head with a chuckle. "Unless you ask nicely."

"Hmm...how nicely?"

She slid one hand behind his neck, resting the other over his heart. A little tug drew his face closer to hers. She brushed her nose against his, once, twice, three times. His heart beat faster against her palm. She tilted her head, drawing their lips a mere inch apart. "May I please have my comb?"

His gaze locked onto hers. He slowly brought the comb down, pressing it into the hand she had on his chest. "You can have anything you want."

His low, hoarse whisper made her heart thump hard. Raw desire flared from his gaze, but he didn't move. A twinge of guilt flitted through her gut. This man loved her. Her playful flirtation wasn't meant to hurt him, but perhaps it wasn't kind to act so without intending to give him something in return.

She swallowed her trepidation. He'd done so much—cared for her, loved her, all without asking anything for himself. If she could get past her fears, the pain of her past...maybe she could love him back.

At least she could gift him a small token of affection.

"Harrison, will you kiss me?"

He inhaled a sharp breath. His grip on her tightened. "Are you sure?"

She nodded.

His lips spread into a wide smile. He took her face in his hands. They trembled against her cheeks as he pressed his mouth to hers in a sweet, tentative kiss.

Tori closed her eyes. Heat burned in her belly. He kissed her gently, almost as if he were afraid to take too much.

That wouldn't do.

She surged up on her toes, pressing into him and taking their kiss deeper. Harrison pulled back slightly, his breaths ragged. He searched her eyes. Tori stared back, holding him tight, hoping he read the acceptance in her gaze.

A fire lit in his. His arms went around her as his lips took hers again. This time, he didn't hold back.

His passion ignited her own. The comb clattered to the floor. She gave back all she got, pouring into him her physical affection, praying that one day she'd be able to love him the way he deserved.

Although...

This feeling. The way they worked together. The safety he offered. Their friendship. Was it possible she already loved him?

Tori gasped, her eyes flying open.

Harrison broke their kiss and smiled at her. He traced her right cheekbone, eyes a bit hazy. "I love you, dear Tori."

Oh, gracious. She thought her heart had already melted with that kiss, but his words turned it to a puddle. How could she not love her most steadfast friend?

She took a deep breath, a smile of her own forming, ready to share her revelation. "I lo—"

He pressed his fingers to her lips.

Tori frowned. What was he doing? She was trying to make a declaration. "Harris—"

"No. Not yet, love."

She blinked and pushed his hand from her mouth. "Why not? I thought you wanted to hear this."

His eyes darkened. "More than anything."

"Then why are you preventing it?"

He pressed a soft kiss to her lips. "Because you're caught

up in the heat of the moment. You're dealing with strong emotions regarding your parents. We just spent a night beside each other. I want..." He exhaled, closing his eyes. "I want you to be sure of your feelings before saying those words."

She stepped back, crossing her arms with a huff. "Honestly, Harrison. Do you think I don't know my own feelings?"

He chuckled. "Give it a day or two. Anyone who'd just been kissed like that might think themselves in love. I want you to be completely sure."

Heat filled her cheeks again. Her gaze dropped to his lips. She closed the small space between them and threw her arms around his neck. "If you're not going to let me say it, let me show you."

This kiss remained gentle and exploratory, but it simmered with passion. Tori lost track of time. When a low groan sounded in Harrison's throat, she barely registered it before he pulled away. Raking a hand through his hair, he grabbed her hand. "Let's sit in the parlor. I don't trust myself alone in this room with you."

He tugged her into the hall. When they reached the parlor, he released her. "Do you want tea? Coffee?"

"Coffee, please."

She settled on the sofa as he prepared two mugs of strong coffee. "You know, I still haven't combed my hair."

"I rather like your untamed curls."

"It's not seemly for a woman to run around with her hair unbound."

He smirked, coming to the sofa and handing her a mug. "You're in our home. No one else is going to see your hair down. Only me." He put his mug on the table, then sat beside her. His gaze went to her hair. "It's beautiful."

Her heart pitter-pattered in quick rhythm. She sipped her coffee, a smile pulling at her mouth. Why had she stubbornly insisted she wasn't in love with him? And when had she started falling?

The revelation felt both sudden and months in the making. She didn't know how to analyze it.

"How do you feel about your parents this morning?"

If anything could douse her fuzzy feelings, that was it. Her lips turned down. "Must you bring them up? We were having such a lovely morning."

He fingered one of her curls. "I know."

Silence stretched. Tori sighed with a shake of her head. "I'm still angry."

"Understandably."

He continued to play with her hair.

Tori leaned into his touch. "I don't want to go to Boston."

Her husband remained quiet, giving her time to think.

She sighed again. Her throat constricted. "What would be the point, Harrison? Why should I go?"

His hand moved from her hair to her back. He rubbed gentle circles between her shoulder blades. "There's a possibility for reconciliation, love. Wouldn't that be worth going?"

"It's not going to happen. My parents are not interested in forgiveness. They've always looked out for themselves."

"You're probably right. But you'd know you did the right thing. You tried one last time. If they reject your love, that's their problem."

"I don't know if I want to offer forgiveness," she muttered. "They don't deserve it."

"Mercy is undeserved grace."

"You sound like a preacher."

"Am I wrong?"

"No." She breathed out a sharp breath. "I don't like that you're right in this."

His hand stilled as he leaned closer. "You have a chance to be free from your bitterness and pain, Tori. You're justified in your feelings. But maybe, if you take this trip, you'll find it in your heart to let go."

She gulped. "What if it hurts too much? What if I break again?"

He kissed her, soft and tender. When he pulled back, he looked in her eyes and cupped her cheek. "Then I'll be here to pick up the pieces."

～

"I can't believe we're actually doing this," Tori said, staring at the train.

Harrison slid an arm around her waist. Hopefully, it showed his support. In the two days since Tori and Ella decided together to visit Boston, his wife had let her mask settle in place once more. She cared for their patients with calm and efficiency, but her heart hadn't seemed in it. Her fears over facing her parents again were strong.

Ella and Cody stood a few feet away, saying their own goodbyes. Harrison leaned close to Tori to whisper in her ear. "I'll be praying for you, Tori. No matter what comes, you're brave. You can do this."

She let out a shaky laugh. "Can I?"

"I've no doubts."

She clutched his free hand. "I wish you were coming with us."

"So do I."

"When that hospital is complete, we need to have a couple nurses on hand so we can travel together when needed."

He smiled, pulling her in for a hug. "An excellent idea."

Tori looked up at him. "I haven't left yet, and already I miss this town. And you."

His heart leapt. Framing her face in his hands, he pressed a kiss to her forehead. "I'll be counting down the days."

The train whistle blew. Tori gulped. "Here goes nothing."

Ella approached, David cuddled in her arms. "Are you ready, Tori?"

"No."

Harrison bit back a laugh. Tori's honesty was one of the many things he loved about her. He gave her a gentle push toward the boarding platform. "The sooner you leave, the sooner you'll be home."

She tossed her head, hand on one hip. "And the sooner I can tell you something *very* important."

Fire pulsed through his veins. He almost begged her to say the three words now but refrained. "I look forward to it."

She took two steps in the direction of the train, then dropped her bag and dashed into his arms. Before he could blink, she pulled his head down for a kiss. His head reeled at the feel of her soft lips. Far too soon, she broke away. "Just something to remember me by," she said, waggling her fingers. "Goodbye, Harry."

He ignored the nickname and smiled. "Godspeed."

The women boarded the train. Harrison and Cody stayed until it pulled from the station and chugged out of sight. He turned to his brother-in-law. "Miss Hattie is helping with the children while Ella's away?"

"Yep. I'm thankful for her. She's staying at the house until Ella's back."

They started down the street. Cody slid his hands in his pockets as they walked. "That was quite a display at the station."

"What display?"

Cody's brows shot up. "That kiss."

Harrison grinned. "Things are looking up, my friend."

"I'm happy for you." Cody slapped his back. "It was only a matter of time."

They parted ways at the hotel. Harrison checked his pocket

watch. His family was likely still abed. He asked the receptionist if they'd been to breakfast yet, and the young man said no. Harrison thanked him and headed for the door.

"Darling, you're up early."

His mother's voice came from the staircase. He turned to see her descending the steps alone. "Mother. Where are Father and Temperance?"

"Sleeping. They'll be up within an hour." She smiled at him, accepting his proffered arm. "Where are we going?"

"You need a proper cup of coffee. We're going to the café."

She chuckled. "Cassie's coffee is the best."

"Indeed."

They walked down the street. The morning hung heavy with warmth, promising a hot day. Sweet flowers scented the air better than any perfumery could.

"Did Victoria head out already?"

He nodded. "She and Ella should be in Boston within a week."

Mother hummed. They walked a little farther before she spoke again. "I fear I may have been overbearing with her."

"What do you mean?"

"Insisting that she visit Crystalline. It wasn't my place. I thought my friend in need of family, but now I reflect on it…" She winced. "Crystalline does not like accepting help. I've tried in the past to offer support, and she always declined. Victoria's reaction does not speak well to her mother's behavior, does it?"

"I'm afraid not."

"I've made a muddle of things." Mother sidled closer to him. "Do you think…oh, never mind."

He nudged her. "Do I think what?"

"Perhaps…would she like to think of me as a mother? You two are married, after all. I'd love to show her a good example of motherhood." A flash of worry crossed her face. "Am I a good mother, Harrison?"

He smiled. They stopped at the café door, and he embraced her. "The best."

Mother's eyes glowed.

He opened the door for her. "You'll have to ask Tori, but I think she'd accept your offer."

"How long will she be gone?"

"Around two weeks." He sighed. "Two long, long weeks."

Mother tilted her head, a knowing smile on her lips. "You love her."

"Very much."

"I wondered when you married so quickly if there was a reason beyond gaining the inheritance." She lifted a brow. "That was why you married, correct?"

He coughed, shifting his gaze away. "Well..."

"Oh, come, son. It's common knowledge that most society weddings are not for love. Your father and I married out of obligation."

"What?" His gaze snapped back to her. "I thought you and Father were in love."

"We are now. But for the first few years, we merely tolerated one another."

He stared, open-mouthed. "What changed?"

She patted his arm. "Coffee first. Then we can talk."

They ordered their drinks. Harrison added on a couple muffins to the order. Once they had everything in hand, they found a table. He took a sip of his coffee and pointed at Mother. "Please, continue. What changed for you and Father?"

She smiled. "Temperance."

"Temperance?"

"When she was born, I saw your father in a new light. The way he worked hard to care for us, how he turned tender any time he held your sister. I started falling in love with him. It took him a little longer, but one day when Temperance was a year old, he proclaimed his own love." She sighed, one hand over her heart. "That sparked a new era for us. I hated that my father made me marry him, but now I can't imagine life with anyone else."

Harrison swallowed a bite of muffin. "You never let on."

"That's because we were well in love by the time you came along." She rested a hand over his. "All I ever wanted for you and your sister was finding love." She leaned back, taking a sip of coffee, gaze never leaving his. "If I ever seemed unsupportive of your dream, it was because I thought you being a physician wouldn't fulfill you the way a good marriage could. I thought the ladies of society would look down on being a doctor's wife." She chuckled. "I'm glad I was wrong. Victoria is a fiery girl, but she's perfect for you."

He smiled, his wife's beautiful face filling his mind. "I couldn't agree more."

CHAPTER 23

Sweat dripped down Harrison's back as he split another log for Wyatt's crew. Six slow days at the infirmary had him itching for work, and Wyatt had been more than happy to let him help with construction, with the caveat that Harrison not injure himself again.

The manual labor felt good. It also distracted him from the fact that his wife was still in Boston.

If train schedules could be trusted, she would have arrived there today. That meant she'd still be gone over a week.

He missed her. A shame the newfangled telephone hadn't found its way west. He'd give anything to hear her voice.

Lord, please let her find the answers she needs. Comfort her and Ella as they seek reconciliation.

He swung the ax again, cutting a log clean down the middle.

"Not bad for a city slicker, Doc." Wyatt walked toward him with a grin.

Harrison mopped his brow with a handkerchief. "I hope I'm not slowing you down."

"Nah. I appreciate the help." Wyatt took the ax. "But it looks as though you're needed in town. The sheriff sent word he'd like to speak with you."

"I'll be back tomorrow, then, if that's all right with you."

"Sure. Thanks, Doc."

The men shook hands. Harrison wiped his brow once more and began the walk to Travis's office. The sun beat down on him. He rolled his sleeves up, thankful for the small gusts of wind to cool his skin. Autumn couldn't arrive soon enough.

When he reached Travis's building, his friend stood in the doorway. He waved Harrison inside. "Would you like some coffee?"

"No, thanks. This heat is brutal."

Travis chuckled. "A glass of water, then? It's not cold, but it should help."

"That would be wonderful."

As he poured the water, Travis pointed to the chair across from his desk. "Have a seat."

"What's this about?" Harrison asked, lowering himself into the chair.

Travis handed him the water. "We got word that Dusty Otterson was spotted a few miles outside Boulder. One of the Marshals shot him, but he escaped capture."

"That's only ten miles from here."

"Yeah." Travis crossed his arms and leaned against the desk. "Considering the amount of money stolen from our bank, I'd wager they hid it nearby. That getaway wagon they used to cart it off would be easy to spot when we started to search. The logical option would have been finding someplace within five miles of town."

"So close? Wouldn't they risk it being found?"

"Not necessarily. There are acres of empty land in the territory, lots of forests and abandoned cabins. It could take years to comb through them five miles in all directions. And that'd be with a team searching full time."

"Which no one will do for one man's stolen inheritance."

Travis stretched out his hands. "I'm afraid not." He scratched his beard. "But with Dusty somewhere close, injured, we might be able to catch him. If we do, we could get your money back."

"Supposing he talks. You said the other brothers have been close-mouthed about it."

"Sometimes it just takes getting the right one. Don't give up hope."

Harrison sipped his water. His gaze drifted to the window. The beginnings of the new hospital stood just in sight. He stared at it a moment, then smiled. "You know, I don't think it would be terrible if we never recovered the money."

Travis hiked his brow. "Oh?"

"If it hadn't been lost, this town wouldn't have come together to rebuild. I've never seen such generosity from neighbors. It's been a blessing." He chuckled. "Of course, if the money is recovered, I'd love to pay everyone back. Especially Wyatt. And I wouldn't complain about being able to buy supplies and equipment without hesitation."

"We'll see what happens. A couple marshals are coming down tomorrow. We're going to discuss the best way to scout the area and see if we can find Dusty. Would you be willing to help, if they ask for it?"

"Can I do that as a civilian?"

Travis grinned. "Consider yourself deputized until further notice."

"If you're sure."

"I am. Doctors are observant. You'll see things through different eyes than law enforcement." Travis straightened, stretching his back. "Cassie asked me to extend a dinner invitation for you this evening. Your family's welcome too. Six o'clock."

"We'd like that. Thanks." Harrison shook Travis's hand. "See you this evening."

He exited the office. Almost immediately, his gaze landed on a couple standing outside the infirmary down the street. He picked up his pace. As he got closer, he recognized Samuel and Lydia. Samuel supported his wife, his brow furrowed and lips turned down in a frown.

Harrison broke into a jog. By the time he reached them, his breaths came in pants. "What's wrong?"

Lydia clutched her stomach with both hands. "We're not sure. It feels like contractions."

"You're five months along?" he asked, opening the door and motioning for them to enter.

"Yes."

Her face creased with worry. Tears sparkled in her eyes. Harrison helped her sit on one of the beds. Samuel sank into a chair beside her, her hand gripped in his.

Harrison took his stethoscope. As he pressed it to Lydia's stomach, he looked her in the eye. "Sometimes first-time mothers panic when pains come on them early. It's possible these are not what contractions feel like."

She swallowed. "I've given birth before, Dr. Blake. This feels very similar to birthing pains."

The stethoscope dropped. "I thought your girls were adopted."

"They are." Samuel cleared his throat. "Our first child died several years ago."

"I'm so sorry." Harrison adjusted the stethoscope again, then paused. Hadn't Tori told him the Allens only married last year? His gaze swung between them. He opened his mouth to ask but decided against it. If they wanted to share their story someday, they would. He didn't want to pry.

"Thank you for your discretion, Doctor." A faint smile tugged at Lydia's lips.

He glanced up. "I'm sorry—"

She shook her head. "Most people would ask right out." Looking at Samuel, she blew out a breath. "We were engaged years ago. I ended up pregnant right before Samuel left for seminary. We were separated for seven years, so he wasn't there for her birth. Unfortunately, our daughter died before we reunited. He never met her."

"Not in this life, at least." Samuel rubbed the back of her hand with his thumb.

"I'm sorry you went through that." Harrison removed the stethoscope and looped it around his neck. "Hopefully, this time around, things are better."

Lydia rested a hand over her unborn baby. "How was the heartbeat?"

"Normal. You might be experiencing false labor pains, or you might need rest. I lean toward the latter."

"What does that mean?"

"It means bedrest, Lydia. For a week to start. If the pains go away, you can try moving around. But if they return, you'll have to confine yourself to your room for the rest of the pregnancy."

Her eyes widened. "The rest of the pregnancy?"

"We'll see if that's necessary. Let's give it a week first. No need for alarm."

"Are you sure?"

"Based on heart rate, the baby does not seem distressed." He patted her shoulder. "I've seen plenty of women through pregnancy, ma'am. This is a common occurrence. Everything should be fine."

Lydia's face relaxed. She smiled at Samuel. "That's good news."

"Indeed," he replied.

Harrison clapped his hand on Samuel's shoulder. "I heard what you did for the new hospital. Thank you."

Samuel shrugged, helping his wife to her feet. "It's the least we could do. We're happy to help however we can."

"It means a lot to me."

Samuel chuckled. "That's the beauty of this town. We take care of our own. I haven't been here a year yet and have already seen plenty of neighborly love."

They said goodbye and left the building. Harrison glanced around the room, hands at his hips. It was too quiet with Tori gone. Hopefully, she'd be home soon.

Hopefully, everything went well in Boston.

~

The sheer mass of humanity bustling around the Boston train station had Tori wishing for the open air and calm pace of life in Harmony Springs. She gasped as a stranger bumped into Ella, making her sister stumble.

"Hey!" she shouted, glaring at the man. "Watch where you're going."

He didn't even look back.

Rude.

She took David from Ella. "Are you all right?"

Ella's face looked haggard from days of travel, but she smiled. "I'm fine, Tori. Let's get to our hotel."

They'd discussed plans for their stay and agreed that staying in a hotel would be preferable to staying in their childhood home. None of the memories in that house were good.

Tori cuddled the baby to her chest while Ella hailed a carriage. He gurgled, chewing on his fingers as they got into the conveyance.

The ride to the hotel passed in silence. When they reached it, they checked into their room and unpacked.

"We should probably go to the house today," Tori said

"I suppose seeing Mother as soon as possible is preferable to putting it off." Ella shoved her emptied carpetbag under the bed. "At least we'll know how long to stay after our visit."

"I hope she gives us a reason to leave."

Ella sat beside her on the settee. "I'm sure this is hard for you."

Brows raised, Tori eyed her sister. "And it's not for you? Mother and Father were harder on you than on me."

"Yes, but I've been gone for a long time. I had time to heal." She put a hand on Tori's arm. "I worry that you're not."

"I'm happy now. Mother and Father have no say in my life."

Ella's green gaze never wavered. "Forgiveness is critical to happiness, Tori."

"You sound like Harrison."

With a laugh, Ella reclaimed her baby. "He's a wise man." She rocked David. "You never explained what that kiss at the station was about."

Blushing, Tori twisted the fabric of her skirt. Ella had been so distracted with keeping David occupied during their trip, she hadn't mentioned the kiss. Now that they were at their destination, though, her sister wouldn't let it go, so Tori opted for the truth. "I think I'm in love with him."

"You think?"

The train ride had given her far too much time to think. Time to convince herself that maybe she had been caught up in emotion. But she'd tried to banish the thoughts. "Love is a choice, right?"

"Every day."

"I'm choosing to love my husband. He deserves it. The feelings are there. I still feel scared, thinking he might one day decide I'm too much." She swallowed, her hands clenching. "But I think loving him is worth the risk. He's a good man. I...I do love him."

"Good."

Ella's simple reply made Tori's brows twitch. "That's all you have to say?"

"Would you like to hear 'I told you so'?" They shared a chuckle. Ella took her hand. "I'm happy for you. Love is a beautiful thing, and I think you and Harrison are good for one another."

Tori's heart warmed. She smiled, tucking a fallen piece of hair behind her ear. "I agree."

Her sister glanced at the clock. She bit her lip and stood. "We should ready ourselves to see Mother."

Rolling her eyes, Tori went to the wardrobe. "Heaven forbid we show up looking as though we just traveled for days." She pulled out a violet dress with lace trim. "Will this do?"

"You'll look lovely." Ella laid David on the bed and stretched. "My dresses are not up to society standards."

"Would you like to borrow one of mine?"

"I think I'll wear my blue flowered dress." Ella smiled, her eyes soft. "That's Cody's favorite."

"And that's what matters."

They dressed and went back outside. Tori looked up and down the street. "Should we get a carriage or walk? It's about half a mile to Mother's."

"Let's walk." Ella cradled David. "If this little one gets too heavy, can we take turns carrying him?"

"Absolutely."

Horses clopped down the street. Carriages rumbled by, drivers shouting at pedestrians. People rushed about. Tori watched the bustle and shook her head. "I don't miss this. How did we live here for so many years?"

"We didn't know anything different."

"Most people would think us crazy for preferring life in the territories to society."

Ella snorted. A passerby looked at her, mouth agape. Tori stifled a smile. "See?"

Her sister chuckled. "We have the better of it. Harmony Springs is home." Her gaze bounced between the brick buildings, cobblestone streets, and fancy carriages. "This feels like a lifetime ago."

Before long, they stood in front of their childhood home. Tori marched up the steps and rapped three times on the door. "Here goes nothing."

It opened mere seconds later. Their butler peered out. "I'm sorry, we are not accepting visitors..." His blue eyes widened. "Oh!"

At least he'd appreciate their presence. Tori smiled, stepping into the parlor. "Hello, Hanson. How are you?"

"Mrs. Blake. I am well." His gaze darted to Ella. "Miss Mountbatten. Er—I suppose that's not your name anymore. My apologies, ma'am." He flushed. "The master and mistress never...well..."

Ella put her hand on his arm. "It's all right, Hanson. I didn't expect they would. My surname is Brooks."

"Mrs. Brooks. Welcome back." He glanced over his shoulder. "Though I'm not sure you will find welcome."

"We didn't expect much," Ella said. "Is Mother here?"

"Yes." Looking at David, the old butler smiled. "Precious child."

"Isn't he?" Ella turned the baby so Hanson could see better. "Cody and I adopted him after his parents died."

"How tragic. Knowing you, ma'am, he's in good hands now." He extended his arm. "Will you take tea in the parlor?"

"Thank you, Hanson. We'd love some."

"Follow me, ladies."

He led them to the parlor. Tori sat on the settee, Ella taking the spot beside her.

Hanson bowed. "I'll be back shortly."

David chewed on his fist, his wide eyes darting about the opulent room. The grandfather clock ticked the seconds away. Tori twisted a handkerchief on her lap. She'd never thought to return here, yet here they were.

Hanson returned with a tray. "Shall I pour, madam?" he asked, directing his question to Ella.

"I can manage, Hanson. Thank you."

He bowed. "I will let Mrs. Mountbatten know of your arrival."

"Wait." Tori half rose from her seat.

He tilted his head. "Yes?"

She sank down again. "Do you know visiting hours at the prison?"

"Ah." He cleared his throat. "I'm afraid the hours are irregular, ma'am. Even if they were not, though, your father has refused to see anyone but his lawyer."

"Oh." Tori ought to feel some disappointment, but all that curled through her was relief.

Hanson bowed again and left the room. Tori's stomach tied into knots. She accepted the teacup Ella handed her, then plopped a couple cookies on her plate. "I have a bad feeling about this."

"At least we don't have to worry about seeing Father. Maybe our visit here won't be so bad."

Raising her brows, Tori sipped the tea. "You're far too optimistic."

"I imagine it can't be worse than the last time I saw Mother." Ella grimaced. "She insisted my marriage to Howard go forward, even after his abominable treatment of me."

"I remember." Tori's blood boiled. "It should baffle me that they responded in such a way, but it doesn't."

Ella sat straighter. "We're free now. Our life in the west is good. We'll be back soon, and all this will be a distant memory."

Footsteps sounded from the hall. Both women stood as Mother entered the room. Her icy blue gaze swept over them, made bluer from the deep sapphire gown she wore. She sat in a chair opposite them. Lifting her chin, she spoke in clipped tones.

"You should not have come."

CHAPTER 24

ori bristled. Her mother's bored, arrogant tone grated her nerves. "Hello to you as well, Mother."

Ella rested a hand against Tori's. Her even expression never changed as she addressed their mother for the first time in over two years. "We wanted to see if you were all right. If you needed anything."

"I have little money and no connections. Your father saw to that."

The lack of emotion in her voice stunned Tori. She and Ella exchanged a glance, unsure what to say next.

Mother's gaze flicked over David. "I suppose that's your child, Ariella?"

"Yes. His name is David."

"I see." Mother sniffed. "He must take after his father. He looks nothing like you."

"Cody and I adopted him."

"Hmm." Mother poured a cup of tea. She took several sips, her nose wrinkled. "Then he's not my grandchild."

Ella stiffened. "I beg your pardon?"

"He's not a Mountbatten. From what I recall, only one of your children are from our line."

"Our line?" Tori tried to keep her voice down as Ella drew her son closer, but she lost the battle. "Every one of Ella's children are as much a part of our lives as if they'd been physically born to her. Adoption is a noble calling, Mother. How dare you degrade it?"

"Because despite your passionate beliefs, his bloodline is not ours. It's quite simple, really. You might choose to acknowledge him as family, but I will not."

"You barely regard us as family." Tori plunked her teacup onto the table. Why had she let herself be talked into this trip? Clearly, they wasted their time. She turned to Ella. "We should go."

"Not yet," Ella whispered.

"Why not?" Tori whispered back. "She doesn't want us here, and she's insulted your children. Why stay?"

Mother selected a cookie from the tray. "I suppose you want to know what happened with your father."

If she'd heard Tori's comments, she didn't let on. How could she change subjects so quickly and dispassionately? They might as well have been discussing the weather. Tori jerked her head toward the door, but Ella shook her head and addressed Mother.

"Yes, we would like to know what happened."

"He was arrested for fraud. It seems he swindled many of his customers over the years. He'll be in prison for some time. I am selling the house. It's the only thing that was left to me after your father's arrest. The sale will be in our lawyer's hands. In the morning, I sail for England." She tipped the teapot toward her cup, frowning when nothing came out. "I shall ring for more tea."

Tori bolted to her feet.

Mother blinked. "Are you ringing for tea?"

"No." Tori threw her hands in the air. "We already knew that about Father. What we didn't know is this trip to London."

Mother reached for a small bell. She shook it three times before setting it down again. "My aunt wrote a few months ago, asking me to visit. I haven't been to London since I was a small girl. This seems a good time to move."

"Move?" Ella gasped. "You're leaving permanently? What about Father?"

Hanson entered the room. "You rang, madam?"

"Yes. Bring more tea."

He bowed. "Yes, ma'am."

Tori plopped back onto the settee. "This is ridiculous," she whispered to Ella.

Mother ate another cookie. Her bored expression never wavered. "Yes, I am leaving permanently. As soon as Archibald was arrested, I filed for divorce."

"*What*?"

Both Tori's and Ella's voices rang out in unison. Tori blinked rapidly while Ella gaped.

"I have thought about it for years," Mother said, leaning back in her chair. "Archibald has never been faithful, and with these fraud charges, it was easier than I expected to obtain a divorce." She smirked. "It turns out these things are simpler when one's husband is a rake."

Hanson arrived with a new pot of tea. Tori's mind whirled with the information they'd received while her mother poured another cup. "You've thought about this for years?"

"Yes."

Still no expression. Tori frowned. She studied her mother, noting the lines surrounding her eyes and lips. Crystalline Mountbatten had never been a happy person.

Why?

"Mother, why did you marry Father in the first place?"

"Our parents arranged it, of course." Mother arched a regal

brow. "He was wealthy, and I came from British nobility. My great-uncle was a duke, you know. Everyone considered it a good match." She placed her cup on its saucer with a shake of her head. "He's no longer useful to me. Divorce is a great scandal, though not as scandalous as your father's arrest. Going to England is for the best."

The pieces clicked in place. "You're going to protect your image."

"Naturally. One's image is everything, after all."

Tori and Ella shared a glance. Ella's eyes misted. She shook her head. "Family is everything, Mother."

For a moment, Mother's gaze wavered. Then it hardened and she stood. "As I said before, you shouldn't have come. I have more packing to do and orders to give about the house. I've no time to visit." She waved a dismissive hand. "See yourselves out."

With that, she flounced from the room.

Ella sat in stunned silence.

Tori's anger burst. She jumped up, running after Mother. "Stop!"

Mother turned, one hand on the wide staircase, brow lifted. "What is it, Victoria? I am busy."

"That's it? Ella and I came all the way from Harmony Springs to see you, despite my misgivings about it all. Harrison convinced me it was a good idea."

"Then he was wrong. I did not ask you to come."

Tori's shoulders dropped. She stared at her mother, a heaviness in her chest. "You never loved us, did you?"

"Oh, for goodness' sake, child. Love is a sentimental notion. You don't get anything from loving another person."

"It's not about getting something. It's about giving."

Mother scoffed. "Even worse."

For the first time, a wave of compassion swept over Tori for her mother. What a lonely existence she'd suffered if that was her view on life. "I'm learning something being married to Harrison. Love is beautiful. It makes life better. Having family around, being with friends in a community that supports you—that's important." Seized by a strange impulse, she stepped closer. "Come to Harmony Springs with us."

Mother jerked back as if slapped. "I beg your pardon?"

"You can experience the same joy Ella and I found there. And you'd have family."

With a laugh, Mother shook her head. "I don't need family. You'll soon find out it's not enough."

"Mother—"

"Goodbye, Victoria."

Spinning around on her heel, Mother disappeared up the stairs.

The weight of silence that descended felt overpowering. Tori trudged back to the parlor.

Ella stood to meet her. "She didn't change her mind?"

"No."

Ella sighed. "I pity her. She's not a happy woman."

"No, I suppose she's not." Tori shuddered. "I fear I was on track to become just like her. Thank God for Harrison."

Her sister smiled. "At least one good thing came out of their manipulations. Neither of us would be married to our husbands otherwise."

"That would be the true tragedy."

Hanson tapped at the door. "My apologies, ladies, but I heard Mrs. Mountbatten go upstairs. Is the visit concluded?"

"Yes, Hanson." Tori gripped his hands. She ignored the flash of surprise on his face. "Do you have somewhere to go?"

He smiled, extricating one of his hands to pat her shoulder. "I do, Mrs. Blake, thank you. Another family hired me directly."

"I'm glad to hear it."

Hanson glanced at the staircase with a shake of his head.

"You two deserve all the happiness in the world. I pray you keep it all your lives."

Tori exhaled a breath, sharing a smile with Ella. "I think we will."

"Very good, madam. Shall I see you to the door?"

"We can manage. Thank you, Hanson."

Both women gave him a hug. He smiled and wished them well, then slipped away to finish his duties. Tori slid her hand in Ella's as they walked to the door. Her gaze flitted around the room. "Is it strange to think this is the last time we'll walk these halls?"

Ella hummed. "No. It might have been where we lived growing up, but it was a house, not a home. Home is Harmony Springs."

"Indeed." Tori's grip tightened. A smile pulled at her lips. "Let's go home."

~

Almost two weeks after Tori's departure for Boston, Harrison kept pace with Travis and two U.S. Marshals as they galloped through a thick patch of forest about three miles from town. Sunlight filtered through the trees in patchy dots. Birds sang happy notes, flying from branch to branch above them.

Marshal Kupp called a halt. His hair, graying at the temples, peeped out from under his hat. He wiped his face before addressing their small group. "Dusty Otterson was last seen a couple miles from here. There are three abandoned cabins within a mile radius. Marshal Tulbert will search the northern one and I'll take the southern. Sheriff Doyle and Dr. Blake, you find the western cabin. We'll meet back here in three hours. If you find anything significant, fire two shots in a row."

"Yes, sir." Travis nodded to Harrison. "Let's go."

They trotted along an overgrown path. Neither spoke. Harrison swept his gaze from side to side, searching for any evidence of human activity. When they'd gone about a mile, he spotted a disturbance off-path. "Travis, look."

Travis reined in his horse. "What do you see?"

Harrison swung his leg over the saddle and jumped to the ground. He walked to a trail of trampled plants. Crouching down, he pointed to dark red stains. "Someone's been here, and whoever it is was hurt. That's dried blood."

"There must be some kind of blood trail. Let's see if we can find it."

"Here's another one," Harrison said, coming to a large tree several feet away. Bloodstains marred the ground around it, and a distinct handprint remained on the trunk. "He is definitely injured."

Travis searched around the area, but no further evidence of blood could be found. "Do you think he patched himself up at that tree?"

"It's possible. Or perhaps he reached the cabin and took care of himself there. Is the cabin close by?"

"Yeah." Travis pointed through the trees. "Can you see it?"

Harrison squinted through the foliage. The cabin came into view. Its logs looked old and weather-beaten, the roof sagging inward. Ripped gray curtains hung from the windows. "Not much of a home, is it?"

"Marshal Kupp said it's an abandoned hunting cabin. Who knows how long it's been uninhabited." Travis took off his hat and wiped his brow. "Let's take a look inside."

They walked their horses into the small clearing and ground tied them. The door to the cabin hung off its hinges, creaking as it rocked back and forth from the breeze. Harrison pushed it open and entered the cabin.

The bits of sunlight coming through the windows revealed a heavy layer of dust in the air. Harrison sneezed twice before pressing a handkerchief to his nose. He stopped a few feet into the cabin. The pallet along one wall lay stripped of blankets, but the wood held dark stains that matched the ones in the woods.

Travis surveyed the pallet, arms crossed loosely over his chest. "How old is that blood?"

Harrison bent down, removing his handkerchief. The smell assailed his nostrils. He put the cloth back to his nose. "I'd say a day or two, if that."

"Let's look for any further clues. All we know right now is that someone's been here. It could be a hunter or trapper who met with injury."

They searched the cabin but found nothing else. Going back outside, they circled the building. Harrison's gaze caught on something white nestled against a tree. He jogged to it. Leaves lay piled against the tree in a way not created by wind. He knelt and scattered the leaves. The dingy white fabric poked out from a hollow in the tree. He tugged. The material didn't budge.

Harrison gripped it with both hands and pulled hard. With a little pop, the material flew out of the tree. He landed on his back in the carpet of leaves.

"Did you find something?" Travis asked, coming up beside him.

"I don't know." Harrison pushed himself into a sitting position and lifted the fabric. "This was wedged into that hollow."

"What is it?"

Harrison laid out the fabric. The white gave way to red-brown stains. Lots of them.

Travis whistled. "Those must be the sheets from that pallet. If Dusty Otterson stayed here, it makes sense he wouldn't want evidence of his stay found." He pulled out his gun and shot twice in rapid succession. "The marshals should be here soon."

"There's something else." Harrison put the bloody sheet

aside. Another white cloth lay inside. He reached for it and maneuvered it out of the tree. The cloth fell open, revealing four bundles of money.

He stared at it. "There must be a thousand dollars here."

"Is there any more?"

The men searched the hollow, but nothing else remained. Travis shook his head. "With that kind of money, there's no doubt Dusty is the one who came here. The question is whether he intends to return."

"Wouldn't the money indicate he does?"

"Possibly. But this is only a drop of the fortune they stole from you. He might have brought this along to pay for anything he might need, while the rest of the money is somewhere else for safekeeping."

Harrison got to his feet. "Should we leave these here in case he returns? We don't want him to know we're on his trail."

"I like that plan, but we'll see what the marshals think."

Kupp arrived a few minutes later. Tulbert came shortly after. Travis explained what they found. Kupp grunted, taking in the money and the bloody sheet. "Good work, men. I agree with the doc. Let's leave it here and set up surveillance on the cabin. I'd bet Dusty returns within the week."

"Assuming he isn't dead." Tulbert planted his hands on his hips. "That's a lot of blood."

Both men looked at Harrison. Kupp took off his hat, running a hand through his hair. "Is that possible, Dr. Blake?"

"There's not enough blood to be life-threatening—at least, not that we've seen. However, infection is a real possibility, and that can lead to death."

Kupp slapped his hat on again. "We'll need to be careful in our search. An injured man is like an injured animal— dangerous and unpredictable. He might enter a town nearby to get help. There's no telling what he'd do to get it, especially with his face plastered on *wanted* posters throughout the territory."

Tulbert grunted. "Since we got a description from the saloon manager in your town, Dusty can't move as freely without risking arrest. He might feel twitchy without his former anonymity."

A chill slid down Harrison's spine. "Do you think he'd come back to Harmony Springs since my wife and I are doctors?"

"There's a doctor a few towns over as well. My guess is, he'd go there rather than risk recognition in your town," Kupp said. "But I'd still recommend keeping a sharp eye out. You never know what outlaws might do."

Travis clamped a hand on Harrison's shoulder. "I'll make sure to have a patrole around the infirmary until Dusty is caught."

"Thanks, Travis."

For the first time, Harrison felt grateful that Tori was out of town. If she stayed in Boston, she'd be safe.

But...what if they couldn't apprehend Dusty in time? She had no idea she could return to danger. His stomach clenched, and he prayed she stayed away until all this was over.

CHAPTER 25

Tori spun in a circle after she and Ella stepped off the train. She took a deep breath of clean, hot summer air and smiled. "It's good to be home."

"Yes." Ella wore a smile of her own, serenity sparkling in her eyes. "I'm glad we took that trip, however badly it went. At least we have answers."

Tori's smile dimmed. Mother's behavior in that short half hour had baffled her. It also scared her. As much as she despised her mother's actions, she knew if left to her own devices, she could have ended the same way.

Shuddering, she pulled Ella toward the livery. "Let me take you and David home."

"Don't you want to see Harrison?"

"Of course, but he'll be here when I get back."

Ella studied her, head tilted. "You've had almost two weeks to think over your feelings. Do you still believe you love him?"

Easy answer. Tori's smile returned. "Yes."

"Once you knew, there was no going back."

"Exactly. I love my husband, and we have the rest of our lives to explore that love."

Ella's grin turned sly. "Does that mean my children will have cousins soon?"

Heat rushed into Tori's cheeks. "Gracious, Ella. One does not discuss things so openly."

"Perhaps not in Boston, but here?" Ella chuckled and nudged her. "I want to be an aunt."

"You are an aunt. Connor Doyle—Travis and Cassie's son? Ring any bells?"

"And I love him dearly. But I want to love on your children, too, my dear sister."

Tori laughed. "We'll see. Harrison and I agreed to have children, but only after we're established in our careers here."

"Mm-hmm. That's your plan, but God might have another."

Longing pulsed deep in her stomach. The sudden sensation made Tori stop in her tracks. She inhaled, hands pressed to her belly. What would it feel like to carry a baby? Not just any baby —her husband's child?

Tingles floated up and down her spine.

Just as fast, dread crept in. She kept it to herself, but after renting a buggy and driving halfway to the Brooks' ranch, Ella spoke. "What's wrong?"

Tori bit her lip, throat working. "I'm afraid of motherhood."

"Why? You're wonderful with my children, and they all love you."

"Yes, but..." She gripped the reins until her knuckles went white. "Mother has always been a hard, cold woman. I'm more like her than I want to be. What if having children makes me resentful? What if I'm a horrible mother?"

"You're not our mother, Tori. You have a compassionate heart. Your children will be well loved." She squeezed Tori's shoulder. "Just the fact that you're concerned about it tells me you want to be different."

"I do want to be different. I want my children to know their parents love them. For so long, I've been concerned about being a doctor. Motherhood was never my goal. Now, I want babies, but I'm worried about my ability to do right by them."

Ella shifted David in her arms. "Do you know how I handle being a mother?"

"How?"

"I take things one day at a time. That's all we can do. Each day, I give the children what I can. Sometimes it doesn't feel like enough. But I love them with all my heart. I do my best and leave the rest in God's hands."

Peace filled Tori's heart. She relaxed her grip on the reins. "Remind me to be more like you."

Her sister chuckled. "Just be yourself, Tori. You can do more than you think. When you have your babies, God will give you the grace necessary to be a mother."

Tori gave Ella a one-armed hug. "Thank you."

She dropped her sister off at the ranch. As Ella climbed to the ground, the front door opened. Her children spilled out with cries of "Mama!" Cody came close on their heels. Tori watched the reunion with a smile. Ella had found happiness. It was time for Tori to make some of her own.

After promising her nieces and nephews to come for supper soon, she drove back to town at a fast clip. The desire to see Harrison grew up inside until it overwhelmed her.

She missed him.

Back in town, she dropped off the horse and buggy, then rushed home. She burst into the infirmary. "Harrison? I'm back."

No answer.

Her shoulders slumped. He wasn't here, and she hadn't the least idea where he might be.

She went upstairs to their apartment, hoping he'd be there, but he wasn't. She unpacked her bag and fixed a cup of tea. Once it was gone, she wandered back downstairs.

Still no sign of her husband.

She planted her hands on her hips. No sense pining. He'd be home at some point. Until then, she'd organize some paperwork.

Going over to the desk, she laughed softly. Why'd she thought to organize the papers? Harrison already had them in perfect piles, arranged by case and patient. She ran a hand over the straight layers. A smile pulled at her lips. She knocked the top of each pile askew.

Footsteps sounded against the walk outside the infirmary. Her heart leapt into her throat. Harrison?

She scurried behind a curtain, hiding her laugh. The door opened to reveal her husband. Her heart jumped again. He was so good, so faithful. How'd it taken her so long to realize her love for him?

What a fool she'd been.

Harrison put his bag away. He headed for the stairs, then stopped cold, his gaze on the desk. "What in the world?"

His jaw twitched. With purposeful steps, he strode to the desk and straightened each pile.

Tori slipped from her hiding spot. She crept up behind him, then threw her arms around him. "Did you miss me?"

He froze. Glancing over his shoulder, his gaze met hers. Shock, then joy filtered over his face. He whirled around and swallowed her in an embrace. "You're home."

She rested her face against his chest. "I'm home."

He pulled back just enough to look at her. His gaze roamed her face, one hand cupping her jaw. "Don't ever leave me again."

With a laugh, she curled her fingers around his vest. "As I recall, you practically pushed me out the door."

"A momentary lapse in reason," he muttered right before pressing his lips to hers.

Tori was thrilled that he felt comfortable enough to kiss her now. She closed her eyes, letting his love wash over her. When he broke away, she knew the time had come. Taking his face in her hands, she looked him in the eyes.

"I love you, Harrison."

His face lit with pure joy. "Yeah?"

"I would have told you sooner, but someone kept stopping me." She winked.

He laughed, but his face quickly turned somber. "I didn't want a spur-of-the-moment declaration, Tori. But this…" He kissed her again. "This is perfect."

She chuckled. "Is it? No grand gesture, no special atmosphere—just a simple, everyday moment."

"Simple and everyday is exactly where our love grew. So yes —it's perfect."

He rocked her gently back and forth for a moment, then his eyes grew large. "Wait…you're home."

She lifted her brow. "We already discussed that."

A look of…panic?…flashed over his face. "You were supposed to still be in Boston."

"Harrison, what's wrong?"

His grip on her tightened. "It might be nothing."

"But?"

He sighed. "We have reason to believe Dusty Otterson is in the area and injured. The marshals think he might try to find a doctor to patch him up. We don't know what lengths he'd go to. You could be in danger."

She frowned. "If I'm in danger, so are you."

"It's possible." He scrubbed his hand against his jaw. "I'm more concerned for you."

"Wouldn't it be risky for him to come here?"

"Yes, which is why the marshals think he will attempt medical help in another town, if at all. Still, Travis promised to have some patrol around here." He took her hand. "Hopefully, it's all worry for nothing. Shall we go upstairs? I want to hear about your trip."

She grunted. "It's not a happy story."

He led her to the stairs. "Then you can cry on my shoulder."

Tori caught her breath. While she and Ella had received nothing but scorn from their mother—a woman related to them by blood—she'd never felt like true family. Not like Harrison. He'd become her rock, her best friend, and the love of her life.

Tingles darted up and down her spine as her husband opened the door to their apartment. Things would be different now that they had both professed their love.

One future—a loveless one—had vanished. What would their new future hold?

~

Once they were situated on the sofa in their apartment, Harrison rubbed his wife's back. "Now, tell me what happened."

Tori leaned into his touch. "Nothing unexpected. We couldn't see Father because he'd refused any visitors. Mother saw us for all of half an hour, announced she was divorcing our father and moving to London, and essentially confirmed that she never loved me and Ella." She barked out a laugh. "Nothing unusual."

He frowned. "Tori, that's exceedingly unusual behavior for a mother."

"It's all we knew."

His heart ached for her. He pulled her into his arms, wishing he could take away her pain. "I'm sorry, love."

She leaned against him. "It's reality. But I learned something through this ordeal." Her gaze met his. "Family can be made. You and I became family when we married, and we can grow a good life together. We can be better parents to our children."

His heart flipped at her casual mention of children, but he attempted to keep a neutral expression. "We can and we will. I promise you I'll be nothing like your father."

"I know." She patted his chest and rested her head on his shoulder. "I trust you."

They talked about her trip a while more. Harrison's blood boiled over some things her mother said and did, but Tori's calm acceptance mellowed him a little.

"It sounds as though you're at peace with what happened."

She tucked her chin with a little nod. "I think I am. There's nothing we can do to change it. You and Ella hoped reconciliation was possible, but it wasn't. Mother is hard, unreachable. We'll probably never see her again."

"And you're all right with that?"

"Yes." She took his hand. "The trip gave me a sense of closure. That chapter of my life is over. My future is here. With you."

He hugged her close. No further words seemed necessary.

When they pulled apart, he remembered something Isaiah gave him the other day. "Come with me."

He led her to his room. A smooth blue-green stone laid on his nightstand. "Isaiah found two stones after church on Sunday. He thought you and Ella might like to have them, since they match and you're sisters. His words."

Tori smiled, running her fingers over the rock. "It's beautiful. Children think of the sweetest things. I'll have to thank him."

He started for the door, then stopped when he realized his wife wasn't following. Her gaze wandered the room, the stone clutched loosely in her hand. "What is it, Tori?"

She ran her hand over his bedspread. "I was thinking—maybe we should turn one of these rooms into a nursery."

His heart slammed against his ribs. "What?"

"You said you want children. They're going to come at some

point. Perhaps we can turn my room into a nursery. And…" She walked toward him, maintaining eye contact. "Maybe I can move in here with you?"

His breath hitched. He took her arms, pulling her closer. "Are you sure that's what you want?"

"Yes."

He folded her into his arms, kissing her forehead. "I'd love nothing more."

Her hands slid to his back, the stone pressing against his spine. She smiled, tilting her head. "Good."

Harrison leaned down, intent on kissing her, when a call came from downstairs. "Hello? Anyone here?"

He sighed, resting his forehead against hers. "Rotten timing."

Tori laughed softly. "We should go see what he needs."

She set the rock on the nightstand, and together they headed down to the infirmary. A young man stood in the room, hat in hand, twisting it back and forth.

Harrison nodded in greeting. "Hello. What can we help you with?"

The man's gaze shot between him and Tori. "I work for Wyatt. One of the trees we felled today caught him. He's in bad shape. Please come right away."

Harrison grabbed his bag. "Of course." He looked at Tori. "Would you mind preparing a bed for him, just in case?"

"I will." Her brow wrinkled. "I'll be praying."

"Thanks." He darted out the door behind the young worker. "What's your name?"

"Clint."

"Are you new? I've helped Wyatt a few times, but I didn't meet all the crew."

Clint shook his head, tugging his hat low. "I've been around a while." He stopped at a hitching post. "We need to take the horses. It's a fair bit to the loggin' site."

Harrison climbed onto his horse. "Lead the way."

They rode to the edge of town. A few minutes later, they entered one of the dense forests. Clint guided his horse through the trees, glancing over his shoulder every so often at Harrison. The silence grew loud the longer they rode.

Harrison nudged his horse side by side with Clint's. "What kind of injury are we dealing with?"

"Huh?"

"The fallen tree. Where was Wyatt hit?"

"Uh—on the head."

"Was he conscious?"

"Yeah. He told me to get the doc."

Harrison frowned. Wyatt was conscious after being hit on the head by a falling tree? "It was a full tree? Not just a branch?"

"Yeah, full tree. He went down like a dead man."

"But he was conscious and talking."

"Yep."

Apprehension slid down Harrison's spine. He reined in his horse. "What logging site are we going to?"

Clint motioned ahead. "It's two miles north. We need to hurry."

Harrison narrowed his eyes. "Wyatt doesn't have a logging site near here. Not north, anyway. You don't work for Wyatt at all, do you?"

The young man sighed. "You ask too many questions, Doc. I hoped it wouldn't come to this."

Before Harrison could blink, Clint pulled a gun from his belt. He pointed the muzzle at Harrison's chest, eyes turning to pools of steel. "No more talking. You're comin' with me."

CHAPTER 26

hey rode for nearly thirty minutes before a cabin came into view. Harrison sucked in his breath. It wasn't the same one where he'd found the bloody sheets and money in the tree, but he'd bet it was one searched by the marshals.

Clint swung down from his horse and grabbed the halter on Harrison's. "Get down," he barked.

Harrison slid to the ground. He grabbed his bag. "I assume Dusty's inside?"

"Yeah, and he needs..." Clint snapped his mouth shut, glaring at Harrison. "No tricks. You didn't hear his name from me."

Harrison refrained from rolling his eyes. "Who else would he be?" He marched to the cabin and went inside.

A man lay on the room's single pallet. His pale face shone with sweat. The stench inside nearly made Harrison gag. His gaze flew to the man's leg, where his trousers had been torn off. A bloody bandage covered the lower half.

"Dusty Otterson?"

The man wheezed. "Who's askin'?"

Clint's voice came from behind Harrison. "I got the doc, Dusty."

Dusty groaned. "I told you, no docs. The feds are gonna find us."

"They've already found the other cabin. It's only a matter of time 'til they find this one. 'Sides, you need help. That wound is oozin' and stinks."

Harrison knelt beside the outlaw.

The man grimaced. "You're the doc we stole from."

"Yes."

"I told 'em not to do it. Said it was too big a risk. We didn't need that much money."

Harrison unwound the bandage. He eyed Clint. "Is there a well around here?"

"Out back."

"Get a bucketful of water and any clean rags you can find." He wrinkled his nose, taking in the state of the cabin and the men's clothes. "Or as clean as you can manage."

When Clint left, Harrison continued unwrapping the bandage. "Where's my money?"

"My eldest brother chose the hidin' spot and gave me and Trent a stipend. I dunno where the rest's at." Dusty clenched his hands. "You're not gonna help me now, are ya?"

Harrison peeled the white strips of fabric from Dusty's leg. "I'm a doctor. It's my job to help people."

Dusty turned his face away. Harrison bit back a gasp as he took in the damage. A jagged wound ate at the side of the man's leg. Angry blisters framed the cut, the skin around it an ugly purple and black. Putrid discharge wet his leg.

Gangrene.

"Is this where you were shot?"

With a grunt, Dusty nodded.

Clint returned with the water. Harrison lifted a sheet from the pallet and dipped it inside. He cleaned the area as best he could, but he fought a losing battle. There was only one way to save this man.

"Do you have whisky?"

Dusty chortled. "Bad time to ask for a drink, Doc."

"Not for me. For you."

"Why me?" Dusty eyed him, wariness creeping over his fever-reddened face. "You gonna pour it over the wound?"

"Yes. And you're going to drink it. Hopefully, it dulls the pain when I amputate."

Dusty bolted to a sitting position. "When you *what*?"

Clint's face paled.

"It's the only option."

Dusty shrank back. "I'll take my chances. Just clean and rebandage it."

Harrison continued to clean off the oozing discharge. "If I don't amputate, the gangrene will spread and you will die. It's just a matter of time." He tossed the dirty sheet to the side and crossed his arms. "What'll it be? You prefer losing your leg or your life?"

Clint cocked the gun and pointed it at Harrison. He jerked his head to the side. "Git to that corner. We gotta talk."

Holding up his hands, Harrison moved to the opposite side of the cabin. He didn't fear the gun. Something told him both these men were all bluster, no bite. The Ottersons weren't known for violence. Still, it would be wise to obey.

Dusty and Clint whispered in frantic tones. The gun lowered unheeded to Clint's side. Harrison eyed it. Could he make a run for it? Probably not. He stifled a sigh. Besides, he couldn't leave an injured man to his own devices. Thief or not.

"You can come back, Doc."

Harrison turned. "Did you decide?"

"How long'll the operation take?" Clint's lips flattened. "We don't got much time. Gotta get back on the trail."

Harrison's brows shot up. "You can't get back on the trail.

This is major surgery. You cannot move him right after an amputation."

"Don't got no choice. My cousin and I are good as arrested if we stay here. Those marshals will sniff us out. Can't stay."

"Clint, if he's moved after this..."

The gun clicked. "Don't make me use this."

Harrison swallowed his retort. He spread his hands. "You don't understand. Dusty will be unconscious from the pain. He won't be able to flee on horseback."

Clint sneered. He pocketed the gun once more. "Good thing we stole a cart."

More stealing. Harrison shook his head. A cart would be easier to track than horses, but he kept his mouth shut.

"How long?" Dusty asked, repeating Clint's question.

"Once I have the necessary tools, less than an hour." Harrison opened his bag. "I have bandages, needle, thread, and a tourniquet. But I don't have a saw."

Clint headed for the door. "There's one out back. I'll get it." He scurried outside.

Dusty pointed to the table. "Whisky's there."

At least they had that. The operation would be miserable for the man, but the alcohol should help. He got up to grab the bottle. "We need to get you some cloth and a stick to bite down on."

"Fine."

Clint burst back into the cabin. "Here."

Harrison stared at the tool, revulsion slicing through him. "I can't use that."

"Why not?"

Reddish rust covered the filthy blade. It looked as though it'd been abandoned to the elements for years. "If I cut through him with that, he'll get an infection."

"We ain't got much choice, do we?" Clint shoved the saw at

him. "Clean it as best you can. This needs to be done within the hour."

Harrison clenched his jaw. There was no point arguing with irrational men. "Fine. Get a stick to wrap for Dusty to bite during the operation." As Clint left the cabin once more, Harrison thrust the bottle at Dusty. "Drink some."

The outlaw guzzled the liquid at an alarming rate. Harrison took the bottle once he determined Dusty drank enough and poured more over the man's leg.

Dusty howled in pain.

Clint raced inside. He tossed a wrapped stick to Dusty. "Here."

Putting it in his mouth, Dusty nodded to Harrison. "Begin."

"The saw needs to be cleaned."

Dusty's eyes hardened. "Then clean it. Get going."

With a grimace, Harrison poured whisky over the saw and hoped it was enough. Then he shut his eyes, praying for guidance.

~

Tori organized the medicine shelf for a second time. She glanced at the clock, annoyed at how slow it seemed to move. Harrison had been gone for three hours. Wyatt's injuries must be grave.

She grabbed the broom and swept until the floor shone. Still no sign of Harrison. She put the broom back and decided a walk was in order. Maybe she could check on some families outside of town. She grabbed her bag and stepped out of the infirmary, pulling the door closed behind her.

"Missus Doc!"

That voice...

She turned, her mouth falling open. Wyatt bounded up the infirmary steps, a wide smile on his face. "The hospital is coming along better than expected. Would you and Doc like to see the progress?"

Tori blinked, her mind scrambled. "But...you're hurt... how...?"

He gripped her elbow. "Are you all right, ma'am? Do you need to sit down?"

"No, I..." Her breathing grew shallow. "Wyatt, someone came to the infirmary and said you'd been hit by a falling tree."

His brow furrowed. "Not me, ma'am. My crew is at the hospital today. No tree felling."

"Do you employ a man named Clint?"

The furrow deepened. "No."

Tears burned her eyes. Harrison's concern about Dusty Otterson sprang to mind. "I need Travis."

"Can I get him for you, ma'am?"

"No. I'll go."

She ran down the boardwalk, not stopping until she reached the sheriff's office. Panting for breath, she tumbled into the building.

Travis rose from his desk. Alarm flashed in his eyes. "Tori, what's wrong?"

She gasped for air, clutching her bag tight. "Someone... took...Harrison. It was...a ruse."

Only then did she notice two U.S. Marshals watching them. One came forward, a stern look on his face. "Someone took the doctor under false pretenses?"

She nodded. "A man named Clint. He said Wyatt was injured and Harrison went with him, but I just saw Wyatt. He's perfectly fine."

The marshals exchanged a look. "That's not good," the stern one said. "We need to start a search."

"The cabin would be a good start," Travis said. "We know he's stayed there before."

"That's where we'll go first." The marshal slapped on his

hat. "Tulbert and I found some money in trees at the other two, about another thousand each. That's what we were about to tell you." He started for the door. "They could be at any of the three cabins."

Travis nodded. "Let's saddle up."

Tori clutched his arm. "I'm coming with you."

"Absolutely not. We don't need you getting caught up in this."

"What if he's hurt, Travis?" She held up her bag. "I can tend him. Or anyone else who might get hurt."

"Might be a good idea, Sheriff," the other marshal said. "Her services could be useful."

"Fine." Travis huffed. "But stay behind me until I tell you otherwise."

Relief curled inside. "Thanks."

He nodded at the stern marshal. "That's Kupp. The other is Tulbert. Gentlemen, this is Dr. Victoria Blake."

"Nice to meet you, ma'am. You the doc's wife?"

She nodded.

"We're going to find him."

Her throat convulsed. "I hope so."

Within ten minutes, they had all mounted horses and raced for the woods. Tori remained near Travis as promised, but she longed to push her horse faster. She'd never known such terror. Her husband could be in serious danger.

She couldn't lose him as soon as she'd found him.

Please, Lord, keep him safe. Let us get to him in time.

In time for what, she didn't know, but Tori continued to pray as they raced along.

The marshals seemed to know exactly where to go. They led the way to a small cabin in the middle of a clearing. Kupp stopped them before they left the cover of trees. "Sheriff and Dr. Blake, you stay here. Tulbert and I will scout the cabin first."

Everything in Tori screamed to go with them, but she

held her tongue. They knew what they were about. She didn't want to interfere and accidentally cause harm to her husband.

The two men dismounted and crept toward the cabin, their pace akin to a snail's. Her hands twitched on the reins. She bit down on her tongue so hard, the metallic taste of blood coated her mouth.

Travis maneuvered his horse close enough to place a hand over her clamped fist. He didn't say anything, just lent support through his presence. Tori blinked back tears of gratitude and fear.

Kupp peered into one of the cabin windows. Moments later, he straightened. "No one's here."

Her shoulders sagged.

Travis squeezed her hand. "There are two other cabins, Tori. He might be at one of them."

"Where is the next one?"

"About a mile east."

"Then let's go."

She nudged her horse into a trot. Travis took the lead, guiding the four of them through the trees. It felt like hours—but was likely only minutes—before they reached the second cabin. The same process repeated, with the marshals going to the cabin at their cautious pace and peeking inside.

Tulbert straightened. His eyes were wide. He motioned Tori and Travis over. They rode up, and her heart twisted at the look on his face.

"What is it?" she asked.

"The doctor is tied up inside, alone...and there's lots of blood."

Tori's stomach dropped. She leapt off her horse, grabbed her bag, and charged toward the cabin. "Harrison!"

As she crashed through the door, her gaze swept the cabin. Her heart pounded when she caught sight of her husband lying on the ground. She dropped to her knees beside him. "Harrison?"

He didn't open his eyes. The jagged gash on his head made her stomach turn. She ran her fingers around the fresh wound. "Harrison, wake up."

No reaction. Tears welled and fell in seconds. Tori pressed a fist to her mouth, stifling a sob.

Travis hurried into the room. "Is he injured?"

"Yes."

The shaky word left her lips as a gasp sounded from Travis. She glanced at him to see he stared in horror at the floor. "Why is there so much blood?"

Fear jolted her as she took in the scene. Bloody sheets, wrappings...and a saw. Her gaze jerked back to her husband. She methodically searched his body for signs of injury.

Nothing other than the gash to his head.

Relief mingled with confusion. If it wasn't his blood, then whose?

The marshals entered the room. Kupp surveyed it before turning to Tori. "We'll get your husband back to town and then investigate here." He glanced at Tulbert. "Ride back and get a wagon so we can transport the doctor."

As Tulbert obeyed, Tori opened her bag. She soaked a bandage in carbolic acid and gently dabbed it over Harrison's wound. He groaned, his eyes flickering open before sealing shut again. When she pulled the bandage away, blood flowed from his cut.

"I need to stitch it."

"Can you do that here?" Travis asked.

"I could, but I'd prefer a more sanitary location, like the infirmary."

"Is it a risk to wait that long?"

"I don't think so. Not if I wrap his head well." Tori bit her lip, gauging the cut. "Let's see what happens with the bandages. I'll need you to lift him slightly while I wrap."

Travis nodded.

She got a long piece of cloth from the bag and wound it around Harrison's head several times. Securing it with a knot, she rested his head on her lap. "Now we wait. If it bleeds through, I'll know to stitch it here."

Waiting was the worst part. Tori ran her fingers down Harrison's cheek, pleading with him in whispers to wake up. Travis joined Kupp in a search of the cabin. She stayed with her husband, praying Tulbert arrived soon with the wagon.

Time passed too slowly. She checked Harrison's pocket watch every few minutes. After forty-five minutes, her ears picked up the rumble of wheels. At the same time, Harrison's eyes opened. He looked up at her, pain etched over his face. "Tori?"

"Shhh." She smoothed her hand over his jaw. Her tears fell on his cheeks as she pressed a gentle kiss to his lips. "You're going to be all right, love. I'm going to take care of you."

He gazed at her, only breaking contact when his eyes fell shut once more. Tori bit back a sob. He had to be all right.

She wouldn't rest until he healed.

CHAPTER 27

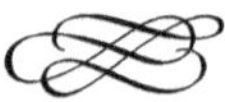

ull pain throbbed through Harrison's head when he tried to lift it the next morning. With a groan, he sank back onto the bed.

Tori leaned over him in a flash. "Where does it hurt?"

Where had she come from? He gave a weak chuckle, closing his eyes. "My entire head hurts, I'm afraid."

"I can mix up some willow bark tea for the pain."

He struggled to a sitting position. Tori helped, climbing onto the bed and fluffing pillows behind him. He smiled despite the pain. "I love you."

"And I you, but right now, I need you to focus."

"Yes, ma'am."

She smoothed the covers over his lap. "Where's the pain located?"

"My forehead. It radiates over my scalp."

"Hmm." She leaned closer, studying the stitches she'd done yesterday evening. "No sign of infection, thank God. But you must have been knocked pretty hard."

"After I amputated Dusty's leg, his friend was intent on them getting away without being caught. He clocked me with his gun as soon as I'd washed my hands. I went down, out cold." He winced. "Does that mean they got away?"

Tori curled up beside him. "No. The marshals followed the cart tracks. They caught up to Dusty and Clint within hours."

"Good." He relaxed against the pillows. "I'm glad that's all over."

"Did he tell you where the money is?"

"No. Claims he didn't know where his brother hid it."

She frowned. "Then where did the thousands come from?"

"They each got a windfall. A big one, from the sound of it, but not nearly what our fortune was."

"It doesn't matter." She cupped his cheeks, gaze roaming over his face. "We have each other. That's enough."

Gratitude swirled in his heart. He rested his head against her shoulder. "It is."

She burrowed closer. "Were you afraid?"

"Not really. They were more concerned about getting away than hurting me. Clint threatened me a few times with his gun, but I got the sense he didn't want to shoot."

Someone knocked at the door. Tori slipped from the room to answer it. She returned a minute later with his family. "You have visitors."

Mother rushed to his bedside. "Darling, I was so worried. Thank God you're all right."

He accepted her hug. Father hovered behind her, relief written on his face.

Temperance sat beside him on the bed. "What was it like being kidnapped by a criminal?"

"Temperance!" Mother gasped.

"What?" She tilted her head. "It's not something that happens often. I want details."

Mother frowned, brows drawn low. "Let Harrison rest. You can get the sordid details later."

Father clapped a hand on his shoulder. "How are you feeling, son?"

"Tired and sore, but thankful to be home." His gaze met Tori's, and he smiled. "Grateful for my beautiful, capable wife."

She blushed.

Mother caught Tori's hands in hers. "Thank you, dear girl, for fixing up our boy."

"It's my pleasure," Tori said, her brown eyes trained on him. "There's not much I wouldn't do for the man I love."

Joy burst in his chest. His heart pulsed double-time. For her to publicly declare her love—that was a big step. He wanted nothing more than to draw her into his arms and hold on tight.

But prudence said that wasn't the right call. Not yet.

Mother pulled Tori a little closer. "Victoria, we had supper with your sister and her family the other night. She told me about your trip...and your encounter at home."

Tori's eyes lost a bit of their light. She pressed her lips together and dropped her gaze. "It went as I expected."

"I am sorry for pushing you to go home. It wasn't my intention to cause you pain."

His wife looked up again. She shook her head, a sad smile forming. "It's not your fault. Mother hid her nature from society. You thought her a good person because you were friends. That speaks to your character, not hers."

Mother's gaze slipped to Harrison before going back to Tori. "There's something I've been wanting to ask you since we arrived, dear. I hope you won't find it presumptuous of me."

Tori tilted her head, curiosity burning in her eyes.

"Would you like to call me 'Mother'?"

His wife's sharp inhale reverberated through the small room. Tears filled her eyes. She pressed her hands to her lips, staring at his mother. "You want that?"

"I'd love nothing more." Mother smiled. "You're my son's

wife, and that makes you my daughter. I would like to be a mother to you as much as I am to him and Temperance."

With a sob, Tori flung herself into Mother's arms. "I've always wanted a caring mother. Thank you. I accept your offer."

Mother smiled, hugging her close. "Then it's settled."

"Touching scene," Temperance whispered to Harrison, wiping a tear from her eye. "You chose your wife well, brother."

"Maybe you'll find someone yourself soon," he whispered back.

She shook her head with a little sigh. "That isn't likely."

A fresh wave of pain throbbed over his head. He tried to stifle a groan. Tori pulled away from Mother, her gaze piercing through him. He shook his head, but she turned to his family. "I think it's time for Harrison to rest. Perhaps we can all have supper at the café tonight, depending on how he feels."

"That would be lovely." Father put an arm around Mother and held his other hand to Temperance. "Come, my dears. We'll see them later."

Once they left, Harrison sank into the pillows.

Tori tutted, tucking the covers around him. "I'm making that tea now. I'll be right back."

He smiled, closing his eyes. "Take your time." Despite the pain, he hadn't been this content in a long time. He was home, his wife loved him, and she'd accepted his family as her own.

"Harrison."

He startled, blinking. "Did I fall asleep?"

Tori sat beside him and chuckled. "You dozed off. Here's your tea."

He accepted the mug. Taking a sip, he wrinkled his nose. "I never liked the flavor of willow bark."

"Not many do, but it'll help you feel better."

He sipped until half the mug was gone, then put it on the bedside table. Raising his arm, he nodded at his side.

Tori filled the empty space. She wrapped her arms around

him as he settled his arm over her shoulder. Her lips brushed softly against his cheek. "I was so scared yesterday, Harrison. When I discovered you missing, my heart stopped. I don't think it beat properly again until we got you home."

"So what you're saying is, you love me."

She gazed at him, a serious expression in her eyes. "With all my heart."

"I'm glad," he breathed, nuzzling his nose against hers. "All my life, I hoped to fall in love. But this is better than anything I dreamed up."

"Is it?" She chuckled. "All the uncertainty and pain I put you through? Losing your inheritance, the hospital...this is better than what you wanted?"

"Yes."

She quirked a brow. "Explain."

"I get to live life with you. That alone makes everything worth it. Hard times and all."

Her light intake of breath accompanied a sweet smile. She cupped his cheek and rested her forehead on his neck. "You're a romantic, Harry."

He chuckled. "Hardly. I just love my wife."

"And she loves you."

The twinkle in her eyes as she looked at him had his gaze dropping to her lips.

Tori shook her head. "No time for romance right now. You need to get better." She picked up the mug and gave it to him. "Drink."

He lifted the mug in a salute. "Yes, ma'am."

Anything to get better if it promised kisses.

~

*O*ver the next couple weeks, Tori kept a close eye on Harrison's wound. She breathed a sigh of relief when she took the stitches out and saw no sign of infection. He was well on his way to complete recovery.

His family left for Boston a week ago, with promises to visit again at Christmas. Tori missed them already—especially her new mother. It still warmed her heart that Katharine offered such love. Thankfully, with summer coming to an end, Christmas wasn't far away. Already, the late-September breeze grew stronger and promised cooler weather.

She washed her hands in the infirmary basin after the final patient left for the day. Harrison sidled up behind her. Before she turned, his arms slipped around her and tugged her tight to him. She leaned her head back against his chest, closing her eyes with a grin. "Hello, love."

"Hello." He nuzzled her neck. "How were the patients today?"

"Fine. Nothing serious, just a few complaints about colds or light fevers." She turned in his arms and wrapped hers around his neck. "How were your house calls?"

"Not too bad. There was one rancher with a horrid cough. I think he has pneumonia."

Tori grimaced. "How did he react when you prescribed rest for recovery?"

"About as well as you'd expect a rancher to react when told to stay still for a week." He shrugged. "We'll see if he listens."

"Hmm. Now that we've established how our days went..." She went up on her toes. "You may give me a proper hello."

His deep chuckle went muffled as their lips met. Tori hummed, tugging him closer. She hoped it never got old, this feeling he invoked when they kissed. She went soft and gooey inside, like one of Cassie's cookies straight from the oven.

It helped that Harrison was an excellent kisser.

When he pulled back, she gave a little moan in protest.

Harrison chuckled, tapping her nose. "As much as I'd love to continue this romantic interlude, we need to get going."

"I suppose seeing our friends will be worth it." She pouted. "But you owe me when we get home."

He grinned and winked. The smolder he sent her way made her stomach swoop with anticipation. She curled her toes. "Maybe they won't miss us if we stay home."

Harrison laughed. He wrapped an arm around her waist. "You'd miss them if we didn't go."

"It's nice of Cassie to host everyone to celebrate David's baptism," Tori said as they left the infirmary. A cool breeze kissed her skin, raising gooseflesh on her arms. After such a hot summer, the break in temperature felt marvelous. She moved a little closer to Harrison. "I don't think she's ever closed down the café since we've been here."

"It's a happy occasion."

Tori looped her hand over his elbow. "How is Lydia? Will she be there?"

"Yes. I visited her and Samuel today, and her pains stopped a couple days ago. She should be fine going about normal duties."

"Will she be at the reception?"

"Yes. She seemed excited about going."

"Good. I haven't had much opportunity to deepen our acquaintance. It will be nice to talk with her."

When they arrived at the café, delicious smells greeted them. Tori inhaled the aroma of pot roast and potatoes with a smile. Light chatter showed the other families were already present—Travis and Cassie, Ella and Cody, and Samuel and Lydia. Their children laughed and played between tables. Harrison bent low to whisper, "Someday, our kids will join theirs."

Tori smiled. She brushed her fingers over his jaw. "I can't wait."

Ella sidled up to them. "Hi, Harrison. Good to see you looking well."

"Thanks, Ella."

She took Tori's arm, pulling her toward a table. "Do you mind if I steal my sister? We have so much to talk about."

"Not at all. Enjoy your time together."

He headed for a corner where the other men stood talking. Ella led Tori to a table where Cassie and Lydia sat. When she'd settled herself, Tori glanced around. "What do we have to talk about?"

"Life." Cassie rested her head on her fist with a smile. "It's been ages since all of us were able to just sit and chat."

Tori reached out to take David from her sister. Once he lay snuggled in her arms, she smiled at her friends. Friends who felt like family. She whispered a prayer of thanks for the wonderful women—and men—in her life who'd shown her what true family was meant to be. "Where do we begin?"

"First," Lydia said, leaning forward and lowering her voice, "we're curious when you might be having a wee one of your own." Her gaze flicked to Cassie. "Right?"

"Absolutely." Cassie's smile grew large. "Lydia and I are already able to commiserate on the hardships of pregnancy, but we'd love a third." She smirked at Ella. "Or a fourth."

Tori and Ella stared at Cassie. Ella spoke first. "Cass, are you having another baby?"

"I am." Cassie squealed. "Isn't it wonderful? Connor is going to have a little brother or sister."

"Was Travis thrilled?" Tori asked.

"Oh yes." Cassie's gaze found her husband, a tender smile on her lips. "I couldn't ask for a better father to my children."

"We've all been blessed with amazing men." Ella sighed, one hand going to her heart. "I'm thankful for Cody every day."

"As I am for Sam." Lydia waggled her fingers at Samuel, who winked back.

Three sets of eyes turned to Tori. She traced a pattern on the table, cheeks heating. "Harrison is wonderful."

"Are you ladies talking about me?" Her husband plopped into the chair beside her.

Tori giggled. "We were, indeed."

"And what's the verdict?"

She leaned toward him. "That you're far too organized."

"Organized?" He blinked, eyes narrowing. "Is that so?"

With an emphatic nod, Tori sighed. "I can't have one paper out of place without you straightening it. Several times over."

He rolled her eyes. "I'm not that bad."

"You certainly are."

"Excuse us, ladies," he said, grabbing Tori's hand. "I need to have a talk with my wife."

She handed the baby back to Ella. As soon as her hands were free, Harrison led her to a secluded corner. Tori hid a grin as he pressed her into the wall. "This isn't very private. Everyone's watching us."

Without a glance over his shoulder, he slid his hands around her waist. "Let them." His voice lowered to a growl. "Now, what were you saying about organization?"

"Not a thing. I thought you were talking with the men."

"I was, but I wanted to ask Cassie about her muffin recipes. You distracted me." He leaned close. "Now, what were you really talking about?"

She reveled in the warmth he emanated. Cuddling closer, she put her hands on his chest. "I told them you're wonderful."

"Hmm. That's better than organized."

She chuckled. "I do love your organization, Harry. It's endearing."

"*Endearing*?"

"Precious?"

He grunted.

Her hands slid around his neck. "Attractive?"

"Now that I like. But you? You, I love."

Heart soaring, Tori pulled him close. "I love you too."

As they shared a kiss, tears of gratitude burned Tori's eyes. What had started as a marriage of convenience to escape Boston turned into more than she'd ever dreamed of. God had taken her anger and pain and turned it to joy, giving her a husband who saw her and loved her as she was, but who wasn't afraid to challenge her, to make her better.

She couldn't ask for a better life.

EPILOGUE

MARCH 1890

ori bounced on her toes as she and Harrison stood beside Travis at the opening ceremony for the hospital. It had taken longer than expected to complete, but months of work had paid off. The Harmony Springs Hospital was fully stocked and ready to open. A ceremonial ribbon stretched across the front door, waiting for the cut.

She grinned up at the blue sky. The temperature hovered around sixty degrees, and the sun shone bright. Perfect weather for their event.

Nearly a hundred people milled about, talking amongst themselves while children scampered between. Tori hadn't expected such a turnout, but it warmed her heart to see so many support the hospital's grand opening.

She waved at her sister and friends in the crowd. Ella waved back, little David in her arms. Lydia stood beside them, holding her own baby boy. Cassie watched from the refreshment table. Cody and Samuel bracketed their wives and children, grinning at the antics of the children.

Her gaze flitted back to the youngest Allen. Lydia had gone into labor in late November. Having not delivered a child since Amanda died, Tori felt a rush of nerves when Samuel requested she come. She tried to send Harrison in her place, but he insisted that she be the one to deliver the baby. Three hours later, Mark was born, healthy and whole, and Lydia recovered well from birthing him. When Tori returned home, Harrison greeted her with a hug and an "I knew you could do it."

Since then, she'd delivered three more babies with no complications.

Tori's heart swelled with gratitude. She loved this community. She might have come here to escape her family, but it had turned into the greatest blessing of her life.

Well...the second greatest.

She beamed up at her husband. He responded by lifting her hands to his lips for a tender kiss. "You ready?"

"I've been ready. This is exciting."

His face gleamed with joy. "It is. Our dream is now a reality. I can hardly believe it."

"One dream achieved." She rested a hand on her stomach. "Another on its way."

Harrison covered her hand with his. "I can't wait to meet our baby. The next six months are going to be long." He threaded his fingers through hers. "How are you feeling?"

"The nausea passed about an hour ago, thankfully."

"Good."

Travis poked his head between them. "Ready?"

Tori nodded. "We are."

"All right." He raised his voice. "Welcome, everyone, to the official opening of our new hospital. I'll have our resident doctors say a few words, and then they'll cut the ribbon."

Tori leaned closer to Harrison. "Are you okay to speak?"

He looked at the crowd and tugged his collar. "I think I need a minute. Do you mind going first?"

"Of course not." She winked. "I am the better speaker."

He chuckled as she addressed the crowd. "Thank you all for coming. Harrison and I couldn't imagine living in a better place. This hospital started as our dream, but it became the community's. We couldn't have done this without you. Your generosity after the fire made this possible. Now Harmony Springs will have access to top medical care. We're honored to serve all of you."

She nudged Harrison. He took a deep breath before speaking. "Harmony Springs is a special place. It's full of caring individuals who work hard and love harder." His voice shook only a little as he continued. "There are a few people we want to thank personally. Wyatt and his team did most of the work, putting other projects on hold to make the hospital a priority. He let me tag along a few times and try my hand at helping."

Wyatt laughed from the crowd. "Hey, Doc, if medicine doesn't work out, you've got a spot on my crew."

Harrison chuckled. His shoulders relaxed, his brow losing its pinched look. "I'll keep that in mind." He waved a hand around the crowd. "To Samuel and Mr. Tolson for organizing those collections, thank you, and a big thank you to all who donated money. Mere words don't feel like enough. We have a modern, well-stocked hospital because of your generosity. What you did made me realize that Harmony Springs is home. Thank you for giving us the opportunity to be part of this town."

The crowd broke into applause.

Travis handed Harrison a pair of scissors for the ribbon cutting. He in turn offered it to Tori. "Do you want to do the honors?"

"Let's do it together."

She accepted the scissors, and Harrison put his hand over

hers. They snipped the red ribbon. The crowd clapped again as the ribbon floated to the ground.

Tori beamed at those gathered around. People grinned and shouted congratulations, streaming forward to walk through the finished hospital. She and Harrison stepped to the side to allow them entrance.

He bent toward her. "This is the beginning of a new chapter."

She leaned her head against his shoulder and smiled, her hand resting over their unborn child.

One dream had been realized. Now, they stepped into another, one she hadn't looked for but that God knew she needed. With a prayer of thanks in her heart, she slipped her free hand into Harrison's.

She couldn't wait to see what the future held.

AUTHOR'S NOTE

Thank you so much for reading the final book in the Harmony Springs series! It's been an honor taking this journey with you. I hope you enjoyed reading Harrison and Tori's story as much as I enjoyed writing it.

If you liked the book, would you please take a moment to leave a review on Amazon and/or Goodreads? I'd greatly appreciate it.

Take care, dear readers. May God bless you.

ACKNOWLEDGMENTS

Writing is my happy place. I am so thankful for readers like you who give me the opportunity to tell these stories.

Thank you to my family, who happily listen to my ideas and suggest ideas of their own when I'm stuck in a rut. Thanks especially to Mom for being my biggest cheerleader.

Thank you to Denise, my wonderful editor. You are amazing, and I'm so thankful for your help.

Thank you to Cappy, who read through this manuscript and gave honest thoughts on the story, thoughts that made it better. Thank you for always being willing to bounce ideas and help me get through writer's block with great suggestions and thoughts on where to take the story and characters. You're a great friend, and I'm so grateful for that.

And finally, thank You to the Lord for the ability to write and tell stories. As the Author of Life, He is the one who wrote the story of all creation, and I am thankful to have a tiny role in mimicking that creative endeavor.

Did you enjoy this book? We hope so!
Would you take a quick minute to leave a review where you purchased the book?
It doesn't have to be long. Just a sentence or two telling what you liked about the story!

Receive a FREE ebook and get updates when new Wild Heart books release: https://wildheartbooks.org/newsletter

Lauralyn Keller loves to combine history and romance in stories that touch the heart. She lives in beautiful Colorado and is a member of American Christian Fiction Writers. When she's not writing, she enjoys cooking, hiking, and reading.

If you love historical romance, check out the other Wild Heart books!

Rescue in the Wilderness by Andrea Byrd

William Cole cannot forget the cruel burden he carries, not with the pock marks that serve as an outward reminder. Riddled with guilt, he assumed the solitary life of a long hunter, traveling into the wilds of Kentucky each year. But his quiet existence is changed in an instant when, sitting in a tavern, he overhears a man offering his daughter—and her virtue—to the winner of the next round of cards. William's integrity and desire for redemption will not allow him to sit idly by while such an injustice occurs.

Lucinda Gillespie has suffered from an inexplicable illness her entire life. Her father, embarrassed by her condition, has subjected her to a lonely existence of abuse and confinement. But faced with the ultimate betrayal on the eve of her eighteenth birthday, Lucinda quickly realizes her trust is better placed in the hands of the mysterious man who appears at her door. Especially when he offers her the one thing she never thought would be within her grasp—freedom.

In the blink of an eye, both lives change as they begin the difficult, danger-fraught journey westward on the Wilderness Trail. But can they overcome their own perceptions of themselves to find love and the life God created them for?

~

A Heart's Gift by Lena Nelson Dooley

Is a marriage of convenience the answer?

Franklin Vine has worked hard to build the ranch he inherited into one of the most successful in the majestic Colorado mountains. If only he had an heir to one day inherit the legacy he's building. But he was burned once in the worst way, and he doesn't plan to open his heart to another woman. Even if that means he'll eventually have to divide up his spread among the most loyal of his hired hands.

When Lorinda Sullivan is finally out from under the control of men who made all the decisions in her life, she promises herself she'll never allow a man to make choices for her again. But without a home in the midst of a hard Rocky Mountain winter, she has to do something to provide for her infant son.

A marriage of convenience seems like the perfect arrangement, yet the stakes quickly become much higher than either of them ever planned. When hearts become entangled, the increasing danger may change their lives forever.

~

Lone Star Ranger by Renae Brumbaugh Green

Elizabeth Covington will get her man.

And she has just a week to prove her brother isn't the murderer Texas Ranger Rett Smith accuses him of being. She'll show the good-looking lawman he's wrong, even if it means setting out on a risky race across Texas to catch the real killer.

Rett doesn't want to convict an innocent man. But he can't let the Boston beauty sway his senses to set a guilty man free. When Elizabeth follows him on a dangerous trek, the Ranger vows to keep her safe. But who will protect him from the woman whose conviction and courage leave him doubting everything—even his heart?